This kiss felt like the culmination of days of wondering and waiting.

"I've never done this before. How am I doing?" Finn's voice was husky, and he hadn't let go of her yet.

Sophie licked her lips. And watched his eyes heat. "You've never kissed a woman you barely know before?"

"I've never auditioned for a play before," he clarified.

She nodded. "Well, just so you know, typically you say words and act out a scene. On a stage. With other people watching."

"We can move this onto the stage if you want," Finn said agreeably. "And you just tell me the words you want to hear."

A bunch of words came to mind. *Sophie, you're amazing. I could kiss you forever. Let's take this into your office.* Wow, that was asking for trouble.

ACCLAIM FOR ERIN NICHOLAS

"Grade: A. It's 'read in one sitting' good."
—SmartBitchesTrashyBooks.com on *Forever Mine*

"Erin Nicholas celebrates geek culture in this upbeat, sexy romance. Looking to connect with his ten-year-old daughter, staid doctor Alex Nolan reaches out to cosplayer Maya Goodwin for a crash course on comics and fangirls. We identified with Maya and her love of superheroes (we've been known to crush on Captain America, too). And we loved the sweetness of this story, which is a perfect escape."
—iBooks Best Books of March on *Forever Mine*

"At its heart, this contemporary romance is about families—the family of friends that Maya has assembled and the family Alex is trying to put together with Charli and her mother—and how the two blend together. This fun and flirty contemporary romance is a fresh and engaging take on the opposites-attract trope, with a lovable cast."
—*Publishers Weekly* on *Forever Mine*

"Fresh, fun and flirty . . . Geeky has never been so sexy."
—Carly Phillips, *New York Times* bestselling author,
on *Completely Yours*

"You can always count on Erin Nicholas for fun, sexy contemporary romance."
—Melissa Foster,
New York Times bestselling author

"Erin Nicholas always delivers swoon-worthy heroes, heroines that you root for, laugh-out-loud moments, a colorful cast of family and friends, and a heartwarming happily ever after."
—Melanie Shawn,
New York Times bestselling author

Totally His

ERIN NICHOLAS

FOREVER

NEW YORK BOSTON

Copyright © 2017 by Erin Nicholas
Excerpt from *Completely Yours* copyright © 2016 by Erin Nicholas

Cover design by Elizabeth Turner. Cover illustration by Blake Morrow.
Cover copyright © 2017 by Hachette Book Group, Inc.

Forever
Hachette Book Group
1290 Avenue of the Americas, New York, NY 10104
forever-romance.com
twitter.com/foreverromance

First Edition: October 2017

Forever is an imprint of Grand Central Publishing. The Forever name and logo are trademarks of Hachette Book Group, Inc.

The publisher is not responsible for websites (or their content) that are not owned by the publisher.

The Hachette Speakers Bureau provides a wide range of authors for speaking events. To find out more, go to www.hachettespeakersbureau.com or call (866) 376-6591.

ISBNs: 978-1-4555-3972-7 (mass market), 978-1-4555-3970-3 (ebook), 978-1-4789-1614-7 (audio downloadable)

Printed in the United States of America

OPM

10 9 8 7 6 5 4 3 2 1

To my favorite "theater geek," Nikoel. And to JH, who saw her light and put it up onstage for others to see.

Acknowledgements

Thank you to my favorite place to see a show, the Shot in the Dark Theater—which inadvertently served as inspiration for the Birch Community Playhouse.

And special thanks for the "cop stuff" goes to David Cuffley and Clyde Lyndsay—the cops who make me want to come up with questions just because I love their answers!

Totally His

*C*HAPTER ONE

*F*inn would have noticed her even if she hadn't been wearing hot-pink lingerie. And nothing else.

He really would have. She was totally his type—brunette and curvy and, apparently, a little crazy. As evidenced by the fact that she was trying to sneak into a burning building. He did seem to be attracted to crazy. No matter how hard he tried not to be.

But maybe she wasn't actually trying to get back into the building. All he knew for sure was that the building was definitely burning and she was definitely acting sneaky. As she pulled away from the crowd, she moved slowly, looking over her shoulder and from side to side, as if checking to see if anyone was watching. She obviously didn't notice Finn. Because he was absolutely watching as she made her way across the street, now acting as if she were just casually strolling along. Toward a burning building. In nothing but a bra and panties.

It made sense that he hadn't seen her before now. For

one, he'd been a little busy evacuating a hundred people, give or take, from the buildings on the block. For another, if she'd been huddled with the crowd, she could have easily been blocked by some of the other spectators. No one seemed inclined to leave, all choosing instead to stand around and watch the real-life drama unfold. She was short, and there were two women in enormous skirts that stood out several inches on each side, a woman dressed in a full-length fur coat and hat—in spite of it being a pleasantly warm September night—and a man dressed as a cow. He was on two legs, but otherwise he was clearly a cow. So there were plenty of big, distracting people to hide behind.

Which might all have seemed peculiar at any other scene, but considering that the burning building was the Birch Community Playhouse and that the onlookers had been in the middle of a production when the alarms went off, it wasn't so strange. Finn had no idea what the play was called or what it was about, but it explained the cow. He hoped.

He watched the woman stop at the east corner of the building, the one farthest from where the firefighters were working. Then he frowned as she slipped into the shadows along the side of the building and out of sight.

Dammit.

He started after her.

As one of the cops on scene, it was his job to keep the area clear for the firefighters and keep the crowd of onlookers safe. If one of them happened to have a great body and be dressed in nothing but a pink bra-and-panty set, well, he'd just call that a perk. And as he jogged across the street, Finn couldn't help but wonder if she was in costume or if the alarm had caught her in the midst of a wardrobe change. If that was her outfit for the show, he might need to buy a ticket.

His foot hit the sidewalk as his cell phone rang. He glanced at the display and then shook his head and answered, "What?"

"You saw her too, you bastard."

The voice on the other end belonged to his best friend and partner, Tripp. Finn grinned. "Who?"

"Seriously?"

Finn laughed. Tripp had a radar for beautiful women. Finn shouldn't have been surprised that he'd noticed the brunette too. "Do we need to flip a coin to see who checks her out?"

"Nah. You go be the mean guy that says she can't play by the burning building. I'll be the good cop later. If you know what I mean."

Finn definitely knew what he meant. And he ignored it. Tripp was a notorious flirt and had plenty of women, but he was also a big talker.

Finn rounded the corner of the building. The streetlights didn't quite reach along the entire length of the building on this side, and it took his eyes a second to adjust. Just in time to see her duck around the back.

Finn sighed. "You sure you don't want to be the bad cop this one time?" he asked his friend, who was assigned to crowd control out front.

"Why's that?" Tripp sounded amused.

"I think she's trying to get back into the building."

"That's perfect," Tripp said.

"Perfect?" Finn asked, heading toward the back of the building after her.

"Sure. 'Hey, you can't go in there' is better than trying

to come up with some charming line to start a conversation, right?" Tripp asked, sounding as if he was enjoying himself. "And maybe you'll get to use your handcuffs."

Finn could practically hear Tripp's eyebrows wagging. He turned the corner to the back of the building and looked around. He didn't see her. She'd gone inside. Dammit. He climbed up the four steps that led to the back door of the theater.

The theater was only one story and wasn't very big. He'd never been inside it, the art studio next door, the trendy new bar on the other end of the block, or the twenty luxury apartments that occupied the upper two stories of the building that housed the bar. This was the artsy part of downtown, just a few blocks off the true theater district. Finn was more the type to hang out at sports bars and, better yet, the sporting complexes around the great city of Boston.

Finn touched the back door and found it cool. It seemed that the flames were still contained to the wall on the other end of the theater, but it was a mistake to assume anything when fire was involved.

Finn yanked the door open and paused.

"You're going in, right?" Tripp asked in his ear, suddenly more serious.

"Yep."

"Okay, talk to me. What's going on? Where are you?"

Tripp was a good guy and a great partner. He was a smartass and a man-whore, but he was a hell of a cop and knew exactly when to be serious.

"Back door. West end. No smoke. No noise," Finn reported, referring to the lack of crackling or other sounds that would alert him to fire nearby.

He stepped inside and pulled the flashlight from his belt,

shining it back and forth. In the center of the room was a huge wooden table cluttered with tape measures, ribbon, lace, and other stuff. There were sewing machines, and the room was filled nearly to bursting with bolts of fabric, mannequins, racks of clothing, and shelves of hats, purses, shoes, gloves, and other accessories. "Looks like this is where they make and store costumes," he told Tripp.

Finn shined the flashlight around, located the door on the other side of the room, and started in that direction. His foot hit something as he rounded the table, and he stumbled. He gritted his teeth, his irritation growing.

"You ever been in a play?" Tripp asked in his ear.

"When I was, like, six," Finn replied without thinking.

"Yeah?" Tripp sounded delighted at the news. "What part?"

"I don't remember." Finn totally remembered. He'd been a Dalmatian in his school production of *101 Dalmatians*.

"I bet Angie has pictures."

Finn could hear Tripp's huge grin. And he knew his friend was right. His mother most definitely still had pictures. And she would happily show Tripp every damned one of them over roasted chicken and potatoes one night without Tripp needing to do anything more than mention the play.

Damn. "You ask my mom about that play, and I might forget to block Duncan next time we play." Tripp was the quarterback for their rec league football team, and Duncan was the huge lineman for the firefighters. Duncan had a tally on the inside of his locker of the number of times he'd sacked Tripp. The number was significantly lower than it would have been if Tripp hadn't had Finn on his offensive line.

"Yeah, well, my ass would tell you that you're not as great at that as you'd like to think."

"Let's find out how great I am," Finn challenged as he reached the door, found it cool, and pushed it open. He stepped into a hallway. It was lit, which was helpful. It was also empty, which was not helpful. Fuck. Now which way? He looked up and down the hall. There were several doors. She could be anywhere.

"Okay, okay, don't get your panties in a wad," Tripp said. "I'm just giving you shit."

Finn grinned. Tripp knew damned well that he needed Finn blocking for him. "I'm in a hallway with a bunch of doors," he said. "These are probably dressing rooms and stuff. Maybe she came back in to get dressed." That would make a little sense, even though it was stupid.

"Or to get something," Tripp said.

Yeah, maybe. People always did shit like that.

Dammit. She was one of those. Convinced that material possessions were worth risking her life for. Finn had no choice but to start searching. He moved up and down the hallway, throwing doors open. "Nothing. And yeah, these are dressing rooms," he reported to Tripp. The lights were all on, and there was clothing scattered everywhere in all of them. "Looks like a tornado hit."

"Well, they were in the middle of a show," Tripp said.

"Yeah, at least everyone bailed and left their stuff behind." That was incredibly intelligent. With the one exception who'd come back in, of course.

After he'd opened every door to every dressing room, a storeroom, and a bathroom, Finn swore. No woman in pink panties. Or any other color of panty.

"Where the fuck is she?" he muttered out loud.

"Keep going," Tripp said. "I haven't seen her come back out."

"I'm heading south. There's an exit sign up here." He headed down the hallway for the door at the end.

"You're at the front?" Tripp asked.

"No. There's no way this door opens to the outside." A moment later, he stepped into the outer lobby of the theater. The empty outer lobby.

"Box office to my left, doors into the theater to my right," he told Tripp.

"Got you."

Finn looked to his left again. "The box office," he repeated. Where the money would be. And the computers.

"You think she's looting the place?" Tripp asked.

"Money or clothes," Finn said. "People also go back in for scrapbooks and photographs, but she wouldn't have any of that here. Why else would she come back in?"

"Check it out," Tripp agreed.

"How are things going out there?" he asked Tripp.

Finn didn't see or smell anything that made him worry right now, but he had no way of knowing if the flames were, at that very moment, licking along the rafters or crawling through the other walls. Finn scowled as he stomped toward the front office. He might be making an arrest here. If nothing else, he was going to chew this lady's ass but good. The ass in the hot-pink...

Fuck. He shoved the office door open, but as it banged against an interior wall, he realized the room was empty. The lights were on, the computer was still running, but there was no one in sight. He also smelled smoke.

Definitely *fuck.*

He turned a full circle, not sure where to go next. It was

a typical office, and there was a safe under the desk in front of him. So she hadn't come for the money. Well, what the hell?

"She's not here."

"She's in there somewhere."

Just then Finn heard a door slam somewhere behind him. He swung toward the sound. "Hang on." He moved back into the lobby just in time to see the woman step out from a room behind the coffee machine.

Her eyes went wide when she saw him.

"Boston PD! Stop!" Finn shouted.

She had covered up. Kind of. She now wore a robe, short, sheer, and unbelted. Which really did nothing to cover his view of her panties and bra. Or all that skin.

And maybe that was why she suddenly took off at a run.

Finn stared after her for a moment, a little stunned. She was actually running from him?

"She's running," he told Tripp grimly.

"You need backup?" Tripp still sounded amused. The bastard.

"Maybe. You know anyone good?" Finn asked, starting after her.

"Ha ha. You need to hang up so you can run? If you huff and puff into the phone, I'll make fun of you."

"If you make fun of me, I'll kick your ass on our next run. Again."

"Go get the girl," Tripp said.

Finn disconnected, mentally calling his friend names. But nothing he hadn't called him out loud and in person.

The woman made it to the other end of the lobby and through one of the doors leading into the main theater before Finn got to her. He grabbed the door as it was swinging shut, nearly smashing his fingers. The lights were off in the inner theater but, as he plunged into the darkness, he got a big whiff of whatever body spray or perfume she wore. He took a deep breath. It was nice. Lemony. Sweet and...

Jesus. Finn scowled and turned his flashlight back on. He was thinking about how she smelled? How about the smell of smoke that was going to be chasing them both pretty soon?

"Hey!" he called into the theater. "You can't be in here. Just come out with me now. No problem. You're not in trouble."

He heard what sounded like papers rustling behind him, and he swung around. He had to lift the beam of light above his eye level. The sound was coming from the room up above the rows of theater seats, where the lighting and sound equipment were. The door to the booth was hanging open, and he heard muttered swearing in addition to the papers.

He started in that direction, but suddenly the door slammed shut.

He strode to the door and banged his fist against it. "You have to come out, ma'am. It's not safe for you to stay in the building."

"Just give me a damned minute!" she shouted through the door.

"I'm sorry, ma'am, I can't do that," Finn said.

"I have to find something. Then I'm coming right out."

"Ma'am, the fire could be spreading. You need to evacuate the building." Finn shined his flashlight on the door, wondering if he could break it down.

"I will!" she called back. "I promise."

"Ma'am, I will have to remove you myself if you don't come out immediately."

"Oh, for fuck's sake!" he heard her exclaim. Something in the room banged—a file cabinet closing, if he had to guess. Then it sounded like she slid something across the floor. Like a chair or a table.

As something heavy thumped against the other side of the door, Finn frowned and grabbed the doorknob, turning it easily. It wasn't locked. He started to push it open and realized that, yes, she'd slid something across the floor—and put whatever it was in front of the door. He shoved hard, moving whatever it was several inches. He could see now that she was bent over a table, a small flashlight held in her teeth as she rifled through a stack folders frantically.

Maybe she wasn't going for the safe in the front office, but she was clearly messing with the theater's stuff. The theater that belonged to his mother's friend Sophia. "Ma'am, this is your last warning. Stop what you're doing and come with me."

She took the flashlight from her teeth and glanced over, her eyes meeting his. She didn't look scared. She looked irritated. Her dark hair lay against her cheek, her mouth was a grim line, and the beam from his flashlight easily penetrated the sheer fabric of her robe, highlighting the curves of her right breast and hip. They stared at one another for several beats, and Finn felt heat sweep through him. Damn, that was stupid. And careless. He was working here.

But she broke the spell a moment later when she bent back over the table, her fingers flying over the folders. Okay, well, he'd warned her. Whatever she'd been able to move in front of the door wouldn't slow Finn down much.

He put his shoulder against the door and shoved. The table scraped across the floor, and as soon as the opening was wide enough, Finn slipped inside.

She straightened, looking even more irritated now. "I have to check one more place."

He shook his head. "No way. Let's go."

"Officer, I understand what you're doing. But I promise you that I'm not going near the fire. I just need to—"

Enough of this. Finn stalked over to her, put a hand around her upper arm, and turned to remove her from the sound booth. And the building.

She dug her heels in, though, pulling against his hold. "Hey, you can't—"

"Oh, yes I can," he told her calmly, careful to keep his eyes off her body. The heat from her skin had immediately soaked through the thin robe, and Finn felt it traveling from his palm up his arm. "I've given you several opportunities to cooperate."

"You're arresting me?" she asked.

"Are you doing something that you need to be arrested for?" he asked, moving her toward the door, even with her resisting.

"No! I need to get something. It's very important. It belongs to a friend of mine. It's irreplaceable."

"Ma'am," he said calmly, "don't make me carry you out of here."

He really didn't want to carry her out. That would involve touching a lot more of her. And the fact that she was barely clothed would become even more of an issue. As it was, he was far too aware of not only her body heat and how much skin was on display, but that the scent surrounding her was definitely lemony. And it was completely inappropriate to acknowledge how badly he wanted to take a really big, deep breath.

"You can't give me two more minutes?" she asked.

"Absolutely not." Finn took a risk and glanced at her. Then he gritted his teeth against the sheen in her eyes. It wasn't as if he'd never had someone cry when he was trying to get them to do something they didn't want to do. But sometimes it got to him and sometimes it didn't. This time it did.

She pulled against his grip and leaned all her weight into fighting the forward motion across the room.

Well, shit. He'd kind of figured it would come to this, but he wasn't sure he was ready to touch her more. Still, it didn't look as if he had a lot of choice. Reminding himself that he was a professional, he bent and hooked an arm behind her knees, looped the other around her back, and lifted her.

She gasped, and for a moment she didn't fight. And he thought maybe the hard part was over. But as he headed out the door, trying to ignore how warm and soft and fucking lemony she was, she started to wiggle.

* * *

"Knock it off."

Sophie frowned up at the cop who was carrying her out of the theater. *Carrying* her. Out of *her* theater. "You can't force me to leave."

"The fuck if I can't."

Of course he could. Obviously. And she'd known going back in had been a stupid, risky thing to do, but she'd thought she'd known exactly where the script was.

She had to get that script.

Angela had finally finished it. And it was amazing. And it was handwritten on pink notebook paper with purple ink. And somewhere in the theater that was possibly burning down.

Sophie squirmed in the cop's arms again. It was the only copy in the world. There was no way Angela could rewrite it if it burned. It had taken her over a year to write it in the first place.

The arms holding her tightened, and with a sigh Sophie gave up trying to get loose. The cop was far bigger and stronger. And under any other circumstances, she would have enjoyed being this close to him. A hot guy carrying her away from danger? Oh yeah, that was good stuff. If only carrying her from danger wasn't also carrying her away from the most beautiful script she'd ever read, written by the woman who was the closest thing to a mother she'd ever had.

Sophie tamped down the swirling emotions that threatened to take over. She needed a plan, not panic. And if she was going to be carried away—literally—she might as well enjoy it. While she came up with what to do after he put her down.

She looked up at him. The cop had dark hair, cut very short, and dark eyes. With the lack of light, she couldn't tell the exact color, but she felt their intensity. He had a strong jaw, because of course he did—just like all the great save-the-day heroes. He also had wide shoulders, large biceps, and big hands. Nice big hands.

She was acutely aware that she was pressed up against his solid, very warm chest. And that one of those big hands was curled around her thigh. Her bare thigh. Which reminded her of what she was wearing. Or what she wasn't wearing. In act two she was in the bra, panties, and robe—until she slipped out of the robe just as the curtain came down. She'd been in the dressing room, about to pull her dress on for act three, when the alarm had gone off. She was smart enough to know that you got out when a fire alarm sounded. But as soon as she'd determined where the fire was and that the firefighters were on it, she'd truly thought she could slip back in, grab the script, and get out again without anyone knowing. No harm, no foul.

She'd kind of forgotten about her lack of clothing. As crazy as that sounded. She certainly wasn't the type to run around in barely-there clothes, and definitely not in her underwear. It was the theater that made her forget the real world. And the wig. Sophie lifted her hand and touched the wig of straight black hair that covered her own blond waves. She really did love wigs and costumes. They allowed her to do all kinds of things she wouldn't normally do.

The cop started for the front doors of the theater.

"Wait!"

He frowned down at her. "What?"

"How about the side door?" she asked. Maybe if she was cooperative and sweet, he'd let her down. And maybe relax a little. And then leave her alone once they were outside.

Then she could slip back into the costume shop, the only other place in the building where the script might be. She'd gone in through that room, but it hadn't occurred to her to stop and look there. Angela had given it to her in the sound booth, saying it was finally done, but Sophie knew that Angie had sneaked it back and had been tinkering with it over the past couple of days. No matter how many times

Sophie assured her that the script was wonderful, Angie was having a hard time letting it go.

"Why the side door?" he asked, but at least he'd stopped walking.

That was good. That was very good.

"Less attention. I don't want to freak anyone out when they see me with the big, bad cop."

He sighed. "If I was so big and bad, you'd be in handcuffs right now."

Sophie felt a bolt of electricity shoot through her unexpectedly. Handcuffs, huh? Well, okay then. She cleared her throat. She must still be channeling her character Beth, Sophie decided. She wasn't a handcuffs kind of girl—not in the bedroom and definitely not in the back of a squad car. She liked things peaceful and easy and very vanilla. She saved all her drama for the stage.

Well, she tried to, anyway. She worked really hard at it, in fact. The more boring things were in her real life, the happier she was.

So she needed to get away from the hot cop, convince him she was going to be good so he would leave her alone... and then be sneakier about getting back in here. This didn't need to be any more dramatic than it already had been.

"Please." She ran her hand up his chest, tapping into her flirtatious Beth on purpose now. "I'm sorry I was giving you a hard time. I know you're just trying to keep me safe. Can we please go out the side door? I don't want my friends to be worried."

His dark brows pulled together, and his jaw tensed.

She'd always been excellent at reading people. Her father had taught her all about body language and tells. It had been important in his... work.

Sophie almost rolled her eyes at even thinking of that word for Frank Birch's way of going through life, but then she pushed all thoughts of her father and his cons out of her head. She'd left her dad and his shenanigans behind her a long time ago. But she'd never been able to stop studying people and figuring out their buttons. And it seemed that her hand on this guy's chest was pushing one of his.

"Your friends should be worried about the fact that you thought coming back in here was a good idea."

She ran her hand over his chest again, noting the hard muscles and the way he swallowed as she did it. She might be doing it to figure out how to get on his good side, but that didn't mean she couldn't enjoy it. "Please," she asked again, softer.

His gaze snapped to hers, and for an instant every plan and idea deserted her and she just stared up at him. Whoa. She had absolutely no urge to get away from him at all in that moment.

"Where's the side door?" he finally asked.

She thought maybe his voice was a little gruffer now. She pointed. "That way." But she didn't look away from him.

Finally he was the one to break the staring contest. As he looked in the direction she'd indicated, Sophie mentally shook herself. *Holy crap.*

"Fine, we'll go out the side door. But you're going back to the front with the rest of the crowd, got it?"

She nodded. "Sure. Of course. But we can't go out together."

He sighed. "I have no idea why I'm going along with any of this, you know."

Sophie bit back a smile. She thought maybe she knew.

He was attracted to her. Attraction made people do crazy things. And he was rescuing her from a potentially danger-ous situation. He was feeling protective of her, or at least responsible for her. So she was getting her way with him. That made her feel a little tingly.

He started toward the side door, and Sophie wondered if he'd noticed that she'd stopped fighting him. That was why he'd picked her up. And as much as she liked being in his arms, she needed to get her feet on the ground before she had a hope of losing him and sprinting for the costume shop.

"You can put me down," she said. "I'm not struggling anymore."

The hand on her thigh squeezed slightly. "Yeah, I noticed."

"So... you don't have to carry me."

He glanced down at her. "You think I didn't notice how quick you were to get sweet and friendly?" he asked.

She narrowed her eyes. "So you don't trust me?"

He gave a bark of laughter. "Lady, you ran from me, hid from me, pushed a table in front of a door to try to keep me out, and fought me every step—right up until you realized you couldn't win that way."

So she'd gotten agreeable too easily. Noted. She frowned. "Well, none of it slowed you down a bit. Why would I keep fighting once you picked me up?"

He hit the horizontal door handle with his hip. "It wasn't that you stopped fighting that made me suspicious. It was that you got all... soft."

They stepped out into the night as he said that last word, and Sophie was hit by the darkness and the gruffness of his voice all at once. Suddenly the moment felt very intimate.

She looked up at him, his face in shadows now. "Soft?" she asked.

"Yeah. You were feisty as hell to start. Then you went soft and sweet." He cleared his throat. "I'm thinking the first is the real you. So I'm not trusting the soft and sweet, thank you very much." He descended the four steps as if carrying another person around didn't require an ounce of extra effort.

Sophie had no idea what to say to his observation.

Soft and sweet. That's what she wanted to be. But that was the part he didn't believe. Which was strange on two levels. One, she'd perfected being soft and sweet. For *years* she'd played the nice girl, the shy girl, the pleaser. Because that made people like her. Especially the women. The trusting, single or widowed, childless women her father had targeted, seduced, and married so he and his daughter had a place to live and someone to take care of them. Frank had blatantly used his sweet, young, motherless daughter to make them trust him and his whirlwind courtships. "Be sweet, Soph," "Let her fuss over you," "Tell her you love her." Sophie could still hear his voice telling her to be a good girl or they'd end up back out on the street.

The thing was, she *had* loved them. All five of them. She'd loved having them fuss over her. The sweetness hadn't always been an act. At least she didn't think it had been. Though she would have done and said anything to stay in any one of those homes.

And now, all these years later, without her father using her to manipulate people, she wanted it to be real. She wanted to be kind and generous, to have people actually trust and love her without all the acting.

But this guy thought the feisty side was real. That was...annoying.

They got to the sidewalk, and the cop stopped. Sophie quickly shook off all her suddenly introspective thoughts. Where had *that* all come from? She thought she'd pushed all of that down deep a long time ago.

He let her legs go, her feet swinging to the ground. Then, when she was on her feet, he let go of her completely and stepped back.

Too bad. The thought flitted through her mind, completely unwanted. But it was colder when she wasn't pressed up against him. She wrapped her light robe around her body and crossed her arms. "Well, thanks, I guess," she told him.

"For saving your life? You got it," he told her with a grin.

And she felt her pulse stutter. That grin. Thank God he hadn't given it to her inside the theater, because now she *really* wanted to be nice and sweet to him. He could have her soft and sweet all night.

Sophie mentally slapped herself. And what was *that*? She wasn't the type to go all mushy for big muscles and a great smile. She was way too cynical for love-at-first-sight or even lust-at-first-sight feelings. That stuff wasn't real. You couldn't know a person within a few minutes of meeting them, and you couldn't trust someone you didn't know. Hell, you couldn't trust a lot of the people you did know.

"Yeah, for that, I guess," she said with a shrug. Act cool, take it easy, let him relax.

Of course, she knew there was no way he was going to leave her on the sidewalk so close to the building. He was going to escort her across the street and behind the barricades. Fine. She'd go along. She'd be easy to get along with, do whatever he said, act contrite even. The sooner he turned his back, the better. Guys like this—the take-charge types that cops needed to be—liked when people just went along with whatever they said.

He seemed to kind of like your feisty side too.

Sophie told the stupid voice in her head to shut the hell up because *that* wasn't helping at all.

They stood just looking at each other for another long moment. It might have been that each was waiting for the other to say or do something first. But Sophie thought it felt a bit like they were both stalling.

Stupid! Get your ass back in that building! She cleared her throat and shifted her weight on her feet.

He nodded, about what she wasn't sure, and said, "I'm going to need you on the other side of the barricade."

Right. Duh. She knew that. "Okay," she said agreeably. Maybe too agreeably. He'd already said he didn't trust her soft and sweet side. So she added a frown and a "whatever."

She turned on her heel and walked toward the front corner of the building, mentally planning how to get to the edge of the crowd without her friends seeing her. Because the hot cop was right that they'd be concerned about her going back into the building. Especially Angie. She'd freak out if she knew Sophie had gone back.

Sophie wasn't the type to risk her life for a *thing*. She knew very well that things came and went. Hell, people and relationships and feelings all came and went a lot of the time too. But the script was special. Besides, she didn't have time for a lecture from any of her friends or fellow actors. She needed to get back inside.

"Hey."

The low, deep voice immediately made her turn. "Yeah?"

"Sorry about whatever you were looking for. But, you know, I had to get you out of there." He seemed to actually mean it.

Sophie shrugged. "It was stupid for me to go back in." That was honest, at least. She knew that it had been a risk. Not a huge one. She wasn't an idiot. If the fire had been anywhere near where she'd needed to search, she never would have gone back in. But she knew that any of the other cops or firefighters would have done the same thing he had. And she was glad he'd been the one to come after her. Being held against him for a little bit had been nice.

"It was," he agreed. "But I get it."

Sophie's eyebrows went up. "You do?"

"Sure."

He didn't strike her as the nostalgic type. But what did she know? She'd just met him. *And he pegged you as feisty right away.*

"Why did you say you think feisty is the real me?" she asked. Stupidly. She couldn't stand around chatting. Plus, who cared why he'd said that? She was never going to see him again. And her feisty side was going to have to stay pushed way down deep anyway. She got that from her father, and she was staying far away from any and all Frank Birch influences now and forevermore.

"You were panicked and in a dangerous situation," he answered. "People tend to be the most real in those moments. No time to filter your thoughts or actions. Just instinct and adrenaline."

She nodded. That was all probably true. Though she was so programmed to put on a show that she wasn't sure adrenaline and panic got to her the way they did to most people. She was shocked by how sad that thought made her.

"Are you okay?" the cop asked, stepping forward.

Sophie pulled herself together. She needed to stop talking to him for multiple reasons now—he was pushing her buttons too. She straightened and gave him a smile she knew looked totally sincere. She'd practiced it and used it since she was six. "Yep. I need to get back out front so you can go back to work."

He frowned but nodded. "Right."

"So give me a minute. I'll go out, and you can follow in a little bit," she said. She had a much better shot at getting back to the crowd without being noticed if he wasn't with her. Not just because of his uniform or size but because she got the definite impression he wasn't very good at sneaking.

Or lying or manipulating people or... She shook her head. No need to think about all of that. The little trick she had planned would irritate him if he found out, but so what? She was never going to see him again.

"I'm going to head around the other way," he said. "Need to check out the back."

Even better. He'd come out on the other side and it'd take him awhile to do it.

Still she said, "Be careful."

He seemed surprised, but he gave her a smile. "Thanks."

The smile was almost as powerful as the big grin he'd flashed earlier, and Sophie had to make herself turn away. It was so typical that she'd meet a guy she had a potent attraction to and he'd be a cop and she'd be in a wig and lying to him.

Because she was definitely lying about going out front and staying there.

She managed to get to the fringe of the crowd without

being noticed. She wove her way between people to one of the shorter girls in the theater company. "Hey, Chelsea."

Chelsea looked up. "Hi, Sophie. Well, this is exciting."

Exciting. Hmm, not the word she would have used. It was a pain in the ass, and she hadn't even started thinking about things like repairs and cleaning and insurance claims...She took a deep breath. "I need a favor."

Five minutes later, Chelsea was wearing the black wig and the robe while Sophie dashed back through the shadows to the back door of the theater. Again. The door led straight into the costume shop, where she and Angela spent most of their time together. Sophie grabbed the first thing on the rack—an evening gown that was two sizes too big and four inches too long—and stepped into it before rifling through the pile of lace and trim on the end of the big worktable. Sure enough, the stack of notebook pages was there. Sophie almost wilted in relief. She grabbed the pages, lifted the skirt of her dress to keep it out from under her feet as she ran, and headed back out. She'd been in and out in less than five minutes. Perfect.

Forty minutes later, the firefighters finally called the all clear. They let the theater company back into the building with supervision, and the crowd of spectators began dispersing. Sophie realized that the script would have been completely safe. But she still clutched the pages to her chest and smiled. It had been worth it to be sure.

As the crowd thinned, Sophie felt a tingle start at the back of her neck, and she stopped to look around, feeling as if someone was watching her.

But he wasn't watching her. The hot cop was approaching Chelsea. Or rather, he was approaching the dark hair and robe.

He was at least fifty feet from her, and there were several people in between them, so Sophie hung back, watching as he put a hand on Chelsea's shoulder, a big smile on his face. A smile that died as Chelsea turned and he realized she wasn't who he'd expected.

Sophie felt a little twinge in her heart at how disappointed he looked. She did not like that she'd tricked him. And she did like that he'd come looking for her. Sophie took a step forward and then caught herself. What the hell was she doing? She couldn't go up to him now. She'd lied to him about going back into the building. She'd also put him in danger in the first place by going in so he had to follow. And now she'd purposefully dodged him. He said something to Chelsea, and whatever she responded with made his lips pull into a grim line. Nope, Sophie decided, any interest that might have been there was now gone.

When he lifted his head and looked around, Sophie had the urge to duck and turn away, but his gaze landed on her before she could. Her breath caught in her chest, and she felt her lips part. His eyes barely lingered for a moment, but his expression didn't change and he didn't come toward her. A few seconds later, he turned away. Sophie blew out a breath. He hadn't recognized her.

What a relief.

Sure, relief. That had to be what she was feeling.

CHAPTER TWO

Sophie stood looking at the black wall and ceiling—both of which had holes in them now—the soaked carpet and chairs, and the front curtain hanging listlessly, having been pulled from some of its tabs by the force of the water. That curtain looked the way she felt . . . limp and bogged down and barely hanging on. This wasn't bad. This was . . . horrible.

She'd heard that a lot of the destruction from a fire actually came from *fighting* the fire. The water and chemicals the firefighters used, not to mention the *axes* they used to punch into the burning walls, all caused their fair share of damage. But seeing it was surreal.

She looked down at the note from the insurance adjuster in her hand. She didn't have a check yet, and wouldn't until the cause of the fire could be determined, but the estimated amount was nothing to sneeze at. Of course, the time it would take to get the theater back in shape would cost her too. If she couldn't put the next show on, their budget would definitely suffer.

Sophie sighed. Fortunately, she knew Rob, Ben, Zach, Alex, Maya, Kiera, and several other friends would help out. She could save a lot of money having her friends and the theater company do the bulk of the work. Rob knew about drywall and stuff, and Sophie knew her way around tools. She'd been building theater sets since she was a kid helping her grandma. They'd get it done, and she'd only have to pay for supplies. Her friends would work for cookies and muffins. She'd have to pay an electrician to come in and redo the wiring, though. And she'd have to replace the lights, several of the chairs, the carpet... It was completely overwhelming to think about everything that would need doing. And relying on her friends meant it would be a part-time job and would take longer. She wasn't sure she could afford more time without a show on the stage.

"Well, this is a damned mess."

Sophie shrieked and spun toward the voice. She'd thought she was alone. Her hand on her chest, Sophie stared at the man standing in the center aisle.

No.

"I heard about the fire and had to come right over and make sure you were okay."

Sophie's heart went from racing in fear to pounding with anger in a split second. "What are you doing here?"

"I told you." Frank Birch came the rest of the way down the aisle. "I was worried about you."

Sophie felt that she was shaking, and she knew she was about three seconds from picking up something heavy and hurling it at her father's head. "Get out."

"Now, Sophia, calm down. That's just adrenaline talking."

No. It fucking wasn't. Sophie closed her eyes and pulled

a deep breath in through her nose and then let it out through her mouth. Then she wondered why she was trying to calm down. He didn't deserve her calm side. She didn't have to be soft and sweet with him. If ever there was a time for feisty, confronting Frank was it. She opened her eyes and stalked toward him. "Get. Out."

Frank's eyes widened, and he actually took a step back. "Soph—"

"Don't Soph me. Don't come in here acting all concerned. In fact, don't come here at all. I've been sending you your money. You have no reason to be here." Except that he did. The realization hit her the next second, and she stopped in her tracks. "The insurance money," she said quietly. He was here because he knew there would be insurance money.

"Have you talked to the insurance adjusters yet?" he asked, tucking his hands in his pockets. "This has to be worth several thousand."

Frank was a selfish, lazy pathological liar. But, ironically, he had never lied to *her*. He wouldn't pretend that he wasn't here about the money. She supposed she should be glad about that.

And she couldn't lie to him about this. Not because she didn't want to or because she felt some sense of loyalty to him, but because he probably knew exactly what their policy said and he probably had a pretty good idea of how much the check she held was worth. Frank worked very hard at not working, and part of that was knowing a little about a lot of things and being incredibly computer savvy. He could find almost anything out about anything or anyone. If he'd turn those skills to something productive, he could make a nice living.

And if he were even a touch more ambitious, he could turn it into a terribly impressive crime spree.

"I have." Sophie crossed her arms. She would love to refuse to give him any of it, but he was a 50 percent owner of the theater. Half of that money was his.

"So how much are we getting?"

Sophie felt her spine stiffen. She knew he thought of all of this as his too. Her grandmother—his mother—had made them partners in her will. It had been the elder Sophia's effort to give her son some purpose, some steady income, and a way to bond with his daughter. The steady-income thing was the only one that had turned out, and it wasn't enough to keep him out of trouble. Or out of the beds of women who were willing to be his sugar mamas.

She could lie to him, but he could call the insurance company and get the information easily enough. "Ten thousand total," she said. "Assuming they can rule out arson." She studied Frank's face. No reaction to the word *arson*. Surely her father wouldn't have set the fire? "After expenses, there won't be anything left," she added.

He frowned at the blackened wall behind her. "Don't tell me you're going to sink it all back into this place."

"Of course I am going to use it to do the needed repairs," she said, holding herself tightly. Ranting and yelling and swearing at him wouldn't do any good. She'd tried all of that. Multiple times.

"Don't be ridiculous," he scoffed. "Tear up the carpet, slap on some paint, replace those seats with folding chairs, and you're good to go."

"Forget it, Frank. That insurance money goes into the theater."

"*Half* of that insurance money can go into whatever you

want," he corrected her. "The other half goes into my bank account."

He didn't care about the theater at all, and it killed Sophie a little bit each month when she deposited half the profits into his account. But it did keep him from messing around in her life.

She narrowed her eyes. "Frank, did you set my theater on fire?"

He appeared genuinely surprised. "Don't you mean *our* theater?"

That was not a denial, and Sophie felt her whole body begin to grow cold. Would he have done this? Would he have taken this away from her for an insurance payout?

"No," she told him firmly. "I mean *my* theater. Did you set the fire?"

He started laughing. "Of course not."

Sophie crossed her arms. "You should understand why I would ask."

"Sure," Frank said, clearly not offended. "But no, I didn't set the fire." His tone indicated that not burning down the theater was like not having a turkey sandwich for lunch. Just a regular, everyday choice that he'd made.

"Really?" she pressed.

"Who do you think is going to be the first suspect, Sophia?" he asked. "Probably the guy with no money in the bank and who is one of the beneficiaries on the insurance policy, right?"

"That's exactly who they're suspecting," she said with a nod. "Along with the woman who is the other beneficiary on the insurance policy."

"Well, did *you* set the fire?" Frank asked. And he didn't seem to be joking.

Sophie scowled at him. "Of course not."

"Then don't worry about it. They have to investigate, but that shouldn't take more than a week or so. Then we'll get the check. But I promise you, I did not do this."

Sophie didn't want to know how he knew about arson investigations. "Why aren't you in Florida?" she asked. "There's no way you heard about this fire from Miami."

"Cynthia kicked me out a week ago," Frank told her.

Ah, Cynthia. Her sixth stepmother, and the first she hadn't met.

"That one lasted almost two years," she commented. That was about average for Frank's relationships. The longest one had lasted five years. Sophie's heart still hurt when she thought about Maggie and some of the best years of Sophie's young life.

"Yeah, well." Frank shrugged, clearly not terribly broken up about his failed marriage. "She wanted to retire, and I didn't think that was a good idea."

Of course not. Retirement would have meant a decreased income and, almost worse, more time together.

Okay, she was done with the small talk. Or whatever this was. "I'll move the money to your account as soon as the deposit goes in," she told him. She started up the aisle past him.

Frank moved in front of her, and Sophie pulled up short. Again her body tensed for a confrontation. Not a physical one—though she definitely felt the urge to throw a punch or two whenever she talked to him—but he didn't use force to get his way. He didn't have to. He was very charming. And manipulative. People sincerely liked him—at least the Frank they got to know. Frank was an amazing actor. He just wasn't much of a human being.

"I need a place to stay."

Of course he did. "Where have you been staying for the past week since you got back to town?" she asked.

"Stayed with a friend in Miami for a few days, then came back here and crashed with Bernie for a few days. But I need my own place."

Which actually meant, "I need my daughter to find and pay for a place for me to stay."

It had been four years since she and Frank had lived in the same city. Four wonderful years. And those four years apart meant a couple of very important things. One, Frank didn't know Sophie's living arrangement, and two, he didn't know her friends.

"It's not like I can afford rent for both of us," she told him.

"You got an extra room?" he asked.

"No." She didn't. The house she lived in was her room-mate Kiera's, and it wasn't just Sophie and Kiera living there. They had another roommate, Maya, and Kiera's boyfriend and Maya's boyfriend were both there almost as much as the girls were. And there was no way in hell she was letting Frank near any of them.

"How about a couch?" Frank asked. "Temporarily. Until we can figure something else out."

"Frank," Sophie said firmly. She hadn't called him Dad in years. "There is no way I'm letting you spend even one night in my house, and *we* aren't figuring anything out. This is your problem."

He sighed. But she knew he'd been expecting that. They had put on acts for other people ever since Sophie's mom had died and it had been just her and Frank, but they had never pretended with one another.

"That house you live in is huge. I can't believe there's not even a corner for me."

Sophie froze. He could be bluffing. But more likely, Frank had looked up her address and gone by her house. "Did you talk to the girls?" she asked. She wasn't going to give him Maya and Kiera's names if she didn't have to. But it was also possible he'd met her roommates.

"No one was home."

So he had tried.

Sophie thought about her strategy for a moment. Did she downplay how much the girls meant to her in the hopes that it would throw Frank off the idea of getting to them because she cared about them? Or did she threaten to end him if he so much as sneezed on one of them? Did she let him see that she'd gladly suffer physical harm, go broke, even go to jail to spare Kiera and Maya any hurt, especially any hurt caused by her father? Or did she play his game of chicken? See if she could get him to blink first?

He wouldn't stay in Boston. He'd get bored and head out eventually. He'd decide it was time to fall in love again. She just had to wait him out.

"There's no room for you in that house," she told him. "And I could never ask them for a favor like that."

Frank watched her carefully, but Sophie wasn't worried. He wouldn't see through her. She was a phenomenal actress. She'd learned from the best.

"You could still convince them to put me up for a while. I'm your father."

Sophie shrugged. "They would probably think it was strange I was asking, actually. They know that you and I aren't close."

"We aren't?"

She frowned at him. "No. We're not."

"We have quite a history. Just you and me all those years."

"You and me and all of my stepmothers," she reminded him, not able to keep the bite out of her tone.

"But really, it always came back to just us," Frank said calmly.

Yes, it always had. Just them. Sleeping in the car and eating at the local shelter until Frank could charm his next victim into letting him and his sweet little daughter into her life—and house.

Sophie swallowed against the emotions that suddenly welled up. She wasn't proud of the cons she'd helped her father with, but she vividly remembered those cold nights in that car, where she'd barely slept because she was afraid they'd be murdered or arrested. She would have done any-thing to sleep in a real bed after even one night like that. After a month or so, she'd been quite willing to put on her manners and sweet smile and be the next woman's dream daughter.

"I am *not* supporting you, Frank. You're not sleeping on my couch, and you will stay away from my roommates. They don't have any money, and they're too young for you to marry."

She almost bit her tongue off as those words fell out of her mouth. Dammit. The idea of one of her friends being romanced by her father made her queasy. Not that either of her roommates would fall for his crap. And they were both, thankfully, madly in love now. But she shouldn't put any ideas into Frank's head. Because there was one friend of hers who was single, and right about Frank's age, and sweet, and a little naive. And Angie had one incredibly important quality that Frank had always looked for in the women he wooed—she loved Sophie.

"Maya is doing just fine with her studio," Frank said. "And Kiera's video game has really taken off in the past two years."

Dammit. He knew their names, and he knew about their work. "You are *not* going to ask Kiera or Maya for money. And I'm not going to ask them for money for you."

He shrugged. "Maybe if I make you miserable enough, one of them will offer me a wad of cash to get me to leave town to make you happy."

That was actually a very real possibility. "So the plan is to make me miserable?" Sophie asked. "How will that be different than what you normally do?"

He didn't seem offended at all. He grinned. "You really want to know?"

"No." She really, really didn't. "What I want to know is how much would it take?"

"To get me to leave town?" he asked.

"Yeah. I didn't realize there was a set price on that."

Something flickered across his face. Regret? But no, that was one emotion Frank Birch had never felt. "Fifty thousand dollars."

She frowned. "That's a very large, very specific amount of money. What do you need fifty thousand dollars for?"

"An RV."

"You're buying an RV?"

"That way I've always got a place to stay, but I can go wherever I want. Expenses will be only food and gas."

For a second Sophie thought she saw something that looked a little like sadness cross his face. He and her mom had traveled around in an old beat-up RV for the first two years after they'd eloped. They'd worked odd jobs here and there, picking up and moving on whenever they felt like it. Then for four years Sophie had lived with her grandmother while her father drifted around in that same rickety RV, mourning the death of the only woman he'd ever really loved. Sophie and Grandma Sophia had been happy, playing pretend and singing songs and making up stories with happy endings every day. Then, suddenly, Frank had shown up on their doorstep, sans rusted-out RV, saying he was ready to be a dad. And he'd taken Sophie to dinner with Karen, her first stepmother, in a brand new four-door SUV. The perfect family vehicle.

"And you really didn't set fire to the theater to get some of that money from the insurance policy?" Sophie asked one more time. But she already believed he hadn't done it. Honesty, even when it was about things she didn't want to know, was the one thing she could count on from Frank.

"Sophie," he said patiently, "if I was going to burn this place to get an insurance payout, I would have done it in the middle of the night when there was no chance of them getting to it before it was worth at least the fifty grand I need."

Sophie didn't concede that that was also a good point. And she didn't want to know how he knew how long the theater would need to burn to pay out a certain amount of money.

"So fifty grand will get you an RV, huh?" she asked.

He nodded. "Saved up about twenty-five thousand, then Cindy gave me twenty-five to move out. Just need fifty grand more."

Cindy had paid him to move out. Nice. And yeah, *just*

fifty grand. But it would get Frank out of Boston and away from the people she cared about. "Sure, piece of cake."

He nodded. "Great."

"I was kidding, Frank," Sophie said with a sigh. "I don't have fifty thousand dollars just lying around." She'd have to look in her notebook to see how much she did have lying around, but she was pretty sure it wasn't fifty grand.

"I know. But if you happen into any extra cash, you now know about my moving fund."

"Definitely noted," Sophie told him. And she was already thinking about ways to get him the money. As much as she hated it. Not because she wanted to help him out, but because it would get him out of her life.

She had extra money. Of course she did. You didn't grow up the way Sophie had and not learn to have a safety net. But she couldn't just give him the money. He'd want to know where she'd gotten it. And she would never tell him that she had cash stashed here and there—at the house, at the theater, and a couple of other places—where she always had access to at least some of it, no matter what happened. She'd tried setting up a bank account that he didn't know about, but when you had to use your Social Security number on something, it was nearly impossible to keep it a secret from someone who knew enough to check those kinds of things.

"And what will you do when you find a girlfriend?" Sophie asked. "You park the thing at her house or does she move into it with you?"

But Frank was already shaking his head. "God, no, that's not nearly enough space for two people."

Sophie didn't comment on the fact that most RVs were made for families of four or more.

"And I'm retiring."

"You're done getting married?" She didn't really believe that for a second.

"You think being a husband is easy work?" he asked. "Keeping women happy has to be the toughest gig around."

She absolutely hated that he referred to his marriages as jobs.

"But I put in a lot of good years," Frank went on. "Now I'm going to kick back. I'll do the RV thing until you marry a guy with a guest room."

She knew this was his plan. But every time he said it, she was a little stunned. "Payback for all of the years you supported me, right?" Because he'd seen being her father as a means to an end rather than what it was supposed to be—his duty and pleasure.

"It's your turn, baby girl," Frank said with a shrug.

Her stomach churned. But hell if she'd show it. "Well, too bad I haven't fallen in love with anyone," Sophie said. "Guess the RV plan is gonna be a longer-term thing."

Frank rolled his eyes. "Be thankful you haven't fallen in love, Sophie. You'll be a lot happier if you don't. Makes it far easier to move on when things go to shit." And in Frank's world, things always went to shit. It was usually his fault, of course, but that was one part of the reality he hadn't quite grasped.

Frank's "retirement plan," as he called it, was one reason that Sophie had stayed away from serious relationships. His goal for his one and only child was for her to marry well—and take him along. If the guy had a spare room and didn't mind buying extra groceries, that was fine, but if she managed to land a wealthy guy who had a spare *wing*, an extra country club membership, and a car or boat he didn't use all the time, Frank would give her the Daughter of the Year award.

"You're young and beautiful, but you're getting older," he said. "You should be married by now, and I should be spending my days in my guesthouse on your property, putting model airplanes together while I watch daytime TV. Waiting for some guy to be the One isn't getting anyone to their goals here."

Right. Because finding love and being with someone for a reason other than money weren't realistic goals.

It actually kind of pissed her off that she was still romantic and thought about falling in love once in a while. Growing up with Frank should have cured her of any such thoughts. But she couldn't help that a little part of her wanted to believe that people could love each other for real and be there for one another.

Still, Sophie was definitely not looking for a long-term, committed relationship. If she thought Frank would sit in a spare room with *The View* on while he harmlessly glued plastic airplane parts together, she might not be so against the idea. But Frank Birch was not, and never would be, harmless and content.

"Anyway, we'll come up with something," Frank assured her, as if she were truly concerned about getting him that money.

But she kind of was. It was almost like an investment. The past few years without him around had been so great. If she could get him to leave Boston and leave her alone, it would be worth fifty grand.

"Until then, I still need a couch," he reminded her.

"Fine, I'll give you all the insurance money, but in exchange, you stop even thinking about getting to know

Maya and Kiera." Sophie hated herself for agreeing, but she didn't know how else to protect her friends. Other than breaking off her friendship with them so Frank had nothing to use them for. And she wasn't strong enough for that. She kind of hated herself for that too.

Frank gave her a grin. "You're a good girl, Sophia Isabelle."

And that just made her feel sick. She really wanted to be the good girl everyone thought she was.

But no matter what, she was Frank Birch's daughter. And that meant she was definitely not soft and sweet.

CHAPTER THREE

"Hey, Ma!" Finn called out as he let himself in through the back door of his mother's house on Saturday afternoon.

He didn't hear a response, but he let his nose lead him. His mother was in the kitchen, surrounded by cinnamon rolls in various stages of completion.

"What's going on?" He propped a shoulder against the doorjamb, not quite willing to go all the way into the kitchen just yet.

Angie baked when she was upset, unlike the milk-and-cookies-after-school stereotype. When they'd been growing up, Finn and Colin had both known they were in trouble if they came home from school to freshly baked cookies. She also baked after an argument with a friend, on the anniversary of their father's death, and when she saw something on the news that bothered her. She'd baked a lot until she'd gained ten pounds and decided to stop watching the news every night.

"Nothing," she told him, without turning. "Just doing some baking."

Uh-huh. "Mom, you have enough cinnamon rolls here to feed the whole precinct." He pushed away from the doorway. "Do I get to take these to the guys, or has Colin already been over?"

Whenever she baked, she eventually felt better and, of course, would need to do something with all the brownies or cookies or pies. Luckily Finn had a whole police station and his brother had a fire station full of people willing and able to help with that. Angie was a mother figure to…pretty much everyone she met who was younger than she was by five years or more. She was quirky and melodramatic and had a hard time knowing when she'd talked too much and overshared, but she was warm and loving and people were naturally drawn to her. Throw in her baking skills and her loud, robust laugh and she'd been adopted as a mom many times over by the guys Finn and Colin worked with.

Angie wiped the back of her hand over her forehead and sighed. "No, these are for the people at the theater."

"You're feeding the whole audience at the theater?" Finn asked, feeling safe about stepping fully into the kitchen since this didn't seem to be about him.

"The people cleaning up the theater," she clarified. "Sophie's friends are all there this afternoon, trying to get things sorted out. It's going to be a huge job."

"Sophie's friends?" he repeated, picturing white-haired men with walkers and tool belts.

"Yes."

The number of pans she produced was also a measure of just how upset she was. A horrible story on the news would get a pan or two. The anniversary of the day she'd buried her true love would get four or five. The night

Finn had been shot and ended up in emergency surgery, she'd produced seven. Today there were five pans of cinnamon rolls covering the countertops. This was something big.

She sniffed. "It's nothing for you to worry about." She kneaded a ball of dough on the countertop. "We've got it handled. Nothing for you to worry about."

Finn frowned. *Nothing for him to worry about* didn't compute. Especially if whatever it was upset his mom. He crossed to the tall chairs at her counter. He kicked one out and sat. "Talk," he told her.

She looked up, and Finn felt a thump in his chest. He'd been expecting to see upset or anger. But this was worse. Her eyes were red rimmed, and her cheeks were rosy. She'd been crying.

"Mom, what the hell is going on?" Five pans of cinnamon rolls and tears. Finn braced himself to hear who had died.

She looked at him for a long moment. Then shook her head. "You wouldn't understand."

Finn felt his scowl. What? Colin was the happy-go-lucky son who made her laugh. Finn was the responsible, serious one who got things done. That's how it was. That's how it had been since Tommy Kelly, the love of her life, had been shot and killed and could no longer make her laugh or take care of her. "Mom," he said firmly. "Tell me what it is."

She sighed and began rolling out more dough. "Finn, I don't want to talk about it. You can't fix this."

Bullshit. He could fix anything. "Angela Marie Kelly."

She looked up, surprised. He was Finn Patrick and his brother was Colin Sean when they were in trouble. He'd never called his mother by her full name before. Then again, she'd never not told him about something that was bothering her before.

Angie put her flour-covered hands on her hips, making white prints on her bright-yellow apron. "Fine."

Finn felt a wave of relief. Five pans of rolls were concerning, but Angie not wanting to talk was downright frightening.

"It's about the theater."

Finn frowned slightly. "The fire?" It had been a dangerous situation for sure, but everyone had come out without injury and the damage had been contained to one area. Overall a good outcome.

For a moment his thoughts flickered to brunette hair and pink satin, but he pushed those images away. He'd rescued someone from the building. Big deal. That was his job. And the hair that he'd been attracted to hadn't even been hers. He felt like an idiot thinking about how she'd ditched him at the scene.

Angie sniffed again, and Finn focused on her.

"Sophia called me this morning. She got an estimate on the damages, and the insurance payment isn't enough to cover things."

Angie's eyes filled with tears again, and Finn frowned. "Okay, well, what's she going to do?"

Angie shook her head. "She said we might have to put off the next show. She doesn't know how long it will take for her to get it all done."

"So she is going to hire someone?"

"She's going to do it herself. With some of her friends. I told her I would help paint, but I know nothing about redoing electrical and..." Angie trailed off and wiped a finger under her eye to catch a tear. "I'm being selfish. This theater is everything to her, and I'm only thinking about myself."

Finn knew that the theater meant a lot to his mother. She spent an inordinate amount of time there and had developed a very close friendship with the owner. But he had no idea what she meant about being selfish. "I think I'm missing something," he told her.

"I just don't want to postpone the next show." She shook her head. "But I'm overreacting. It will be fine. It's not about me."

Finn was used to not quite following his mother's conversations. She often had them more with herself than with the people around her. But this time it felt as if he needed to know the details.

"Mom." He reached out and covered her hand with his. "I don't understand. Fill me in here."

She met his eyes, and the sadness in her gaze made Finn determined to make this okay, no matter what. He gritted his teeth and made himself smile.

"The next play we were going to do at the theater was...something I wrote," she said.

He had to admit that he hadn't been expecting that. "You wrote a play?"

Angie nodded. "Sophia's been teaching me about scriptwriting and encouraging me to finish. It's taken me a long time. But it's finally done and she wanted to produce it right away." Angie gave a little laugh. "She was afraid I'd chicken out."

"Wow, Mom," Finn said, relieved that she was laughing instead of crying now. "I had no idea that you wanted to write a play."

"I didn't either, really," she said. "Until I met and started working with Sophia." She gave him a small smile. "But that theater..." Then the smile died, and her eyes went sad. "It means so much to me. More than the play. Even if we can't put the show on for a while, I can't stand the thought of Sophia having to deal with the fire damage like this. The theater barely makes ends meet. She does so much already to keep it going. For us. And now she's going to have to tear the walls down and put them back up. With her own two hands. Literally."

Finn took that with a huge grain of salt. As he did most things his mother said. Angie was a happy person. Eternally optimistic and bubbly. Unless she wasn't. She was an equal-opportunity drama queen. Things were always amazingly wonderful or horribly awful.

He wasn't diminishing the fact that the fire had done some damage to the theater and would set the production schedule back a bit, but it was a business. A business that produced plays. If it wasn't producing plays, it wasn't making money. Or so he assumed. He actually knew nothing about the theater business. But it was also a place that his mother loved dearly, and as with everything she did, she gave it 1,000 percent.

Like her painting. And her baking. And her projects.

Finn loved his mother more than any other person or thing on the planet. But Angie was...unconventional. And bighearted. And had a little bit of attention deficit disorder. She needed to be occupied and to have a project. Or she would make up projects.

Like the time she went to the local homeless shelter and got all the people staying there into the kitchen with the idea that they'd have a bake sale and raise some money for the shelter. Or the time she'd started art classes for kids of single parents who couldn't afford after-school care so they would have a positive way to express themselves and something to do rather than causing trouble. Or the time she'd gotten teens involved in babysitting at the local women and children's shelter to show them what it was like to take care of babies.

Finn hated when Angie did that shit. Some of the places she went and the people she tried to befriend were dangerous. But, much to his chagrin, the projects worked. At least kind of. The baking at the homeless shelter hadn't gone far. People, for some reason, didn't want cookies made by guys who huddled around Dumpsters in alleys some of the time. But the art classes and the babysitting project were still going on. Colin thought it was great and encouraged it. Finn...didn't.

But the theater. That was a whole other thing. There Angie not only *could* be dramatic—it was required. And Sophia seemed to be a very positive influence. And, if nothing else, it gave Angie a place to be and something to do. The theater specialized in unknown plays by amateur playwrights and novice actors and actresses. At least that was Finn's impression from what his mother had told him. But Angie loved it, and she hadn't come up with her own community help project in almost a year. Finn was a fan of the place for that, if nothing else.

"Ma, Sophia isn't going to literally repair the theater with her own two hands," he said. "I'm sure she'll hire help. And I'm sure the insurance company gave her what she needs. They'll at least make sure the walls are rebuilt and things are cleaned up."

But Angie was already shaking her head. "They won't.

She told me she needs ten thousand dollars. She has friends who can help, but they all work full-time so the work at the theater will have to be on the side and will take some time. She's going to have to *close* for a while."

Finn looked at his mother. She was sincerely distraught.

"But I was thinking I can help Sophia with the drywall. I was watching some videos online," she said.

Finn resisted sighing. The last time Angie had used YouTube, she'd attempted to build a coffee table out of old wooden pallets. It hadn't gone well. And she'd needed stitches.

"I know how to do drywall," Finn said. Exactly as he knew she'd expected him to. She knew him. And she knew that he would never let her near drywall paste. But she didn't have to talk him into this. That theater mattered to her, so it mattered to him. And she'd written a play that was actually going to be performed onstage. He was still amazed by that. "You know you can just ask me," he added.

She was frowning, though. "You don't have to do that."

"It's not a problem."

"I don't think it's a good idea," Angie said. "We'll work it out. I shouldn't have said anything."

He looked at her. Okay, what the hell was going on? She always wanted—or at least accepted—his help.

"Well, I'm involved now," he said resolutely. "Tell Sophia she's got two more big strong guys coming to her rescue."

"Finn, I really don't—"

"No worries, Ma," he said. "I'm on it."

He heard her heavy sigh as he headed for the front door. Now he was really curious about this theater and the people there.

He pulled his phone out and dialed his brother as he strode to his truck. Angie didn't like to bother them at work, so she wouldn't call Colin right away. Probably. But Finn wasn't taking the risk.

"What's up?" Colin answered a moment later.

"Whatever Mom says, your answer is, 'I'm with Finn.'" Colin chuckled. "Always."

"I'm serious."

"Okay. What happened?"

"Well, how do you feel about doing some manual labor for a good cause?" Finn asked. "And I should inform you, your answer is, 'Sure.'"

* * *

The front door of the Birch Playhouse was unlocked, but there were no people in the lobby when Finn stepped inside.

"Hello?" It was pretty quiet, but he heard the sounds of…birds chirping. He frowned and headed deeper into the theater. As he drew closer to the office door where he'd seen the computers and safe last night, he also heard the sound of a rushing stream. What the hell?

He stepped through the doorway. "Hello?"

No answer, but the birds and water were much louder now, and he also heard crickets. Really loud crickets. He turned the corner to an inner room and came up short. There was a woman sitting on a pink yoga mat next to the desk, her back to the door.

She was dressed in a sports bra and shorts, her blond hair piled on top of her head in a knot. And she was not at all the older, grandmotherly type he'd been expecting to find at the theater.

Not that he was complaining.

She had her legs crisscrossed, her hands resting on her knees. He'd seen the pose before and knew it had something to do with meditation.

He didn't want to interrupt or startle her, so he decided to wait.

He knew he should go out in the lobby. Or that he should leave and come back. Or leave and call later. But he hesitated in the doorway. It might have been that he didn't want to risk his mother getting to Sophia first and convincing her friend not to let him and Colin pitch in. Or it might have been that there was a lot of creamy skin on display and he was, after all, a guy.

But he only lingered for another thirty seconds. Or so. He was just turning away when he heard, "Just *fucking breathe*, for God's sake."

For a moment Finn thought she was talking to him. It was good advice. But then he realized that she was self-coaching. Or something. She was talking to herself, anyway.

He propped a shoulder against the door frame. Yeah, he was going to wait. Right here.

She pulled in a deep breath, her shoulders rising, and rolled her head. Tendrils of long blond hair escaped the bun on top of her head and brushed against the smooth skin of her neck. Her hips flared below the curve of her waist, and the muscles that bracketed her spine were taut. And Finn wanted to run his hand over them.

That was a very strange and out-of-character urge. But out-of-character urges were becoming uncomfortably common in the past few hours. He'd been thinking about the woman from last night and all her gloriously smooth, bare skin far too much. And now he wanted to touch this woman too? He wanted to feel her muscles flexing, the warmth of her body, and the satiny texture of her skin. That was really creepy and stalkerish. He straightened. It was one thing to notice a woman was beautiful...and not wearing many clothes. It was another to watch her without her knowing it. And imagine touching her. A lot. Yeah, he was going to go now. And quite possibly *not* come back after all.

"*Dammit.*" Suddenly the woman slumped forward, her forehead to her mat.

He paused midturn. Was she okay? Should he...

"Fuck, fuck, fuck." She bumped her forehead against the mat as she said each *fuck*.

Finn couldn't help but smile slightly. Clearly the meditation wasn't going that well.

"Screw this," she said, pushing herself up from the mat. She stomped to the stereo system and hit a button. The gentle, if loud, nature sounds were instantly replaced by the pounding sound of good old hard rock. AC/DC to be exact.

Finn felt his eyes widen as she turned toward a freestanding punching bag in the corner of the room. He hadn't noticed it before now. Of course he hadn't had his eyes off the woman and her back—which was still weird—so he hadn't noticed much about the office. She pulled on boxing gloves and began to punch and kick at the bag with impressive form. This was obviously not a new activity. Her punches and jabs were perfect, and her kicks were spot-on.

And if he'd liked her firm, smooth back muscles in a sitting position, watching them stretch and tighten as she kickboxed was so much better. The punches showed defined shoulder and upper back muscles as well. The kicks drew his attention to her hips, which were curvy but firm. And her footwork brought his attention to her calves and thighs and ass, and yeah, he wanted to touch those too. It didn't help that Brian Johnson was singing about American thighs just then.

He was going to wait in the lobby. Because even though he wasn't as creepy as he seemed at the moment, if she saw him, she'd not only assume he was weird, she'd probably also kick his ass.

Just then she pivoted to the other side of the bag, punched twice, and then lifted her leg for a roundhouse kick. But as she balanced, she must have caught him out of the corner of her eye. She gasped, and her leg completely missed the bag. She stumbled, her momentum making her pitch forward. She caught herself with her hands flat on the floor, but Finn had already taken a first instinctual step toward her. Before he could say or do anything, however, she righted herself and pushed her hair back from her face. She stared at him for a moment.

And he knew instantly who she was.

The crazy woman from last night.

This was the woman who'd gone back into a burning building and then ditched him in the crowd after he'd saved her ass.

And she was a blonde. The rest, however, was exactly as he remembered it. Curvy, firm, with smooth, creamy, pale skin. The skin he'd just been obsessing over was the same skin he'd been obsessing over since last night. And the memory of it was seemingly seared into his palm and his mind. And damned if that didn't sound creepy as hell too.

He frowned. She frowned. And then she turned and jabbed a finger at the stereo, cutting AC/DC off midwail.

"You scared the shit out of me."

"Yeah. Sorry. I knocked but you didn't hear me over the...crickets." Which was kind of funny, actually, considering crickets generally signified peace and quiet.

When the corner of her mouth curled slightly as well, Finn relaxed a little. He remembered her feistiness from the night before, the way she'd given him a hard time and had then gone all soft. He was, of course, suspicious of the soft side, as he'd told her, but he couldn't help but like it.

"I was..." She looked around. "You heard the crickets too?"

He nodded.

"How long have you been standing there?"

Downplay the creep factor, Kelly. "Just long enough to know that the deep breaths weren't doing the job."

She sighed. "Yeah. There's something wrong with me. Kicking the crap out of a punching bag relaxes me, and chirping birds are like fingernails on a chalkboard."

He laughed. "If it makes you feel better, I don't think I could get my legs crossed into that position on the floor if there was a million bucks riding on it. Not everyone is made to meditate."

She studied him for a moment. Then said, "You don't seem too irritated."

"Irritated?" He was horribly distracted, actually. He was having a hard time not staring at her stomach. And wondering just what in the hell was wrong with him. He wanted to run his hand over her abs too.

He was a perv. He'd always thought he was a nice guy who respected women and considered physical attraction natural and normal. And he'd always thought he was an ass man. Now, with this woman, he was weird and into backs and abs.

"You're not here because I dodged you last night after the fire?"

Right. The giving-her-wig-and-robe-to-someone-else-to-throw-him-off thing. "I didn't love that, but I can take a hint. I didn't know you'd be here today," he told her.

He had briefly thought about the fact that, if she was a regular at the theater, he might run into her over the days it would take to do the cleanup and repairs. But then he'd reminded himself that she had gone to great lengths to be sure he didn't find her after the fire was out. So he'd written her off. Or tried to, anyway. Apparently her *skin*, for fuck's sake, had made a deeper impression than he'd realized.

"You didn't come to talk to me?" she asked.

"I came to talk to Sophia, actually," he told her. "Or maybe to warn her." He gave her a little smile.

She frowned in return. "Warn her? About what?"

"I've mobilized a group of volunteers to come help with the cleanup and repair," he said. "They'll do great work. But they're kind of rowdy. Just thought she should be prepared. And I realize I should have asked her, but things tend to kind of snowball with these people."

That was an understatement. Not only was Colin a firefighter, but three of their cousins were as well. Michael, Ian, and Matthew had agreed to help, as had five other guys on the crew. Not to be outdone, Finn had called Tripp, and they'd recruited six more cops. As soon as his uncles and other cousins heard about the situation, they'd easily have five more guys.

"You mobilized a group of volunteers?" she asked with a frown. "Why would you do that?"

"This place is really important to my mom, and she has a lot of people who care about her and who owe her favors of one kind or another." Angie cooked, sewed buttons back on, visited people in the hospital, gave advice about everything from birthday gifts to girlfriends, and generally just made everyone feel better. "So they want to help get things fixed up so that the next play can go on as planned."

She was staring at him now. "When you say a group of volunteers, what are we talking here?"

"Probably twenty guys, give or take."

Her eyebrows rose. "And they know what they're doing? Tools and construction and stuff?" she asked.

"Absolutely."

With that she gave him a big, stunning smile. And Finn felt like she'd punched him in the gut. Holy crap. That was the kind of smile that made a man want to keep doing whatever caused it, over and over and over again.

"That's amazing," she said. "Honestly. I don't know who your mom is or why you have so many friends with hammers, but I'm so grateful. I don't know what to say."

She didn't have to say anything. If she kept looking at him like he'd just saved the day, he was going to be very happy he'd come down here.

"You might know my mom," he said. "She's here a lot. Angela Kelly."

The huge, bright smile dropped away instantly. "*Angie* is your mom?"

He nodded. Uh-oh. She didn't look thrilled anymore. What was the problem here? It was rare that someone didn't like Angie. But Finn could imagine that her propensity for meddling and butting in could rub someone the wrong way. And not all of her advice was solicited. "You do know her then?"

"Well, yeah, of course I know her," the woman said. "But you're her *son*?"

"Finn," he said.

"*You're* Finn?" she asked, looking even more alarmed now.

"Yes." He frowned. "Is everything okay?"

"But you're..."

He waited for her to finish that thought, but instead she just started shaking her head.

"No way," she finally said. "No way."

"Sorry." He shrugged. "It's true."

"But the way she talks about you..." The woman trailed off again.

But she was not getting away with that. "What does she say about me?" He didn't like this a bit. First his mom had acted strange about him coming down here to help out, and now this woman, who clearly knew Angie well enough for her to have been talking about her sons, was obviously flabbergasted by his offer to help. What the hell?

She finally seemed to really look at him and notice that he was scowling.

"She just said that theater isn't really your thing and that you weren't interested in coming to any of the plays," she said. "She told me she doesn't share much about all of this with you, so I'm surprised you'd be here to help us get back on our feet."

He was insulted. "Well, apparently it's true that she doesn't share much about it because I had no idea that she would be so broken up about you having to cancel some shows, but she was. So here I am. Now can you please help me find Sophia so I can clear all of this with her?"

The woman crossed her arms. "I'm Sophia."

He frowned at her. "Seriously? Come on."

Her eyes widened. "Excuse me?"

"Look, I can tell that you're feeling protective of my mom and maybe you feel that way about Sophia too, but I promise you, I'm here to help."

She shook her head. "I am Sophia, Finn. Everyone calls me Sophie. But I'm the Sophia you want to talk to."

He stared at her. "But..." What? That made no sense. Except... why didn't it? She'd been here last night. She'd known her way around the theater. She was here now. She knew his mom. Oh yeah, because in his head she was supposed to be seventy-plus years old.

"You're the Sophia Birch that owns this theater?" he asked.

"Yes."

"But I...looked you up," he finished, realizing he might sound like an idiot.

One of her eyebrows arched. "You looked me up?"

"I looked up Sophia Birch. After my mom started spending so much time here," he said. "I wanted to know who she was hanging out with all the time."

"And what did you find?" she asked.

"A sweet woman with white hair and a big smile and... eyes just like yours." There, *now* he officially sounded like an idiot.

She gave him a small smile. "That was my grandmother, Sophia Birch. She owned this theater for almost forty years."

"And then passed it on to you."

"Yes," Sophie said with a nod.

"I'm sorry," he said sincerely. "I've been thinking about Sophia, my mother's friend, as a much older woman."

Sophie nodded, but she looked as if she was fighting a smile. He had to ask. "What?"

"Just that...you're a cop, right?"

"Yes."

"And you did some research on someone to make sure your mom was safe."

"Yes."

"But the research didn't include the fact that the woman you were looking for has been dead for three years?"

"I—" But he had nothing to say. She was right. "I looked up the theater, saw her name was associated, figured it was all legit, and yeah, I guess I didn't dig very deep."

"I'm not saying you should have," she told him. "Your mother is a grown woman, capable of making decisions about her activities and relationships, right?"

"You would think," he said, almost to himself.

But she heard. "You don't think she's capable?"

"Well, now that I'm talking to one of her best friends, I should probably watch what I say."

Sophie nodded. "Probably."

"Because your loyalty is definitely with her," he said, watching her face.

"Definitely."

She said it firmly, her eyes meeting his directly, and Finn decided he really liked her. She was a loyal friend to his mother. Even if she was forty-some years younger than he'd thought. "So I'll just say that my mother lets her heart lead her more often than her brain," he said.

Sophie's face relaxed into a smile. "Yes, she does. It's one of the things I love most about her."

"And it's one of the things that makes me worry about her the most."

"I can understand that."

"You don't worry about her?"

Sophie's smile grew. "I don't have to."

"No?"

"She's got you."

He couldn't explain what was happening, exactly, but he felt *something* happening between them. Sharing a love for his mother—was that something that would make someone more attractive to him? Apparently. He had never met a woman who already knew his mother this well. Someone who was protective of her, even to the point of defending her to *him*.

"She's talked about me a lot?" he asked.

Sophie laughed. "*A lot*. Colin too."

"And you've known her for how long?"

"A little over a year."

"She talks about you a lot too," he told her.

"Clearly she doesn't talk about how young and energetic I am," Sophie said drily.

He laughed. "The funny thing is, she probably has. The image in my mind was of an older woman, but someone with tons of energy and enthusiasm."

Sophie looked touched by that. "That's really nice."

But something was bugging him. The more he thought about how often his mother mentioned Sophia and how much time she spent with her, the stranger it became that he had never actually met this woman. "Do you think it's odd she's never introduced us?" he finally asked.

"No," Sophie said.

But that was all she said.

"Really?"

"Really."

He should probably leave it at that if she didn't want to elaborate, but he was a Kelly. Kellys didn't leave things alone. "Why is that?"

Sophie lifted a shoulder. "Because you have a great big family and your mom wants you to meet someone special and fall in love and get married and have a bunch of grand-babies for her to spoil."

"Well, um, yeah. I guess."

"And she knows that I don't...do that."

"Do what?"

"The whole family thing."

Finn frowned. "So you think she just figured there was no point in introducing us if you didn't want to get married and have kids?"

"And because I have pretty firm personal rules about getting involved with guys who are close to their families."

"You like jerks who are loners?"

She smiled. "Kind of. Yeah."

Well, that ruled him out. He was a nice guy—he couldn't help it. And he hadn't been alone since...he could barely remember. He lived alone, but between work and family things, he was rarely there when he wasn't asleep. "But you do date?"

"Yes."

"Even though you're not interested in anything serious?"

"Yes. And most of the guys are fine with having a lot of sex and not introducing me to their mothers."

Wow. Finn coughed slightly. "Okay." Then he shook his head. "Really? You just date for sex?"

"Dating can be fun. Especially if the guy isn't interested in getting married either. So I also date for...fun." She smiled. "But I don't really need a boyfriend. I have the theater and my friends here to share my work and interests, and I have my roommates for companionship, and so... yeah, mostly for sex."

"And my mom knows this?" They were *really* good friends in that case.

Sophie laughed. "I've never said it quite that way. She just knows that I cut her off pretty quick when she started talking about her handsome, sweet, successful sons."

"You specifically didn't want to meet me?" He felt... offended, he supposed.

"Or Colin. Or any of her amazing nephews, if that's any consolation," Sophie said with a smile.

So she was...cold. Or incredibly introverted. Or shallow. But none of those really seemed right. Which was crazy. He didn't know her. But Angie knew her. And, more, loved her. There was no way Sophia Birch was cold or shallow.

And what the hell did he care if Sophie didn't want to get married or have kids? She was a beautiful woman with a kick-ass uppercut, but that didn't override the rest. He hadn't been serious about anyone in a long time, but he had definitely not ruled out marriage and kids and all of that. In fact, he had always just kind of assumed that would all happen. Eventually.

"Besides," Sophie said, "you're not into theater at all. Like to the point that your mom has never invited you to see a show she's in. I own a theater. This is what I do for a living. We don't have a lot in common."

Well, that was a good point. But suddenly he had an urge to watch a musical or three. Yep, this day was really weird.

"I think I'm being judged unfairly," Finn said.

"Oh?"

"I just think I haven't had the right exposure to theater before this."

"What's your exposure been?" she asked, looking amused.

"Playing a puppy when I was six." He couldn't believe he'd admitted that. Again. "Crawling around on hands and knees, barking. Traumatizing stuff. So much so that I've blocked most of it out."

She nodded. "I understand. You probably need to give it another chance."

Maybe she'd give *him* a chance. The thought flashed through his mind. Maybe he'd like theater. Or maybe this was an opposites-attract thing. That seemed more likely. Or hell, maybe they could just date for the sex.

"Okay, yes, I'll go to a play with you sometime," he said. "I'll even buy. But you have to sit close and explain stuff to me that I don't understand."

She looked confused for one second, and then her lips curled. "You thought I was asking you out?"

"Oh, you're *not* dedicated to helping people learn about the theater and fall in love with your greatest passion?" he teased.

She tipped her head. "You like chocolate martinis?"

"Um…what?"

"Those are probably my greatest passion."

He chuckled. "Never had one of those either."

"Hmm, so many things to help you learn to be passionate about."

Heat streaked through his gut. Yeah, he definitely wanted to try something new. Like dating for sex. In fact, that sounded like a hell of an idea. "So it's a date."

"Well, it would be, except for one very important detail," she said.

"What's that?"

"I don't date guys with huge families who are involved in everything they do. And whose mother I adore."

"Okay, I get it," he said honestly. "That could be messy." He sighed. "Especially with *my* family."

"I haven't met any of your family, but I've heard stories." She was grinning again.

"They're all true."

"You should still really try a chocolate martini and a play sometime, though."

"I have a feeling I won't like either one without you."

She gave a little snort. "You just met me."

"Yeah, weird, right?"

"Yeah."

He shrugged. "It's been a weird day. I'm kind of getting used to it."

"Do you always just say exactly what you're thinking and feeling?"

"Do you mean am I always honest?" he asked.

She hesitated and then nodded. "Yeah."

"Yes."

She gave him another bright smile, but it was smaller than the one that had kicked him in the gut. It still made him feel as if there were less oxygen in the room, though.

"Then I'll be honest too. This is the first time I've wished I didn't love your mom so much."

"Sophie! We're here!" someone called from outside the office.

"Be right out!" she answered, her eyes still on Finn. "My friends. The cleanup crew *I* recruited," she told him.

"Got it. My guys should be here any minute too." He was disappointed they were no longer alone. Which was stupid. Then he thought about that. "Hey, were you here alone before I showed up?"

"Yes."

He frowned. "You were here, all by yourself, front door unlocked, stereo turned up so loud that I was able to watch you for...a while...before you even knew I was here?"

She arched an eyebrow. "For a while? How long were you standing there, anyway?"

"Long enough. Doesn't matter. It would have taken a fraction of that time to hurt you. Are you here alone often?"

She shrugged. "This is where I work. The rest of the people in and out of here are volunteers."

"I don't like it," he said flatly. He felt his frown deepen. "Anyone could walk in off the street and do God knows what." Finn was shocked by how tense he suddenly felt. Sophie could kick the stuffing out of her boxing bag, but he could have clocked her over the head or grabbed her from behind before she had even a prayer of doing any damage of her own. "You need someone here with you. Or the door locked. At least. Where do you park? Do you call someone before you leave so they know you're on your way home?"

Sophie's eyes were wide. "I...do lock the door. Sometimes. And I park on the street."

"Do you know the people who run the other businesses

nearby? And please tell me you're not out after dark on your own."

"Finn, I—"

"Do you always have the music that loud?" He scowled at the stereo. "That's not safe. It's better than earbuds, but keep it down. And lock the damned door."

God, if she was anything like his mother, then she was a sunny optimist who believed the best about everyone else and went along in her own little world, never thinking something bad could happen to her. Fuck. He hated when his mom went out on her little missions, and now there was Sophie, his mom's BFF, to worry about too.

"But...my friends were on their way," she finally said carefully, as if anticipating another lecture.

"So they could be the ones that called the cops when they found your dead body?" he asked.

Her mouth dropped open, and Finn swore under his breath. Dammit. He was getting all worked up. He sucked air in through his nose and then blew it out slowly. "I just mean, you really shouldn't be here alone with the door unlocked. As a cop, I need to say that."

Right. But he hadn't been talking as a cop. That realization was unavoidable. He would have likely said the same things to anyone, but he was pretty sure his heart wouldn't have been pounding this way with anyone else.

There were several beats of silence, and then Sophie said, "So this is the real you."

"What?"

"Last night when you were hauling me out of here, your jaw was tight like it is now and you were all bossy and growly. And now this."

"I was doing my job—last night and now."

She didn't look convinced. "Last night you said you were sure the real me was the feisty side because when people react emotionally, that's when they're most true. So the real you is this bossy, protective side."

Well, shit. He could hardly deny it. The flirting and asking her out had all been real too, but yeah, he was much better at being bossy than he was at being charming. "You really need to lock your door when you're here alone," he repeated.

"Yeah, I heard you."

"Are you going to do it?"

"Are you going to come by and keep an eye on me every night if I don't?"

As if someone had touched a match to a wick, something flared between them. Hell yeah, he'd come by and keep an eye on her. Both of them. Not to mention his hands. "You in the market for a bodyguard, Feisty?"

She looked him up and down. Slowly. Blatantly. "Well, that would be one way to see you that wouldn't involve dating your whole family and potentially upsetting your mother."

Damn. That was the best plan he'd heard in a really long time. "Couldn't drink chocolate martinis if I was working."

"Then I might just have to go further down my list of passions to teach you about then."

"Sophie, let's go!" a man's voice yelled from the lobby. "We need the lights on!"

That seemed to shake her out of...whatever this was. She blinked and took a deep breath and then reached for a zippered hoodie hanging on the back of her desk chair. As she slipped into it, Finn realized he hadn't taken a deep breath for several minutes. This woman had him all twisted up. And he'd known her for maybe a half hour. But Sophia Birch had been doing the unexpected since he'd first seen her in the crowd last night. "Maybe we should talk about this later," he said, not quite ready to let it go.

She smiled. "Hmmm. I guess. If you promise to never propose, you might even get me to lock the door."

CHAPTER FOUR

*W*hat the *hell* was she doing? Sophie wondered as she stepped past Finn and out into the lobby where Kiera, Maya, Rob, and Zach were gathered. She hadn't even wanted to meet Finn. For a year she'd avoided him and his whole family on purpose. And now she was flirting with him? Stupid, stupid, stupid.

"Hi, guys," she said, pulling the zipper up on her hoodie. "I'll get the lights on."

But no one moved. They were all looking over the top of her head. At Finn. She sighed.

"Hey, everyone," he greeted. "I'm Finn Kelly."

His deep voice made Sophie want to sigh in a whole different way. Which took her right back to how crazy she was acting. One minute she was telling Finn all the reasons she couldn't have chocolate martinis with him—all very legit, honest reasons, by the way, including that she didn't know how to do the family thing and Finn Kelly, by all accounts anyway, had big-loud-overly-involved family in his blood. And the next minute she was telling him she'd be happy to be locked inside the theater with him after hours. Which was also honest.

What. The. Hell.

"Hi, Finn. I'm Zach Ashley. You look familiar," Zach said as he stuck out his hand for Finn's.

"I'm with the BPD," Finn told him, taking his hand. "You're an EMT, right?"

And the cop thing did it for her too, Sophie acknowledged.

Zach nodded. "Yep, that's it. I don't think we've ever met formally, but I've seen you around. Nice to meet you."

"You too."

"So what are you doing here?" Zach asked. "Are you investigating the fire?"

Finn glanced at Sophie. "No, but have you heard anything? I can make a call to see who was assigned to it."

She shook her head. "The insurance adjuster and the fire investigator have both been here, but I haven't heard anything back from either of them." She'd been eager to get the visit over with. She needed that insurance check. She'd been surprised when the investigator said that it was going to take a few days to finish his report.

"I'll check into it when I get back to the station," Finn promised. He frowned slightly but didn't say anything more.

"So if you're not here about the fire, why are you here?" Maya asked.

Sophie shot her a look. She could hear the tone of Maya's voice. The tone that said Maya had her own ideas about why Finn was here.

"He is here about the fire," Sophie said. "Kind of. He

was here last night, and he came by to offer some help in
the cleanup."

"My brother is a firefighter," Finn added. "We both got
some buddies to come and help out."

"Wow," Zach said. "That's really great of you."

"It is," Maya agreed. "But why? Do you guys do this
often?"

"My mom is really involved in the theater," Finn said.
"She was pretty upset about all of this and the fact that
Sophia—Sophie—might have to push some shows back."

Sophie caught Maya watching her with round eyes.
Yeah, yeah, Finn was really hot. She knew exactly what
Maya was thinking. "This is Angie's oldest son," Sophie
said, giving Maya the big round eyes right back.

Everyone knew Angie. And Maya and Kiera would understand why it didn't matter that Finn was big and hot and
bossy. They didn't know all the details of her childhood
and her father's shenanigans, but they knew about her mom
and her stepmoms. They also knew that the one thing she
wanted more than anything else was a mom-daughter relationship. And that she'd found it with Angie.

"You're Angie's son?" Kiera asked with a little laugh.
"Well, that explains a lot."

Sophie frowned at her, but Kiera was watching Finn.
Sophie wanted to watch Finn.

Thankfully, he was behind her, so she wouldn't embar-
rass herself in front of her friends by acting all starry-eyed
over him. Because she would have. And they'd have noticed. It just figured that the first guy she'd been attracted
to in way too long would be Angela Kelly's son.

Actually, it did figure. Angie was wonderful. Of course
her son would be wonderful. It was startling how many

things Sophie knew about him already, both from what Angie had told her and from things she just assumed because she knew Angie.

"It explains a lot?" Finn repeated. "Uh-oh."

Sophie could tell he was smiling. She'd known him for a little over an hour total and she could already hear the smile in his voice? Crap. She could *not* develop a crush on Angie's son.

Kiera shook her head. "I mean that as a total compliment. Your mom is always taking care of Sophie. It doesn't surprise me that she asked you to come and help out."

Angie *was* always taking care of Sophie. And Sophie loved it. After not letting anyone take care of her for years, Angie had swept into Sophie's life and loved her in spite of Sophie's insistence that she didn't need it or want it. How Angie had done that still baffled Sophie. When she'd met Angela Kelly, she hadn't been a vulnerable little girl who just wanted a mom to read her bedtime stories. She'd been a jaded adult who had convinced herself that she was better off without family. But Angie didn't stay at arm's length. Literally or figuratively. She'd enfolded Sophie in a hug within five minutes, and Sophie had felt her cynicism and stubbornness melt away.

So she absolutely could not risk breaking Angie's son's heart…or falling for him and having her heart broken. Which was a crazy thing to think was even a chance after just meeting him, but yeah—it seemed possible. Very possible.

"Funny you should say that," Finn told her. "My mom has actually never once invited me down to the theater, and I realized today that she's purposefully kept me from meeting Sophie."

Kiera looked surprised, but Maya grinned.

"You must be a womanizer or something," Maya said.

Sophie frowned at her friend, but she heard Finn laugh. The sound was husky and rolled over her like a soft touch. She consciously worked not to shiver in delight.

"Why do you say that?" he asked.

"Well, like I said, Angie takes care of Sophie. There must be a reason she hasn't introduced you," Maya said. "Do you drink, gamble, sleep around?"

"On occasion, no, and define *sleep around*," Finn replied.

Sophie wanted to turn around and see the grin she knew was stretching his face, but she kept her feet planted. "Maya—"

Maya waved her hand in a shushing gesture. Sophie sighed. If Maya wanted to give Finn the third degree, then she'd give him the third degree. And there was no way Kiera, Zach, or Rob would step in to stop her. They all looked highly entertained.

"Okay, let's see...a different woman every night," Maya said.

"Then no."

Sophie couldn't help it. She was a little interested in this.

"Okay, the same woman for a few nights but you don't even know her last name," Maya said.

"Always get a last name," Finn replied easily.

He didn't sound offended. And Sophie supposed that if he was, he could always leave, which would make her life a lot easier.

"Okay, so you see the same woman for at least a few nights, you know her last name and even where she works, but you never talk about anything deeper than the weather and you basically just go straight to the bedroom?" Maya asked, mischief in her eyes.

Sophie felt a very unwelcome and completely idiotic jolt of jealousy shoot through her at the idea of Finn going straight to the bedroom with anyone, and she frowned harder at Maya. Maya needed to stop giving Finn a hard time. And she needed to stop giving Sophie things to be idiotic about.

"You think my mother didn't introduce me to Sophie because I'm not creative enough to use other rooms of my house?" Finn asked, sounding amused.

Sophie pulled in a quick breath and then worked to cover the fact by coughing lightly. She wasn't opposed to hot sex on the living room couch or even the kitchen table, of course, but she didn't think she'd complain much in Finn's bedroom.

And those were *exactly* the kinds of thoughts she shouldn't be having.

Maya grinned. "Okay, fair enough. But you never introduce the women you . . . get creative with . . . to your mother, right?"

Sophie almost groaned. She didn't want to listen to this. But she really, really did at the same time.

"You're right on that one," Finn agreed.

Maya looked intrigued. Hell, Sophie *was* intrigued.

"Well, there has to be something wrong with you," Maya concluded. "Angie loves Sophie like a daughter. If she's keeping you apart . . ." She trailed off. "That's it," she said. "She thinks of Sophie as a daughter and you as a son . . . Obviously she can't handle the idea of you two being together like that."

Like that. Two simple words, a vague phrase, but Sophie felt heat curl through her stomach. She wanted to be with Finn *like that.* And she'd just met him. And had a hundred great reasons not to. Maybe she'd inhaled a bunch of toxic fumes in the fire. That would make more sense than all of this.

Before either of them could address Maya's comment, the front door of the theater banged open, and the lobby filled with guys. Big, loud guys. With tools. And they just kept coming, until the lobby was crammed full with noise and muscles.

Typically Sophie would have shared a holy-crap look with Kiera and Maya at a time like this. But she was having a hard time looking away. She assumed Kiera and Maya were similarly afflicted. Of course, they were both madly in love now. Maybe that kept them from looking at other men.

For some reason her gaze skipped to Finn. And she realized that her friends could absolutely appreciate all the guys surrounding them like a wall of testosterone while still really only wanting one man.

Sophie shook her head. Wow. She'd never before felt anything close to the spark she felt with Finn. This had to be a case of wanting what she couldn't have. Or the things Angie had told her about Finn. Or his smile.

That smile broke over his face as he greeted his friends. Yeah, it was at least in part his smile.

Finally Finn quieted them down. He turned to her. "Sophie, these are my friends and family and coworkers. Guys, this is Sophie. She owns the theater."

"Wait. Sophie?" one of the men asked. "Like short for Sophia?"

The man asking was at the front of the crowd and looked a lot like Finn—dark hair, good-looking, and built tall and solid. But his smile seemed to come more easily. And he had his mother's eyes. She nodded and smiled. "I'm Sophie Birch. And I'm guessing you're Colin."

Colin laughed, the sound low and husky. And it did nothing to make her heart beat faster the way Finn's did. Which was good, Sophie told herself. He was Angie's son too, so also off-limits. But one of the *other* guys could have a sexy voice and a great ass and gorgeous dark eyes, couldn't he?

"So you're Mom's Sophia."

Sophie's attention swung back to Colin—making her aware her eyes had wandered to Finn again.

She was Angie's Sophia, and that made her heart beat faster too. In a whole other way, of course. But she loved Angie, and more, she was loved by Angie. Sophie gave Colin a big smile. "Yes."

"And that means you know that I'm the sweet one," Colin said, moving in and extending his hand as if he wanted to shake hers.

Sophie laughed and took his hand. She did know that, in fact. "You're also the big talker." Colin was the charmer, the joker, the laid-back, easygoing one. Finn was…none of those things. He was the serious, responsible one. Except that in her office earlier he'd seemed a little flirtatious. Until he'd gotten all gruff and protective.

Again her mind wandered to the big guy a few feet away. She could feel his eyes on her in spite of the other guys talking and laughing with him, and knowing he was watching her made her feel jittery. Not in a bad way. At least not entirely. But she got the impression that Finn didn't miss much, and she wasn't sure she wanted him figuring her out. She was sure, however, that he wasn't missing the fact that his brother was flirting with her.

Flirting was fine. Colin was, no doubt, also a great guy. But she liked gruff and protective and responsible and serious better. She'd been raised by a laid-back charmer who was quick with a joke and flirted with anyone who'd give him two seconds of their time. And it was all fake. She had a hard time trusting charm and flirtation.

"So she did tell you all about me," Colin said, still just holding her hand. "She told me about you too. How funny and imaginative you are," he said. "I gotta admit, I have a thing for girls who like to be...creative."

Creative. The word made her thoughts bounce to Finn and the rooms in his house. And yes, she was creative, as a matter of fact. Blatant flirting and innuendo were exactly what she'd expect from Colin based on his mother's stories. Sophie opened her mouth to respond but suddenly Finn was there. Right there. Nearly on top of them and pulling their hands apart. Literally.

"Knock it off," he muttered to his brother.

Colin smirked at his brother, not seeming at all surprised that Finn was insinuating himself into their introduction. "I feel like I already know Sophia here," Colin said. "This is more like a reunion than a first meeting. Don't you agree, Soph?" he asked. "It feels like we can just skip all the small talk and get-to-know-you stuff and just jump into more serious things."

Sophie was far more intrigued by Finn's glowering at his brother than she was by Colin's invitation. "More serious things?" she asked.

"Yeah, like where you see yourself in five years, if you want a big or small wedding, how many kids you want."

Sophie wasn't even looking at the man who wanted to talk about weddings and children. She was watching his brother's jaw tighten and his eyes narrow. Yeah, apparently serious did it for her. "I want a huge wedding and a dozen kids," she said absently.

She realized what she'd said when Finn's head snapped around and his gaze met hers. She did want a huge wedding and a bunch of kids. Deep down. Deep, *deep* down. But wanting and having were very different things. She also wanted to be able to eat an entire cheesecake by herself and lose weight. That didn't mean that she could make entire cheesecakes a part of her life plan.

So why had she said that? It was never going to happen. Not as long as she had to be worried about their grandfather conning their lunch money out of her kids. And sleeping in her guest room and sponging off her hardworking, bighearted husband who would love her more than anything. For real. Forever. Because *that* was really what she would go for. Serious or charming, responsible or carefree—none of those mattered if the guy made an honest living, cared about others, and truly, deeply loved her.

Sophie's heart felt as if it had jammed itself into her throat, making it hard to breathe and think. She stared at Finn. His family would insist on a huge wedding. And that was the craziest thought and stupidest thing to make her stomach flip over, ever.

"Having a dozen kids takes a lot of practice," Colin said.

She nodded, her eyes on Finn. It did. *A lot* of practice.

"Get to work," Finn said, his voice low and firm.

She knew that he wasn't talking to her, even though he was looking at her. Sophie felt her eyes get wide, but Colin chuckled, clearly not a bit concerned by his brother's

annoyance. Sophie wasn't exactly concerned by it. More...
captivated by it. Why was he angry about Colin talking about
how many kids she wanted to have and the practice it would
take?

But she thought she knew. This...whatever...between
them was not going to be easy to ignore or brush off.

"Okay, come on, guys," Colin said. "We've got work to
do." He gave Finn another little smirk and then winked at
Sophie. "We're here for you, Soph. No worries."

"And stop calling her Soph," Finn practically growled.

That simply made Colin grin wider as he turned and
headed toward the inner theater doors, followed by the herd
of men.

Sophie was only then aware that not only had Finn
witnessed the whole exchange with Colin and Colin had
witnessed Finn acting sort of possessive—or definitely
possessive—but so had all the other guys. And so had
Kiera and Maya.

She resisted looking at her friends. There was no good
way to explain any of this. Except for the toxic-fumes
thing. Or that Frank had stirred all of her emotions up to
the point that she wasn't sure what she was feeling and for
who. And it didn't matter. It was all moot. Finn could act
possessive of her all he wanted. She wasn't his and never
would be. The pang in her chest at that thought was probably just heartburn or something.

Finn watched over his shoulder until the door bumped
shut behind them. Then he focused on her. "Don't flirt with
my brother."

She arched a brow. "I think he was flirting with me."

Finn gave a single nod. "He was."

"And you didn't like it."

"Not even a little."

She felt a swoop in her stomach but tried not to show it. "Because it would upset your mom?" The mom who was the reason she shouldn't step closer to him.

"My mom would totally expect that from Colin," Finn said.

"So you didn't like it because your brother is mostly full of crap and didn't mean it and you don't want me to be let down?"

His eyes narrowed slightly. "He is mostly full of crap, but I think he meant an awful lot of that."

"So why didn't you like it?" And why was she poking at this? It. Didn't. Matter.

"Because I saw you first."

Oh, *that* was why she was poking. She'd really wanted to hear him say something possessive. Which was ridiculous. She shouldn't like that. She certainly shouldn't encourage it. But no one had ever been possessive of her before.

"But I told you that nothing can happen," she reminded him. And she realized she kind of wanted him to argue with her. And convince her that it would be okay.

He took a deep breath and let it out. "Yeah."

Her heart sank. Also ridiculous.

"But that doesn't seem to matter when I see another guy holding your hand."

And her heart bounced up again. A little. With caution.

"I won't hold your brother's hand anymore," she said.

"Or anyone else's."

Sophie fought a smile. "Ever?" Again with the poking. What was she doing?

Finn's eyes darkened, and he took the tiny step that

brought them closer. The one she hadn't been willing to take. "That would be preferable, yes."

"You shouldn't say stuff like that to me."

"I know."

There was that raw honesty again. That put-it-all-out-there. Damn, she liked that too. There was no guessing with Finn.

Then he headed into the theater.

Sophie watched him go. This was so, so bad. She could not have a huge, all-at-once, raging infatuation with Finn.

But she did.

"What was that?" Maya demanded from behind her.

Crap. Her friends were still there. Sophie turned slowly to face them. "What was what?" she asked. But no way did her voice sound as casual as she wanted it to. Not even a little.

"The holy-shit, sexual-tension, no-other-guy-can-have-you thing with Finn," Maya said.

"It's just...lust," Sophie said. She could hardly deny that there had been major sparks pinging back and forth between them. Maya and Kiera were way too observant not to have noticed, not to mention in love themselves.

"That was the hottest thing I've seen in a long time," Kiera said.

"He's very..." Maya trailed off, and Sophie filled in a few adjectives mentally.

Hot, big, bossy, intense.

"...not your type."

Sophie blinked at Maya as her friend finally finished her sentence.

"No?" Sophie asked.

"Well, actually," Maya said, seemingly thinking out

loud, "I don't know if that's true. Because I've never seen you look at a guy like you were looking at Finn."

How had she been looking at him? With drool on her chin?

"But when you do date," Maya went on, "you go out with serious, white-collar guys who are super sophisticated."

She did. For sure. She went for men completely unlike her father. They were employed in office jobs that required a lot of brainpower and gave a lot of stability. They were also very nice men, but they weren't flirts, they weren't especially funny, and they had almost no impulsiveness. She knew some women loved surprises and spontaneity. She'd had her fill of the unexpected by age sixteen.

But Finn didn't seem spontaneous. At all. He seemed... solid. Not physically—well, not *just* physically—but in that his life had a very firm foundation. He was a cop because his dad had been a cop. His whole family was in Boston and always had been. He had people who counted on him, and he never let them down.

Finn was the opposite of her father in almost every way. But...

She hated the *but*s. There were always *but*s. *But* she was single and had no plans to change that. Her father was enough of a wild card in her life. Sophie hugged herself. She simply didn't know if she could ever fully believe that someone else could give her the absolute stability she craved.

"It doesn't matter," she said, needing to end all of this before her friends put even more craziness into her head. "He's Angie's son."

"Yeah, that kind of sucks," Maya said.

"But Angie would love to have a dozen grandkids," Kiera, the gamer-girl-turned-hopeless-romantic, said.

Sophie felt her cheeks heat at the reminder of how she'd blurted out the dozen-kids thing. Then she instantly shut down every thought of just how much Angie would love that and what an amazing grandmother she'd be.

"Look, it's obviously possible to want to do dirty things to another person within five minutes of meeting them." *Or five seconds.* "But I'm not seeing baby nurseries and family Christmas photos with Finn, okay?" That damned heartburn came back, tightening her chest as she thought about babies and holidays.

Damn Frank. If only he'd just been a loser jerk who had never been able to get a girl. But no, he'd gotten them. He'd had Christmases with them. Sophie didn't remember her nursery, but she'd had a pink princess room at Maggie's. And she wanted all of that again. She wanted the home, the dinner every night, the family movie nights on the couch, the huge birthday parties.

And at the same time, she was scared of having it all...and losing it.

"But it could work out," Kiera said. "I mean, I never thought I'd fall in love either. And not with someone like Zach. But here I am."

Oh God, is Kiera thinking about baby nurseries? Sophie made herself breathe and not let on how hard the wave of jealousy had just hit her. Like a monsoon. And something else hit her too—Kiera and Maya were both moving on. They'd be getting married soon and thinking about, then having, babies. Kiera and Maya were going to have families. Homes.

Sophie took a deep, shaky breath. She was so, so happy for her friends. She wanted them to have everything they wanted and deserved. But they were *her* family. They'd been her permanence these past few years. And that had been incredibly naive of her.

The three of them weren't going to live together as roommates forever. Of course life would move on and they'd fall in love and make families and homes. And they'd leave her.

Sophie didn't resent it. But she did envy them. Deeply.

She forced a smile. "The chances of Finn being my Zach or Alex are slim," she told them. That was reality. The probability of her meeting a guy she could love and trust like Kiera and Maya did Zach and Alex was small to start with. The odds of that guy being Finn Kelly were... a billion to one. And she wasn't a gambler.

CHAPTER FIVE

Twenty minutes later, Sophie had showered in the tiny shower she'd installed in the back dressing room and was in clean clothes. Her stomach was growling, but food was going to have to wait. She needed to check on things in the theater and see what the status was. There might be several big strapping men in there, but she knew that didn't mean this was all going to be an easy fix. With the way her luck ran, it was going to be anything but.

Still, she felt warm when she thought about how Finn had rallied his friends and family to help. Sure, it was technically for Angie, but Sophie's heart didn't care when it flipped over in her chest as she remembered how triumphant he'd looked when the guys had showed up.

And then thinking about Finn, in any capacity, quickly turned the warmth she was feeling to hot.

The idea of a sex-only fling just wouldn't leave her alone. It was a horrible idea, of course. She already liked him too much for that. From what she knew from Angie and what she'd already seen, liking him for only his body was not possible. No matter how spectacular that body was.

She pulled the door to the theater open, telling herself she was eager to get inside to see what was going on with her theater, her pride and joy. It had nothing to do with the big cop who was now up on a ladder, his shirt off, pounding a hammer against the drywall.

But *damn*. The sex-only-fling idea took root again immediately.

It was hot in the theater, and he wasn't the only one without a shirt and with muscles bunching and skin glistening. He was, however, the only one she wanted to lick.

"Sophie!"

She started when Maya called to her and felt her whole body flush when Finn twisted to look over his shoulder at the sound of her name. She made herself focus on where Maya and Kiera were seated, in the third row in the section of seats closest to the wall the guys were working on. There was no way he'd caught her ogling him. And no way he could tell what she was thinking from clear across the theater. And yet she had the very weird impression that he did, in fact, know all the naughty things that were tripping through her mind.

"I swear to God, you should just sell tickets to this," Maya said as Sophie took the seat next to her. Maya was holding a bag of microwave popcorn, munching away as she watched the men work.

"Why aren't you helping?" Sophie asked.

"We don't know what to do," Maya said with a shrug. "I don't know anything about drywall or electric stuff or whatever."

"Me neither," Kiera said. "I did some sweeping and picking stuff up, but they kept making it dirty again and I threw out some stuff they needed, so I just got out of the way." Kiera reached for a handful of popcorn. "And I'm not complaining about just watching. Seriously. I know lots of people who would pay big for this. Mostly female people. But still."

Sophie focused on the scene in front of her from the perspective of a woman who wasn't obsessed with the forearms—and okay, the rest of—the hot cop on the ladder.

"Not a bad way to pass a couple of hours," she had to agree. Hot men sweating, swinging tools around, and knocking things down. And laughing and talking and joking as they did it.

"This is like going to a Chippendales show but with tools and actual, you know, work," Maya said.

"Have you been to a Chippendales show?" Kiera asked, her eyes on the stage. And not just on her hot boyfriend.

"I have. But it was a little...not this," Maya said, gesturing toward the guys.

"Not this?" Sophie asked.

"It was choreographed, and the guys were oiled up and shaved, and they were kind of in-your-face."

"Isn't that what women like?" Kiera asked. "Abs and asses in their face?"

Maya laughed. "I guess. But this is *real*, you know?"

Sophie didn't know about Kiera, but *she* knew. This was real alright. Very real. "They sure didn't hesitate to take their shirts off, did they?" Sophie asked.

"It's really hot in here," Maya said. "I mean, literally." She chuckled. "But there's also a lot of testosterone in here."

"I noticed," Sophie muttered.

"So once one of them stripped down, the others had to," Maya said.

"After Maya gave him a whistle, of course," Kiera added with a grin.

"Oh, they love it. They're firefighters. They love the you're-my-hero stuff," Maya said.

"Like world-renowned pediatricians?" Sophie asked, nudging Maya with her elbow.

Maya winked. "Alex is humble."

"But he loves when *you* tell him he's a big hero," Sophie teased.

"Well, yeah. But I show my admiration in very special ways," Maya said.

Sophie looked at her friend and felt her heart warm. Maya lit up from the inside when she talked about Alex. And Sophie was so happy for her. Everyone deserved that kind of love.

"Well, I don't think the firefighters mind being half-naked and ogled," Kiera said. "They do those calendars all the time, right?"

"I've bought one every year," Maya said, tossing three kernels into the air and catching all of them in her mouth.

Sophie thought about the hot guys who didn't mind being shirtless onstage. She couldn't sell tickets to this. Could she? Well, no . . . but it was actually a brilliant idea. In theory, anyway. She couldn't quite bring herself to exploit their kindness and hard work—and she was proud of resisting that, considering her lineage—but she couldn't help that her wheels were spinning a bit. She needed money since Frank was taking half of the insurance payment, and she had no idea where it was going to come from. She couldn't just dip into her savings for all of it. But if she could do some kind of fund-raiser...

The back door to the theater banged open, and Sophie pivoted in her seat. It seemed that the doors around here were banging and thumping a lot lately. Ever since Finn had showed up.

There had also been a lot of people here since he'd shown up, she thought, as several strolled down the middle aisle. A couple carried toolboxes, but one carried a huge portable CD player and the rest all had dishes, plastic bags, and cardboard boxes in hand.

"Hey, food's here!" one of the guys from the stage yelled.

That got everyone's attention, and all Sophie could do was sit back and watch as the newcomers—men and women, a handful of younger boys, and three teenage girls—seemed to take over the space. They set dishes and casserole pans, loaves of bread and cookies, and bottles of water and a case of beer on the edge of the stage. The girl carrying the CD player looked around and found an outlet, and soon country music filled the air.

"Dammit, Zoe, *not* country!" someone yelled at her.

She propped a hand on her hip. "Why not?"

"We need rock and roll."

"Why do you need rock and roll?" Zoe asked, her ponytail swinging against her shoulder as she tipped her head.

"We're knocking shit down. You can't do that to country."

"Not even Jason Aldean?" she asked.

"Jason Aldean is drinking music," the guy said. "We're using sledgehammers here. We need Guns N' Roses."

Sophie couldn't help but nod. Guns N' Roses was an

excellent choice. If you didn't have AC/DC or Joan Jett or Mötley Crüe. She didn't even know who Jason Aldean was.

"So all country music is for drinking?" Zoe asked, grinning in spite of the fact that her music pick was being disparaged.

"Hell no," the guy said, not even bothering to watch his mouth around the girl who couldn't have been more than sixteen. Or the little boys who weren't any older than ten or eleven. "A lot of country music is for fu—loving." Ah, there, he'd caught himself.

Sophie laughed softly.

The girl rolled her eyes, clearly unfazed, and one of the guys called out, "A lot of rock music is for that too."

Sophie couldn't disagree with that either. AC/DC again. Def Leppard. The Rolling Stones. They all made her list of great sex songs. And, as was becoming quite predictable, her eyes found Finn among the crowd of hot male bodies. He was looking at her too.

"So what do you listen to when you roll out to a fire?" Zoe asked.

The firefighter grinned. "*Slippery When Wet.*"

Zoe lifted a brow. "Bon Jovi?"

Sophie was impressed a girl her age would know Bon Jovi's older stuff.

"Of course. We're all livin' on a prayer each time," the guy said with a grin.

"Aw, you guys have love songs to work to together," Zoe said.

"We've got each other, and that's a lot," another said, and all the guys laughed.

"That's kind of lighthearted for going out to a fire, isn't it?" Zoe asked.

"Yeah. And we do what we do so that the people affected by the fire can have more lighthearted times too," Colin said.

Everyone just nodded to that, and Zoe gave Colin a big, sincere smile.

"What is this?" Maya leaned in to ask.

Sophie shook her head, making herself look at her friend. "Looks like Finn's posse is even bigger than we thought."

"And they have brownies," Kiera said. "Huge frosted brownies."

They did. Along with lettuce salad, what looked like macaroni salad, mixed fruit, and, amazingly enough, not just lasagna but what appeared to be some kind of chicken Alfredo casserole.

This wasn't just people showing up with sandwiches and chips and delivery pizza the way Sophie sometimes did for the volunteers who worked on sets after hours at the theater. This was a full-on three-course dinner. For at least fifty people.

"I don't remember the last time I saw this much food," she murmured to Maya, as her stomach growled.

Maya grinned. "At a restaurant, maybe?"

Exactly. This wasn't a normal family dinner. Then again, maybe it was. This had to be Angie and Finn's family.

There was more laughing and joking as paper plates, plastic silverware, and napkins were pulled from bags and distributed. Zach pulled Kiera out of her seat to join him, and Maya got up to follow them.

"You coming?" she asked Sophie.

"Yeah. In a minute." She just needed a second to observe before she dove in. She needed to let everything kind of sink in. The theater was never this...alive. She loved the players who had a passion for acting and for this theater in particular. She loved the work that went into building sets and making costumes and staging a show. She loved working on lighting and music. But this was different. And she knew exactly what the difference was. It was the same thing that Maya had mentioned that set these guys above the Chippendales dancers. This was real.

Sure, the work that went into making a show come to life was *real*. They hammered real pieces of wood together and painted and decorated with real paint and supplies. They really sewed fabrics together to make costumes. All of that was technically real. And the people involved got along and enjoyed it. They joked and laughed and worked hard too. But it was a side project, extracurricular to their real lives—jobs, families, friends. The work they did created imaginary worlds that were temporary and brought people together who didn't spend time together outside the playhouse. There were regulars who knew one another well by now, but they still didn't have relationships in which they could call one another dumbasses or tell another member of the cast to fuck off.

These people *knew* each other. This—all of this noise and commotion and all of these relationships—was their real life. They worked together, they socialized together, many of them were related to one another. The feeling of family and familiarity was thick in the room, and Sophie felt overwhelmed by it. As well as very, very tempted.

She had a group like this with Maya and Kiera and Rob and Ben, the guys next door. Their circle now also included Zach and Alex as well as Zach's sister and even his parents at times, along with Alex's daughter and her mom. Their group also sometimes included the people who worked at Maya's martial arts studio. When they were in town, Kiera's best guy friends and bosses, Pete and Dalton, were also there.

But none of them were Sophie's.

They never made her feel left out or unwelcome, of course. She enjoyed them all and could depend on them. She considered them her makeshift family. But, maybe more than ever, she wanted to bring someone into the group who belonged to *her*, who was there because of her.

The guys loaded their plates, jostled for the brownies and cookies, kissed the cheeks of the women who'd brought the food, and acted as if eating lasagna on a theater stage with drywall dust and soot streaked on their faces and clothes was perfectly normal. Or at least no big deal.

"Hey."

She looked over her shoulder, her heart in her throat. Finn was standing in the row behind her, two plates in hand.

"Hi." She gave him a smile and wondered if it looked as wobbly as it felt.

He handed her a plate. "I didn't know what you'd like."

The paper plate was filled with a sample of everything offered. The smell of the tomato sauce, garlic, and oregano hit her, and her stomach rumbled happily.

"Any of it. All of it," she said, reaching for the plate eagerly.

He chuckled as he handed it over, and that made her hungry too—a different hungry.

"Thanks," she said, balancing the plate on her lap. "But you didn't have to do that."

"I wasn't sure if you were still over here because you

weren't hungry or because all of these jerks scared you off, or what."

He settled two seats to her right in the row behind her. She wished he'd sit closer but was also glad for the space. He made the normal-size seat look kid size, and she knew his knee would have been pressed against hers. Which would have been sweeter than the frosted brownie on her plate. And that was saying something. But why tempt herself? Finn's big, hard knee—and the rest of him—was off the menu.

Sophie shifted in her seat, turning sideways and hooking a leg over the arm of the chair so she could look at him as they ate. She ran a finger through the chocolate frosting and lifted it to her mouth. It was rich and fudgy and perfect. And she might need fifteen more if she couldn't indulge in Finn.

She heard him clear his throat, and she glanced up. His eyes were on her finger—and her mouth. That look on his face made everything in her clench. She sat up straighter. How long was this cleanup job going to take? She wasn't sure how long she could deal with this heat between them.

"Not scared off," she said, going back to what he'd said before about his family. "They're just—"

"A lot."

She smiled and nodded. "But in a good way."

Finn looked over at his family and sighed. "Ninety percent of the time I'd agree."

"Your mom says seventy-five percent."

He grinned. "That's because her house is the biggest and everyone congregates there. That means everyone can leave when they've had enough. Except her."

Sophie laughed and then took a bite of pasta salad. It

was the best pasta salad she'd ever had. Whether that was because it really was the best pasta salad ever, or because she just hadn't had a lot of pasta salad in her life, or because she was feeling included in something big and warm and familial at the moment, Sophie wasn't sure. But she was definitely feeling warm and included. And the pasta salad was amazing.

"I can't believe you asked them to bring food."

"Oh no," Finn said quickly. "This is not totally my fault. I asked my brother to bring a sledgehammer. There was no mention of lasagna."

"Ah, so I should be grateful to Colin?" she asked, taking a bite of said lasagna.

Finn's eyebrows slammed together. "*No.*"

Was it strange that when he used that tone she could feel a tingle where his hand had been on her thigh the night before?

"Then who should I thank for the twenty shirtless men, the three-course dinner, and Bon Jovi?"

The guys had all slipped their shirts back on, though a few of them hung unbuttoned, but she didn't think that would last. And, okay, she was hoping it wouldn't last. Finn was one of the guys wearing a T-shirt, so his six-pack and pecs were covered at the moment. But that didn't mean she couldn't close her eyes and conjure up the vision again in a heartbeat.

"You know how phone trees work?" he asked. "Where one person calls five people to give them news or ask for something, and those five people call five more and on and on?"

"Sure."

"That's what happens with my family."

"That's...efficient," Sophie commented, feeling equally overwhelmed and fascinated by the idea.

"It's scary," Finn said. "I think about that first phone call really hard before making it. Because nothing's ever private in this group."

"But it's nice," Sophie decided. These people weren't here to be in the way or cause trouble. They were here because they cared. One of them needed something, and the rest showed up.

"It's loud."

Well, it was that. She smiled. "But these aren't all Kellys, right?" she asked. She knew Angie was very close to her husband's family, even though he'd been gone for sixteen years, but Sophie also knew that Angie's family, her four sisters and their families, were in Boston as well.

"Nope," Finn said. "There are some Patricks and some Sullivans and some Derbys and some Hatches here too."

Wow. That was a lot of names. And people. Sophie watched them all laughing and talking. They all mingled as if one big, happy family. They also touched a lot. There was back slapping and shoulder bumping and hugging. It seemed that no one had any personal space. Or that it wasn't respected, anyway. And no one seemed to mind.

"You have that look on your face again," Finn commented.

She looked back at him. "What look?"

"That wide-eyed stare that makes you look curious... and terrified at the same time."

She laughed lightly. But he'd nailed it. "Curious and terrified" summed it up nicely.

So she'd stayed firmly away from Angie's extended

family. As soon as the stories had started and Angie had pulled up photos on her phone, Sophie had been out. She wouldn't go to Angie's house for dinner; she hadn't attended Angie's birthday party; she hadn't let Angie introduce her to any member of her family. And, because she didn't want to hurt her friend, she'd confessed to Angie early on what was behind all of that. Angie got it, and she enjoyed having the theater be her own little quiet place away from her family. It had worked for over a year now and, if not for the fire and Finn showing up like the cavalry, it would have kept working.

"I'm not used to the big-family thing," she said lightly. "I don't have any brothers or sisters, and my dad was an only child. And we're . . . not close."

Finn sighed. "Only child. Sounds like heaven."

She could tell he was only half-joking. "You don't love all of this?" she asked, waving her plastic fork in the direction of his family.

"I do. Of course," he said. "But those twenty or so people? They're only a portion of the group that not only knows everything about me, but thinks it's their God-given right to meddle in my life."

Sophie bit back the wistful sigh. Her friends were there for her, gave her advice, pep talks, whatever she needed. But they never pried. They never just showed up and burst in and took over. She should appreciate that. But instead she was jealous of Finn.

"They care about you," she said.

He nodded. "They do."

"That's nice."

"That is one word for it."

Sophie looked at that grin and realized that it was great

he was from a big, raucous family. Because *everything* else about him totally did it for her.

"So you seriously never date guys with families?"

She fought a smile. He wasn't officially asking her out, but she knew that he was feeling all the chemistry between them. It was important to nip this in the bud. She nodded. "They might have families, of course. But I never meet them. I like things quiet and low drama. I like it to just be the two of us. I don't like all the meddling."

That wasn't completely a lie. She thought she might actually kind of enjoy a little meddling, but she didn't meet the families of the men she dated. She didn't want to get close to them and then never see them again. In fact, her best relationship had been with a guy who'd been an only child and an orphan who'd grown up in the foster system. That sounded terrible, but it had worked for her not to have parents and grandparents and siblings to get attached to. She'd dated him longer than any of the other guys she'd been in relationships with. Every once in a while, a guy would decide he wanted it to go beyond the sex-only thing and have her meet his mother. That was Sophie's cue to end things.

She grimaced as she thought about her past boyfriends. She hated that it seemed like she'd inherited her father's allergy to long-term commitment. But she didn't seek out men because of what they could give her. That was the one thing saving her from stopping dating altogether.

"Well, I get not wanting to get everyone all mingled," Finn said. "I never introduce the girls I date to my family anymore."

Sophie felt her eyes widen. "Really? How do you avoid it?"

He shook his head. "My family agrees that it's a good plan."

"Really?"

"Had a bad experience with a fiancée that got very attached to them and vice versa, and when we broke up it was...bad."

She could imagine. "A fiancée?"

He nodded. "It was five years ago. But it was hard. And I realized that it's easier to just not get everyone involved in everything."

"Yep. Makes sense." She took another bite and tried to just enjoy the food. But she could admit, to herself only, that she was *really* interested in the woman Finn had been engaged to.

"So you're right that we should definitely keep it to sex only," Finn said.

Sophie almost swallowed macaroni down the wrong pipe. She coughed hard. "What?"

"Well, you've now met this bunch of yahoos, and you already know my mom. Really well."

"I do know your mom," she said with a nod. "Really well." And she needed to remember that.

"So we can't date," he summarized. "We'll have to just—"

"'Whoa, oh, oh, oh...for the longest time...'"

Sophie whipped around at the amplified sound of Billy Joel booming from the theater's sound system.

But not just Billy Joel. Colin was now crooning along with Billy Joel, looking completely at ease at the center of the stage. The guys had obviously found the sound booth and a microphone.

"Boo! Somebody shut him up!" someone shouted.

"I'm awesome, and you know it!" Colin called back.

"You suck!" someone else yelled.

Everyone laughed at that. Colin held out his hand to Kiera. "Come karaoke with me."

Sophie watched Kiera blush and decline. Emphatically. She was not the spotlight type. But Colin clearly was.

"Thank God it's not real karaoke!" someone said, turning the music up to cover Colin's singing.

Colin pulled one of his aunts onstage instead of Kiera, and they swayed and sang together as a couple of cousins came in on the background *ooh ooh*s.

Sophie glanced back at Finn. He was watching with resignation and a touch of amusement.

"You sing too?" she asked.

"Fuck no. Which is good because we've got plenty of attention whores in the family," he said.

Sophie watched Ian and Michael join Colin at center stage and couldn't help but think of Maya's words about selling tickets. This was almost better than watching them work. Hot guys without shirts on were great. But hot guys goofing around and unabashedly making fools of themselves in the name of fun was really even better.

"They're always like this?" she asked.

"Always," Finn confirmed. "Not one ounce of self-consciousness."

"They know how to have a good time," Sophie said. "That's great."

"Is it?" he asked.

"Uh, yeah. Guys who can laugh at themselves are hot."

He looked at her for two heartbeats. "Well, that's Colin. And that means he's the first one I throw out of here on his ass."

She laughed. "What? Why?"

"Because I don't think I can handle you thinking he's hot."

Sophie smiled. Colin was hot. But Finn was...more. The fun-loving type was great, but the tough-cop type was making parts of her tingle she'd almost forgotten she had.

Her thoughts were interrupted as Finn's phone rang, and he pulled it from his pocket. He answered without even looking at the display. "Kelly."

He frowned and shifted in his seat, his eyes on Sophie, and she found she couldn't look away. "Okay, I got it." He paused, listening. Then his eyes went to the charred wall behind her and he said, "Yes, we're helping out. Cleanup." He paused again. "Yeah, I understand." His gaze back on her, he said, "I can do that. Okay. Thanks."

He disconnected and took a deep breath.

"Everything okay?" Sophie felt compelled to ask.

Finn lifted a shoulder. "That was Chuck, the fire investigator."

Sophie frowned. "Is there a problem?"

"He wants us to stop work on the wall and wiring for now. He's coming back for another look."

Sophie felt her stomach twist. "Oh. Why?"

"He isn't completely confident about ruling out arson," Finn told her. He took another deep breath and then asked, "Speaking of family, is your dad in Boston?"

Her stomach knotted tighter. But no, Frank had told her he hadn't done this. The timing and his need for money were suspicious, she could admit, but he didn't lie. And, as he'd said, he was smart enough to have set the fire in the middle of the night rather than during a performance, when it had been detected quickly. Hell, the man had keys to the place. He wouldn't even have had to sneak in. He could have walked right in the front door with a can of gasoline and a box of matches.

She nodded. "He is. He's been living in Miami, but he's been back in Boston for a couple of weeks."

"Has he been here? Have you talked to him?"

She frowned. "Yes. This morning."

Finn shook his head. "I'm sorry. I just... The investigator had some questions, and he heard that I was helping out down here with the other guys, and he wanted to know what I know."

"What you know?"

"About you and your dad."

"Are we suspects?"

Finn sat forward, resting his forearms on his thighs. "You're the only two that stand to profit from the fire."

In spite of the fact that he was questioning her about possible criminal activity, she could still appreciate his honesty.

"And since they haven't ruled out arson, of course we are," she filled in.

Finn met her gaze steadily. "We just have some questions."

We. Finn and the police department and the fire department. Sophie took a deep breath. "Okay."

"Your dad hasn't been living in Boston for a while?"

She shook her head. "Four years. He was in Florida with my stepmom. He just came back to town about two weeks ago. I didn't know he was here until this morning. He came by to... check on me and the theater after hearing about the fire." Sophie realized she'd tripped a bit there and hoped Finn wouldn't notice.

But he did. "So he stopped by this morning. What did you talk about?"

She sighed. "The insurance money," she admitted. "And how to spend it."

"What did you decide to spend it on?"

"The theater." Sophie paused. No. She didn't want to lie to Finn. "Actually, we argued about how to spend it. I wanted to spend it on the repairs. He...didn't."

"What did he want to spend it on?"

She knew how bad this was going to sound even before she said it. "He's buying an RV."

Finn didn't react. Clearly he'd questioned people before. "So he came by right away and wanted the money, but not to reinvest."

Sophie nodded. "He never has invested in the theater. He doesn't care about it."

Yeah, that sounded bad too.

"So it wouldn't bother him if it burned down?" Finn asked.

She shook her head grimly. "No."

Finn leaned in a little. "Sophie, is there any chance that your father started the fire? Or had something to do with it? I know he has a record and doesn't stay in one place long, doesn't have a real solid work history."

"Or marriage history. Or any solid history of any kind," Sophie said. Then she sighed. "I know how it looks. I really do, Finn. But I flat-out asked him and he said that he'd had nothing to do with it."

That answer did get one of Finn's eyebrows to rise. "It did occur to you then?"

She gave a humorless laugh. "Definitely. Not much about my dad surprises me. But he didn't do it."

Finn was watching her carefully. "No?"

She shook her head. "Nope."

"How can you be so sure?"

"Because he told me."

Finn paused. "He told you. That's it? You believe him?"

"I do. My dad has done a lot of stupid, selfish things, and he's lied to a lot of people, but he's never lied to me. It's the one thing he's always given me—the truth."

Finn didn't really react to that, outwardly anyway, but he didn't reply right away either.

Sophie shifted in her seat so she was facing him more fully. "Seriously, Finn. If he'd told *you* that he didn't do it, I would be skeptical. But he told me. Just me. One-on-one, to my face. He's never lied to me like that. Not even in the midst of things being as crappy as they could possibly get."

"Sophie—"

"I know how it looks. I do. I get it. And in your shoes, I'd probably think the same thing. But you can trust me. He didn't do it." She knew it. She couldn't explain it. Having faith in Frank seemed so stupid. And the funny thing was, she *didn't* have faith in him. Not really. She didn't trust him with her friends; she didn't trust him not to take money right out of the safe in the office; she didn't trust him to not try to emotionally manipulate her into supporting him. But he'd also never promised her *not* to do those things. Because he couldn't keep that promise.

That was the thing—Frank didn't always do what she wanted him to do, he wasn't there for her, but he would also never make her promises he didn't intend to keep. He'd promised that he had not set the fire, and she believed him. Every time he'd promised her it was the last night they'd be sleeping in the car, it had been true. Every time he'd promised her that she would not spend Christmas in a shelter, it had been true. Every time he'd promised her that she would definitely be able to spend the entire year in one school, it had been true. And the times when it hadn't been true—the year she'd moved schools three times and the year she'd spent Christmas in a shelter with one single present donated by the Salvation Army—he hadn't made the promise.

"Sophie, I want that to be true, but—"

"Everyone's already here? Unbelievable."

The pronouncement cut off whatever Finn had been about to say. Angela Kelly had arrived, in a swirl of multicolored scarves, tinkling bracelets, and the scent of lavender.

Sophie breathed deeply of the scent that always made her smile and felt some of the tension ease out of her body. "Hi, Angie."

"Hello, darling," Angie said to Sophie. Then she turned to her son. "Finn."

"Hi, Mom."

"You just ran right over here, didn't you?" Angie asked.

Clearly unmoved by her irritation, Finn asked, "When have I ever said I was going to do something and then not done it?"

Sophie blinked at Finn's words. They were almost identical to what she'd just been thinking about her father.

Finn shoved to his feet and faced his mom.

"I'm serious, Finn. I'm not happy," Angie said.

"Okay, let's go," he said, starting down the row of chairs toward the far aisle.

"Where?" Angie asked.

"To have the conversation we're about to have in private

so that Sophie can keep believing we're both nice and reasonable."

"Why would she not believe that?"

"Because we're about to fight over her, right?" Finn asked.

Sophie felt her eyes widen. They were going to *fight*? Over her? What? "Um—" She glanced up at Angie.

Angie didn't look surprised by Finn's statement. She sighed. "Dammit. We are? Already?"

Finn nodded. "Yep." Then he continued down the row.

Angie looked back to Sophie. "Do you mind?" She pointed at the brownie on Sophie's plate.

Sophie honestly didn't know what to say or do...or think. She lifted her plate. "All yours."

Angie picked up the brownie. "If I didn't have chocolate, my family would have made me a drunk a long time ago."

"Uh, Angie?"

"Yeah, sweetie?"

"Are you and Finn really going to argue?"

"Oh yeah. And I'm very sorry they're all here like this," Angie said.

"Don't be," Sophie said quickly. "It's...great."

"Yeah. I was afraid of that," Angie said grimly, turning to follow her son.

* * *

Finn didn't want to fight with his mother. He rarely even talked back to her. His goal was to make her life easier and happier. But the idea that she'd purposefully kept him and Sophie from meeting was nagging at him more than it should.

"You tried to keep Sophie and me from meeting?" he asked, as Angie joined him at the back of the theater.

"Yes."

"Because she doesn't like guys with big families?"

Angie sighed. "Because I saw her first."

He lifted a brow. "What?"

"I already love her. So you can't mess with her."

He knew it. "So this is about Sarah."

"Yes," Angie said.

Finn knew that Angie hadn't totally forgiven him for breaking up with Sarah. She'd been the daughter of Angie's best friend, Mary. He'd known Sarah his whole life, and when things turned romantic between them, their mothers had been thrilled. They'd had the whole wedding planned by the time he took Sarah to their first prom. They'd been together for six years. Hell, even he and Sarah had thought they were going to get married. But he hadn't left her at the altar. He'd broken up with her at their engagement party.

He'd seen it in her eyes when they'd been listening to her father's toast at their party. They loved each other, but they weren't in be-together-forever love. She'd cried when he told her he thought they should end things, but not because she was hurt or angry. In relief.

Of course, her father had seen her tears and had punched Finn in the nose. That had gotten Finn's cousins and Sarah's brothers riled up, and more punches were thrown. Angie had thrown beer in Sarah's brother's face to get him off of Colin. That had caused Mary's protective instincts to flare, and she'd pushed Angie, and they'd gotten into a huge argument. A couple bloody noses, black eyes, insults, and tears later, the families had also broken up.

Angie wasn't over it. Then again, Finn wasn't completely over it. He was over Sarah, but not over their families' friendship being ruined.

"You're afraid I'll break her heart," Finn said.

"I'm afraid you'll break *my* heart."

Right. In this scenario, Sophie wasn't Sarah. She was Mary. The friend Angie had lost.

"And yes, hers. She's...had a lot of loss in her life, Finn. I don't want you and our family to be more."

Finn's whole body tightened. He was already suspicious of Sophie's father, and with the discovery that Sophie had some pain in her past and that she tried to avoid family involvement, he was having a hell of a time tamping down his curiosity and his protective urges. Hell, she was also a suspect in a possible arson. He shouldn't be feeling anything like that for her.

"I can't just be her friend?" He could do that. He could just...be there. And want to kiss her every time she smiled. Dammit.

Angie gave him a *seriously?* look. "I've got the friendship thing handled."

Finn regarded his mother for a moment. "You're protecting her."

"Yes. She needs a mom more than she needs a guy."

He stared at his mother for several long seconds. He swallowed hard. Angie was taking care of Sophie. And his urges to take care of Sophie made no sense. Stepping aside and letting Angie be the one to protect Sophie was the right thing to do.

"So I just need to let it go," he said.

"That would be wonderful."

He started to nod. His gut twisted with the idea of letting

Sophie go, but his brain was telling his gut to just chill out. Fine, he'd let her go. He'd finish the theater repair for his mom's sake and then walk out and forget about Sophia Birch. Unless, of course, he was sent to arrest her for setting the theater on fire.

He shoved a hand through his hair. She hadn't done it. He had no proof one way or another, but he had his gut, and it was telling him that Sophie would never do anything like that. Sure, she had a feisty side and, apparently, a past with some darkness in it, but no, her love for this place was evident.

Speaking of the theater and people loving it...

"Okay, so let's talk about this theater thing," he said.

"What theater thing?"

"That this place is really important to you and yet you've never invited any of us to get involved or help out or even see a show. Sophie needs help getting this place back on its feet, but you were fighting me about coming down here. That's ridiculous. We have the manpower and skills to get this done."

Angie crossed her arms. "I didn't think you would really care."

"Well, that's bullshit," he said easily. "You got interested in rescuing miniature dachshunds. I ended up with seven dogs in my house. All at the same time. You got interested in an after-school sports program for kids who have parents in jail. I coached three seasons. You got interested in making your own whiskey. I still have supplies in my basement."

Angie didn't deny any of that—she couldn't—but she stubbornly refused to agree with him.

"Mom," he said, his voice gentler, "why haven't you asked me to be involved here? And don't tell me it's because I suck as an actor because I *acted* interested in dachshunds, after-school sports programs, and whiskey."

"You still have one of the dogs," she finally said. "And you liked that sports program."

He smiled. He did have his Rosie, and he loved her. "You're right. But you didn't know that before you got me into all of it. So you really wanted to keep me away from Sophie this badly?"

"When she said that she wasn't interested in making this a family affair, I agreed," Angie said. "It came up the first time that I invited her over for a family dinner."

"She actually asked you not to invite any of us to shows?" Finn asked.

"No, not that," Angie said. "She didn't want to get involved in our family stuff. But, of course, she would have been fine with you all coming to shows."

"So what gives?"

"I just…" Angie took a deep breath. "This just isn't your thing. Even more than dachshunds and whiskey. And," she added when he started to protest, "honestly, it was nice having something that was just mine. In this family, that's pretty hard to find. I could just come here and there were no interruptions, no extra opinions, no crazy questions. I could just be here and…not share it."

Finn frowned. "You didn't want to share it?"

"Not really." Angie gave him a smile.

Finn wasn't sure what to do with that. He got it. Alone time, having something that was just hers, was understandable. It was easy to lose yourself in a big, dynamic group like the Kellys. But it was strange for him to think of his mom having things—projects and people—he wasn't involved in.

"I don't like that you would keep our help from Sophie when she obviously needs it," he finally said. He hated the idea of Sophie doing it alone. Or having her doors unlocked. Or having sex-only dates. And it was absolutely crazy that he cared.

Angie nodded. "Okay, I might have been wrong there."

"But I really don't like that you didn't think you could trust me to be a good guy."

Angie frowned. "Of course I trust you to be a good guy."

"But you didn't think that telling me to stay away from her would be enough."

His mother studied his eyes, clearly trying to gauge his sincerity. And Finn really wanted her to see it. To see that he understood that she and Sophie both had good reasons for him to keep his hands to himself and that he could respect that because he *was* a good guy. Who could probably not pull off a sex-only date with his mother's best friend...because he wanted to feed her and make her laugh and listen to rock and roll with her. Even if she'd set her theater on fire.

He ran a hand through his hair and then down over his face.

"Is it enough?" Angie asked then. "Now that you've met her? This is drywall and brickwork only?"

Sure. It could be drywall and brickwork only. It *should* be. He could help his mom's favorite place get back on its feet and ignore the blue-eyed blonde who made every protective instinct he had flare to life in spite of the fact that she ran her own business, kickboxed, and completely owned her sexuality. It didn't matter that she had no family to speak of, wanted a dozen kids, and made the most amazing sounds when licking chocolate frosting off her fingers.

But then a cheer went up from the front of the theater... and Finn's life got more complicated.

He pivoted in time to see his brother take Sophie's hand and pull her to the center stage, where he proceeded to twirl her around, then fold her in his arms, as Van Halen belted one of its greatest love songs. As Colin sang along. As they danced. In the spotlight. As if they were in some damned romantic movie and this was the scene where the guy finally gets the girl.

And *that* unfortunately mattered.

He just stared at the sight for three seconds and then said to his mom, "Okay, it might be a little more than drywall and brickwork."

He heard her mutter, "Dammit" as he started for Sophie.

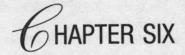

CHAPTER SIX

*H*is mom was right on his heels as Finn stomped to the front of the stage and planted his hands on his hips. The song ended, and Colin stepped away from Sophie with a huge grin.

"How'd I do?" Colin asked.

"That wasn't exactly what I was expecting," Sophie told him. But her cheeks were bright pink.

"I told you I'm perfectly comfortable in the spotlight," Colin said.

Sophie nodded. "You did say that."

"What's going on?" Finn scowled at his brother.

"Maya is a brilliant woman," Colin said.

"That's Sophie," Finn said, pointing at the blonde his mother had just warned him away from. Who was also *not* going to date his brother.

"Yes, but the idea for a play starring firefighters and cops to raise money for the theater was Maya's," Colin said.

A play? With these guys? Finn looked around. It was

a horrible idea. "Cops and firefighters can't act," he said. "Who wants to see that?"

"Everyone," Maya said with a grin. "Cute guys onstage hamming it up? Oh yeah, big-ticket money."

Finn looked at her. "Seriously?"

"People pay stupid money for firefighter calendars," Maya pointed out.

"And at the bachelor auctions," Kiera added.

"But they're just standing there. They don't have to have talent for that," Finn said. He hated this idea, but he wasn't entirely sure why. It probably had to do with the idea that Colin might be dancing with Sophie again.

"That's what makes it fun," Kiera said. "This theater is known for amateur productions and people discovering the theater for the first time. This is perfect. It will highlight the guys who saved the place, who are working to restore it, *and* the mission of the theater all at once."

Finn's frown deepened, but he didn't have a great argument against it.

Finally he looked at Sophie. He hadn't made eye contact with her since seeing her reaction to his brother twirling her around like they were freaking Fred and Ginger. He'd known that, if he looked directly at her, he'd want to grab her and show her that Colin wasn't the only one who could get her heart racing.

And he'd been right. The second their gazes connected, he wanted to get his hands on her. But he didn't dance. He tended toward more horizontal activities.

Sophie pulled her bottom lip between her teeth, but her eyes met his directly. Finn felt his jaw tighten and then relax. "You okay with this?"

"It's a good idea, if they're willing," she said. "I could

use some extra money for everything. And the guys..." She trailed off.

"The guys what?" Finn asked.

"Look good onstage and are fun," she said with a shrug.

"So what play are we going to do?" Colin asked.

Finn looked over to find Colin looking back and forth between him and Sophie.

"I don't know," she finally said. "What do you all think?" She looked at Angie as his mom came to stand beside him in front of the stage.

"Something with a lot of parts," Angie said.

Sophie nodded. "A lot of male parts."

"Something big," Colin said. "A popular show. Something people really want to come see."

But Sophie was already shaking her head by the time he finished. "No, it can't be something big."

Colin frowned slightly. "But you want to sell a lot of tickets. If we do something...like *Beauty and the Beast* or, oh! *The Book of Mormon*, that has a lot of male parts."

Sophie shook her head again. "No way. For one, we can't afford the rights to those shows, and two, this theater is known for small, independent plays."

Colin stepped closer. "But we want this to be huge, right? A big success? Lots of money coming in?"

"We'd love to make a little profit on this, and I appreciate all of you being interested in helping. But I'm not going to change what we do here." Sophie looked at Angie again. "For one, the people who know us and come here for the type of experience we provide would be disappointed. For another, the people who come to a big, popular play would later be disappointed to find out that's not what we really do here. It's better to stick with what we know."

"But I just think we need to—" Colin tried again.

"If we use firefighters, get some news coverage, and do a romance, we'll be golden," Angie interrupted her son.

Sophie's smile was bright. "I agree."

"You like the idea?" Maya asked Angie.

"I have to admit, it's pretty great. We could use the extra money for sure."

Her use of *we* didn't escape Finn's notice. She really was involved here. He hated that he hadn't known how much. Then he glanced at Sophie. Something had gone on with her in the past that made Angie protective of her. And damned if he didn't want to know all about it.

Of course he did. He hadn't wanted the dogs. Yet he now had a cupboard full of toys, and dog food was a regular item on his grocery list. He'd wanted Sophie almost on sight. So of course he'd dive right into everything going on with her. And he wanted to make it all better.

Dammit.

"A romance?" Colin asked with interest.

Angie nodded. "Everyone loves a romance. Especially our female patrons. And who brings the most people to the theater? Women. They'll bring their husbands, their friends, their sisters. We put on a grand romantic show with a bunch of good-looking firefighters running around and we don't have to worry about whether people have heard of the show before."

Sophie's smile grew, and Finn shifted his weight as his palms tingled, remembering how it had felt to hold her. Was it weird that her smile seemed to trigger a reaction in his hands? Yeah, it was. But he was beginning to think weird was par for the course.

"Okay, I'm game," Colin said.

"You're game?" Vince, another of the firefighters, asked.

"Sure," Colin said. "We want this show to be a huge success, and we don't have much time. Makes sense that I play the male romantic lead and Sophie does the female part."

"How does that make sense?" Michael asked.

"I'm the most comfortable onstage," Colin said. "And Sophie and I clearly have some chemistry."

Finn narrowed his eyes, but his brother wasn't paying any attention.

"And I've been in more plays than all of you," Colin went on. "I did a bunch in high school, and oh yeah, I did that one commercial that one time."

A bunch of the guys groaned at once. Colin had been cast in a local commercial for a blood drive over the holidays two years ago, but you would have thought that it was a starring role in a blockbuster movie the way he wouldn't shut up about it.

"You smiled at the camera and let the nurse poke a needle into your arm," Dan said with a laugh.

Colin gave him the finger and then turned his charming smile back on Sophie. "We'll probably need some one-on-one time," he said. "And I just want you to know that I'm willing."

"Gee, thanks, Colin." She was blushing again.

"You don't even know what the play is," Vince said before Finn had to chance to interrupt. "What if it's a gay romance?"

The guys all laughed, but Finn was watching his mother and Sophie. They were plotting. By only exchanging looks...and apparently reading one another's minds. It was spooky. And fascinating. He knew Sophie made his mom happy, and he'd been grateful to her even without knowing her. Now to put a face—a gorgeous face—with the name and knowledge was...strange. But he was quickly adjusting. One of his mother's best friends was a young, beautiful blond woman who smelled like lemonade. Who no way had tried to burn down this theater.

He knew, somehow, watching Sophie and his mother silently communicating, that the show *was* going to be some big, full-blown, sappy romance, gay or otherwise. His mother was a huge, hopeless romantic who still loved the only man she'd ever given her heart to, even though he'd been dead for sixteen years. And if Sophie was close enough to Angie to share her love of theater and art, then chances were Sophie was equally starry-eyed.

"I know the perfect show," Sophie announced to the group. "It's a brand-new, never-before-seen independent script that is the most beautiful love story I've ever read."

Nailed it.

"With one male and one female lead?" Colin asked.

Everyone laughed again. Sophie nodded. "Yes."

"And kissing? Will there be kissing?" Sean, another of the firefighters, asked in a singsong voice.

Sophie grinned. "There will be kissing."

Colin reached for Sophie's hand and twirled her around again. "I can't wait for rehearsals to begin."

Sophie blushed but smiled. And pulled her hand away.

"So no auditions then?" Finn asked. "Colin just gets the part?"

Everyone, every single pair of eyes, focused on him. The ones he could feel most were his mother's, Tripp's, and Sophie's. Not necessarily in that order.

He didn't look at his mom or Tripp. It wasn't as if

he wanted to be in the play. But, well...no one else was going to be touching Sophie Birch. She was his. As stupid and strange and out of character and risky as that sounded.

"Does someone else want to audition for the part?" Angie asked Finn, giving him a look that said, "It better not be you."

"Yes. I'm auditioning," Finn said, earning him a scowl from his mother that was on par with the one he'd gotten the time he'd confessed to wrecking her brand-new car two days after she'd gotten it home.

He'd been in a hell of a lot of trouble with that stunt. She'd been upset with him for days.

He had a feeling that was nothing compared to this.

"I think I should handle this one," Colin said. "The sooner we open the show, the sooner we'll have money to cover what we've paid for repairs and supplies."

"We'll have insurance money to get started, and we'll be doing most of the work, so costs will be low," Finn said. Well, they'd eventually have the insurance money. Provided Frank Birch hadn't set the fire. And yes, he had said "we." As if this was all his concern as well. He was aware. And if he hadn't been, Tripp's gaze boring into the side of his head would have reminded him. He couldn't meet his partner's eyes. Because he had no idea what he was doing right now either. "And I thought all the fireflies here were going to be helping out too? Unless you can't handle swinging a hammer and learning your lines at the same time?" Finn asked, looking the group of firefighters over.

What was he doing? Challenging them? Really? Over a play no one had heard of that was going to be performed at a theater that almost no one had heard of? Why? He needed to shut the hell up.

Colin straightened to his full height, which was still two inches shorter than Finn's. "We can handle whatever you throw at us," he said. "And you know it."

And they were officially in a pissing contest. Over a woman Finn had just met. Who his mother had practically begged him to leave alone. The only thing he really knew about Sophie was that she smelled good. And that she was kick-ass behind closed doors. And that she didn't have a family. And that that bothered him more than it should. And that he wanted to kiss her.

"Good," Finn said, also drawing to his full height. "The sooner we get this place back together, the better."

"So you're auditioning," Colin clarified. "For the lead."

Well, if the lead was going to be kissing—or dancing with, touching, or smelling—Sophia Birch, then yeah. But he wasn't just auditioning. He was getting that part.

"Definitely," he said.

He was here to put this theater back together for his mother. And there was no way in hell he was going to be able to be in that theater and watch Sophie kiss anyone else.

He didn't even care that he was acting like a jealous kid fighting over a shiny new bike. The bike didn't belong to anyone. It was just there. Looking gorgeous and up for grabs. And he probably shouldn't ever admit to anyone that he'd compared Sophie to a bike.

And if Tripp was a good friend, he'd get Finn out of here. Now. Before he did anything else ridiculously stupid. Finally Finn turned to look at his friend.

Tripp was grinning like an idiot. Until he met Finn's

gaze. Then he also straightened, cleared his throat, and lost his stupid grin. "Hey, Finn, we should get going if we're going to pick up the rest of the supplies we need," Tripp said, as if reading Finn's mind.

"Yeah, probably." Finn looked at his mother. "We need some more...stuff...for the wall."

"So auditions will be tomorrow night then," Colin said. "We don't have a lot of time."

Finn nodded. "I'll be here."

"What did you just do?" Tripp asked as they hit the sidewalk and the door closed behind them.

As if the spell had been broken the moment he was out of sight of Sophie, Finn was suddenly wondering the same damned thing. He scrubbed a hand over his face. "Fuck, man, I don't know."

"Well, it looked to me like you offered to measure your dick against Colin's on a stage in front of a bunch of firefighters."

That was pretty much exactly what he'd just offered to do.

"Of course there will be cops there too," Tripp said.

Yeah, Finn had figured that. "What am I going to do?" He couldn't play the romantic lead in a play. Hell, he couldn't play any kind of anything in a play.

"Well you have to show up now." Tripp opened the door to the passenger side of Finn's truck. "And you can't blow it."

Finn slammed his door behind him. "How the hell am I not going to blow this?"

Tripp looked over with a grin. "I think you'll be okay."

"What?" Finn asked, bracing for his friend to tell him what a dumbass he was.

"It's the romantic lead opposite Sophie Birch."

"So?"

"So that means you basically have to act like you're crazy about her."

Finn scowled at him. "This isn't helping."

Tripp laughed. "I saw how you looked at her. If the part requires you to act like a lovesick teenager, you've got it wrapped up."

Finn started the truck and shifted it into gear. He'd known Tripp for eight years. They'd been partners for five. Tripp had saved his ass a dozen times. And vice versa. There was absolutely no lying to the man. Or denying that the man was telling him the truth.

"Colin has a thing for her too," he decided to mention. And Colin was his brother. But his mother didn't want either of them with her.

"Well, she didn't look at him the way I look at chocolate-dipped bacon."

He thought about that. "She looked at me like that?"

"Oh yeah."

Chocolate-dipped bacon. Huh. That was Tripp's favorite thing in the world. Like he'd-give-his-left-nut-for-it favorite thing in the world.

Finn pulled onto the street, telling himself to keep his damned mouth shut for a change. But by the time they'd pulled into the hardware store parking lot, he couldn't help it. "She really looked at me like that?"

* * *

What had just happened?

Sophie watched the door bump shut behind Finn and Tripp as they left the theater.

Things had gotten way out of hand really quickly. That was what had happened.

Maya's comment about the guys being so easy to watch and then all of them hamming it up onstage had finally made the idea that had been floating around in Sophie's mind click into a place. A play. With the firefighters and cops. And then Maya had said it out loud. And the guys had jumped on the idea. Well, Colin had jumped on the idea. But the rest had seemed willing. Or willing-ish at least.

But then Finn had jumped on the idea too. Or something. She didn't think he was actually chomping at the bit to audition for the lead role in a romantic stage play. But he hadn't seemed to like the idea of Colin doing it either.

Sophie noticed Angie starting up the middle aisle as the guys all got back to work on the wall.

"Angie, can I talk to you for a minute?" Sophie called after her friend.

Angie turned back. "Of course."

Sophie made her way off the stage and followed Angie partway up the side aisle. "I'm so excited we're going to be doing *Tony and Angel*," Sophie told her when they stopped where Angie and Finn had been talking. "You're sure it's okay?"

Angie gave her a bright smile. "Of course it's okay."

Tony and Angel was the script Sophie had rescued from the fire. It was Angie's play. The story of her falling in love with her husband, Tommy.

"I think it's wonderful that your boys want to be involved," Sophie added, gauging Angie's reaction.

Angie sighed. "I hope so."

"You don't seem convinced."

"I just...I knew this would happen. They'd all come down here and mess everything up."

It didn't feel like things were messed up, but Sophie nodded. "I wasn't expecting this. But it's...fine."

"It's not fine." Angie's gaze was on the crowd of people behind Sophie. "You wanted to be kept out of all of this, and I understand why, but now...this." She sighed.

"Angie, really, they're just trying to help. I appreciate it. As soon as the theater is back together, they'll move on. I know that. I don't have any big expectations here."

Angie's eyes found hers again. She seemed to hesitate and then asked, "Can I be honest with you?"

Sophie felt her gut tighten. "Of course."

"My family...my boys in particular...Finn in very particular...don't understand acting."

Sophie swallowed. "You've mentioned that they're not really into live theater before."

"I don't mean the theater scene," Angie said. She seemed to be trying to figure out how to say what she wanted to say. "I mean biting their tongues, fudging the truth, telling white lies, having a poker face. Finn can't not demonstrate exactly how he feels and say exactly what he thinks."

Sophie couldn't help it—she liked that. A lot. She loved not having to guess and not having to try to read someone else's thoughts and feelings. "Is that a bad thing?"

Angie shook her head. "Generally no."

"I value honesty, Angie," Sophie said. "Deeply. After all those years with my dad, not knowing if what he was saying was true or if it was to get something out of someone, I would love spending time with people who just let it all out."

Angie's expression softened into an affectionate smile. "I think that's true on a level," she said. "But honey, you don't like personal relationships. You do, however, love connecting with people. That's what you do here. It's a way of interacting with people. And you get to laugh and cry and get angry and fall in love. But it's safe because you're playing a part. And you have a script. You know what to expect. You know what they're going to say and do, and you know how to react, because it's written down right in front of you."

Sophie pulled in a long breath and let it out slowly. That was all... exactly right.

"Yeah, I guess so."

"After all those years of guessing what was going to happen next and having your life dictated by someone else and everything up in the air and subject to change on a dime, here you feel in control."

Angie wasn't wrong. This place was not just the way Sophie made a living. It was also where she got to have full control, where she was the director, where she wrote the stories. Most importantly, where she wrote how those stories ended.

"I want you to hold on to this theater," Angie said. "I want you to have more in your life too, of course. But you need this place and I want to help be sure you always have it."

"Thank you," Sophie said softly.

Angie smiled.

"But I don't understand what that has to do with your family being here and Finn being a really honest guy," she said.

"Well, you love the control and knowing what comes next. You also get to tell people when they're overdoing it."

"Okay."

"None of that will happen with my family," Angie said drily.

"What do you mean?"

"Nothing happens according to any kind of plan or schedule with the Kellys. There are no scripts, and they rarely do what's expected. They don't hold back. It's... chaos... about ninety percent of the time."

Sophie smiled. "It's just until the theater is cleaned up and the show is done."

Angie didn't look convinced. "They're all very unpredictable."

"Even Finn? He seems very steady and predictable," Sophie said, without thinking. But it was true that the big, sexy cop seemed the epitome of stability.

Angie frowned. "Well, that's what has me worried the most. He is. He's the rock, he's the one that keeps everyone else grounded, the one we can count on, the guy behind the scenes. So imagine my surprise when he said he was going to audition for a play. A leading role in a play, no less."

Sophie's heart thumped. "You really think he's going to audition?"

"Between Colin challenging him and your big blue eyes?" Angie said with a little laugh. "Yes."

"And that would be bad." Sophie didn't ask it as a question. It would be bad. Because she and Finn would spend more time together then. A lot more time.

Angie must have seen something in her face. "He's drawn to drama." She laughed lightly. "Ironic since this whole theater thing isn't really his cup of tea. But he does love real-life drama. He'll say he doesn't," she added, "and he'll say he wants a break from the family's issues and melodrama. But it's not true. He likes to be the calm in the eye of the storm and the guy that keeps things from going totally off the rails."

If that was the case, Finn wouldn't be able to resist getting involved with Sophie. Because in spite of her best efforts at a normal, even-keel, happy life, Frank was back in town, and her livelihood had almost burned down, and she needed money like yesterday, and she now had an entire herd of people stomping around her theater and a new production to put together in only a month's time with a bunch of amateurs. And the two sons of one of her best friends fighting over her. That was all definitely very dramatic.

"So we shouldn't do the show?" Sophie asked her.

Angie sighed. "I really like the idea of putting the fire-fighters onstage," Angie said. "I do think that will be a draw, and I think we can get you the money you need. I also like the idea of showing these guys what theater is all about."

Sophie smiled. She and Angie shared a passion for introducing people to the theater. "So we *should* do the show?"

Angie nodded. "I think we should."

"You're really okay with us doing *your* show with *your* family?" Sophie asked.

"I am. I guess," Angie said. "I mean, they're here now. There's no getting rid of them once they get excited about something."

"And Finn in the leading role?" Sophie asked.

Angie shrugged. "Well, he did take really good care of those dachshunds."

Sophie raised an eyebrow. "Dachshunds?"

"He's always there when someone needs him," Angie said. "I got involved with the dogs, fell in love, got in over my head, and he fixed it."

Sophie felt her heart thump again. She didn't need fixing. She would figure all of this out for herself. As always. But she wouldn't mind having Finn Kelly around a little longer.

"So I'm like a dachshund?" Sophie teased.

But Angie didn't smile. "You're something that's important to me, so you'll automatically be important to Finn."

Ah, okay. Finn would be interested in her and her problems because of Angie. And nothing more. Good to know.

"Well, don't worry," Sophie said, forcing a smile. "I think in this analogy the theater and this play are the dachshund."

Angie seemed to consider that. "Maybe," she finally said. "But you should know that he still has one of the dachshunds."

Sophie felt her stomach flip but then realized she wasn't surprised by that at all. "So he gets easily sucked in."

"He puts his whole heart into the things he does."

She cleared her throat. Twice. "Okay, well, maybe Colin is a better choice since he's done theater before. Or even one of the other guys." Colin, after all, seemed to really want the part. Finn was just auditioning to be generous... and maybe to annoy his brother. And maybe someone else would step up and knock her socks off. That would actually be great. Not being enamored with a guy who very likely saw her as a community service project would be great.

Angie pulled her into a hug. "I love you, you know."

Sophie squeezed her back as the words did what they always did—seeped into her heart and made her feel warm and wanted. And Sophie was reminded that with Angie it was about even more than feeling loved. It was being able to love Angie back without fearing having her heart broken. She didn't have to worry about Frank picking them up and moving them away. She didn't have to worry about that inevitable day when Frank screwed up and the tears and accusations started. She didn't have to worry about losing Angie. Ever.

At least as long as she didn't get involved with Finn.

* * *

Finn hadn't auditioned. She was disappointed. She shouldn't be, she knew. It was better this way. Or at least things would be easier. But Sophie had kind of wanted him to want to audition.

She made her way through the lobby on the way to the office. Then stopped and cocked her head. Was someone still here? She headed down the hallway, the noise growing louder as she neared the greenroom.

The TV was on. Someone must have forgotten it. But as her hand connected with the doorknob, she realized who was inside. She pushed the door open. Sure enough, Frank was stretched out on the couch, feet up on the arm, watching television. And the room smelled like lasagna.

She planted her hands on her hips. "Seriously?"

Frank looked over from where he was stretched out on the couch, feet up on the arm, a plastic container that had been full of lasagna balanced on his stomach. The container now only held a plastic fork and a few streaks of tomato sauce.

"Hey, honey."

Sophie walked into the room. "You ate my leftovers?"

"They were amazing." He pushed up to a sitting position.

He held out the container to her. The empty container. Her stomach growled, and she realized this was her own fault. She never should have left the lasagna in the fridge. She should have known Frank would go poking around.

"That was my dinner," she informed him, crossing her arms. She certainly wasn't going to clean up after him. "I take it you decided to stay here?"

He set the container on the floor by his feet. "You wouldn't be making meatloaf anytime soon, would you? I love your meatloaf."

Her meatloaf recipe was actually Nancy's meatloaf recipe. Stepmother number four. And it was definitely amazing. "I didn't make the lasagna. And I'm not making you meatloaf, Frank. I'm not feeding you. The food in the fridge is mine. You can get your own."

He sighed. "I'm tired of burgers and pizza."

Sophie rolled her eyes. The poor guy. "Maybe you should, I don't know, get an apartment and start making your own food."

"I'm fine here," he said, looking around the room. "Couch, TV, bathroom with a shower, fridge, microwave. I'm set."

He was. She had been expecting this. Because it was all free and she couldn't kick him out. He was half owner of the couch, TV, fridge, and microwave. Technically, anyway. But this was way better than him showing up on Kiera's porch or finding stepmother number seven. "Guess it's microwave burritos and soup then." She started to turn away.

"You always hated the microwave burritos," he said.

Sophie stopped and squeezed her eyes shut. Dammit. "Yeah, I did." She didn't face him.

"That's why I was always working on the next place to stay, Soph."

Sophie braced herself. She knew what was coming next. "Don't, Frank."

"I could have eaten burritos for months if I'd had to. I didn't mind sleeping in the car. I moved on to the next woman each time for *you*."

Sophie wanted to throw something. Or punch something. He always did this—put all of it on her. And worse, it worked.

But it wasn't her responsibility to take care of him now because of that.

Was it? Was some strange, misplaced sense of duty why she'd made sure the heat in the building stayed at a decent level overnight, and that there was a pillow and blanket on the couch, and that there were extra supplies in the bathroom? Because she'd known he'd show up here and she could do at least that much, right?

She needed to get to her office and do some kickboxing. "Okay, on that heartwarming note, I'm going to go, Frank. Stay. Leave. Whatever. But leave my food alone."

"So if you didn't make the lasagna, who did? Maybe I need to get married again after all," Frank said, rubbing his stomach with a smile.

Because getting married for lasagna seemed funny, of course. Until you got to know Frank Birch. And she knew him *well*. She sighed.

Without the theater, Sophie wouldn't be tied down any-where. She could move around. She could stay ahead of Frank. He wouldn't know exactly how to find her when he needed something. He might even have to go back to sleep-ing in cars or shelters.

She squelched all the emotions stirred up by those thoughts. She wasn't staying in Boston, running a barely-making-it theater, so that her dad would have a place to come to between wives. She wasn't. Not even deep down in her psyche. Probably.

Maybe that was why she'd always avoided therapy. She didn't really want to dig around in the depths of her thoughts and emotions. She didn't have enough AC/DC to work through all the self-directed rage that might result.

"Did you know that the police think maybe one of us set the fire?" she asked.

He nodded. "Of course they do."

"That doesn't bother you?"

He shrugged. "Not much I can do about it. The theater that I'm a fifty percent partner in had a fire. Makes sense they'd wonder."

"Has someone talked to you?"

"Yep. Stopped me outside of here yesterday."

"But you said you didn't do it and they believed you?" Sophie pressed.

"I said I didn't do it. Not sure that they believed me." Frank seemed legitimately unconcerned about all of it.

"Because you *didn't* do it, right?" she asked.

Frank sighed. "I told you, I didn't do it. Do you know how much work insurance fraud is?"

Of course. He hadn't set the fire because it would be *work*. Not because it would be a terrible thing to do.

Sophie shook her head and started for the door. "Okay...so...try to stay out of the way. I have a show coming up."

"Yeah, heard about that."

She turned to face him. "You did?"

"I heard something about casting a bunch of firefighters? I think that's great. Should bring in some big money."

Sophie narrowed her eyes. "Money for *repairs*. That's the whole reason they're doing it, Frank. They'll know if the money doesn't go back into the theater."

Frank just shrugged.

"And there are cops too," she added. "Not just firefighters." Not that him taking half of the money that came in was illegal. Technically it was his. It was just...an asshole thing to do. Then she frowned. "What do you mean you heard it? We just decided to do it last night and just had the auditions tonight."

"I saw the end of the auditions and put two and two together when they were all talking about work."

He'd seen the end of the auditions? "How long have you been here?"

"Where am I going to be?" he asked, swinging around to lie back on the couch again.

Right. "So you just hung out in the theater?"

"Back row center," he said. "I even had popcorn."

He'd eaten her popcorn too. Sophie rubbed her forehead. "So can I expect that you'll be dropping into rehearsals as well?"

"You never know," he said, turning his attention back to the TV. "It's probably time I get more involved with the theater. Since I'm back and all."

Terrific. Not that she'd ever longed for Frank's presence,

but this would be the absolutely worst time for him to be around. She didn't want him to get to know her friends or the Kellys or the firefighters who were here doing a good deed or...anyone he could potentially swindle. Which was...pretty much anyone. It wasn't only the women who were at risk. Frank had messed with plenty of other people over the years too. Those were smaller things and much less frequent—a dinner here or there with the idea Frank would pay next time and he just never got around to it, a couple of "loans" that never got paid back, a poker game that just magically went in Frank's favor every hand—but Frank always came out better than his pals.

"Frank, I would really appreciate it if you'd stay out of the way and out of the rehearsals."

He just waved a hand at her. "No worries, Soph. It'll all be fine."

She couldn't deal with him. Because he honestly didn't care what she thought or what she wanted. "Whatever," she muttered, and turned on her heel.

She made her way down the hall to the lobby, her mind whirring.

It would be very important for her to downplay her relationships during rehearsals, in case Frank was hanging around. She couldn't let on how much she loved Angie or how close they were. He'd hone in on that in two seconds. She couldn't let Kiera and Maya come help out. She had to be friendly but not warm with the guys. This had to be all business. Frank couldn't get the idea that anyone here had a soft spot for her. So she couldn't let on that there was anything between her and Finn.

She rolled her eyes. That one didn't matter at least. He hadn't auditioned. Maybe he'd come help with the repairs again, but he wouldn't be around all the time. And they wouldn't be kissing as Tony and Angel. Which was good. Because she wasn't sure she was a good-enough actress to act like that was just a part. And according to Angie, Finn didn't hide his feelings well at all. And whether or not it was a good idea, there was real chemistry between them. Very real.

"Your door was unlocked again."

Sophie gasped and spun, her heart racing.

"Finn!"

CHAPTER SEVEN

As if she'd conjured him with her thoughts, there Finn was, leaning with his shoulder against one of the thick white columns on either side of the lobby as if he owned the place. The columns were decorative, but as she took in the sight of him beside it, her imagination made him into a Roman centurion using his strength to hold up the crumbling walls and ceiling of a cathedral as she scrambled to safety.

Good grief. Sophie reined in her fantasies and gave him a smile. "You came to check on the lock?" Her mind really wanted to run with that as well. Finn as her bodyguard. He'd have to be with her 24-7. He'd have to be here at the theater but also at home with her...

"I came to talk to you. But I wasn't pleased to find you in here alone with the door unlocked." He pushed away from the column with a frown.

"What did you want to talk about?" she asked. She wasn't about to admit that she wasn't alone.

He came toward her until he nearly stood on her toes. "You need to lock that damned door."

Ah, no distracting him. She hadn't really thought that would work. She nodded. "Yeah. Okay. You're right."

She had so many people in and out of here that she just didn't bother a lot of the time. And sometimes she really did forget. She'd had self-defense training at Maya's martial arts studio, and she and Maya and Kiera practiced a lot. She also had a mean right hook, a strong roundhouse kick, Mace, and a stun gun. And lots of places to hide in the theater. She simply wasn't that concerned about her safety. This was home. She felt completely comfortable here. But yeah, Finn had a point.

And maybe Frank had left it unlocked. She'd almost forgotten for five seconds that he was now living here. She resisted sighing or growling.

Fidgety because of the way Finn was looking at her, she crossed the lobby to the panel of switches for the overhead lobby lights. It felt as if he was trying to read every one of her secrets and vulnerabilities. And as if he'd be successful if she gave him a full minute of eye contact.

"So, what did you want to talk about?" she asked, hitting the off switch.

The overhead lights went out, but the security lights by the front door gave them enough illumination to easily move around and see one another.

"The play."

The play he thought of as a community service project. Except that he hadn't even bothered to audition. Whereas he'd not only taken in a bunch of dachshunds, he'd even kept one.

Sophie shook that off. She was *not* jealous over the

fact that he'd gotten fully involved with other projects but hadn't with the theater after all. She didn't need his charity. She didn't need his help, and she'd rather not think about him feeling sorry for her.

"What about it?" she asked, fussing with the leaves on one of the plants by the office door.

"I...had to work tonight."

"Did you?"

"I picked up a shift. Because I thought that it would be better than coming to audition."

"You picked up a shift to avoid auditioning? You thought your brother would drag you down here or something?" she asked, aware that she was more annoyed about the whole thing than she should be. The auditions had gone well, and Colin and a guy named Mike had showed some promise. She figured she'd need to decide between the two.

"I picked up a shift because I wanted to audition and I was trying to keep myself from doing it."

"Because your mom asked you not to?"

"Yes. Partly. And because I'm more the behind-the-scenes guy than I am a spotlight guy. And because—" He took a deep breath. "Because she's already taking care of you and..."

He trailed off as Sophie came to stand in front of him again.

She felt that strange draw when she got within five feet of him. That feeling that she could tell him anything and everything. That feeling that he was there for her. Not in the sense of him agreeing to be there to help with the theater cleanup or to make the play happen. But there for her. There *because* of her somehow.

The dim lighting wasn't helping. She should have left the lights on. Sure, he might be able to see her eyes and expressions more clearly then, but there was something about the dark that revved her imagination to intense stupidity.

It was because nighttime had been her dreaming time as a kid. She'd lie in bed and come up with story after story. They were all romances, and nearly every one of them involved her dad and current stepmother being in love forever, staying together, even making Sophie some siblings. And family vacations and huge blowout birthday parties and parents' nights at school when she had two parents sitting in the front row. And a dog.

Sophie reeled all of that back in somehow and swallowed hard.

He had trailed off with "She's already taking care of you," implying that it had crossed his mind that *he* might need to take care of her.

"What's your dachshund's name?" she asked.

She'd clearly surprised him, but he answered. "Rosie." The slight curl to his mouth was definitely a sign of affection.

"Was Rosie the runt of the litter?" Sophie asked. He seemed the type to pick the runt.

He looked puzzled. "No."

"But you kept her, out of all of them, for a reason."

He nodded slowly. "They were all rescues, and they were with me for about two months. She'd...had it the hardest. She needed the most stability. I didn't think that sending her to a new home just as she'd gotten settled would be good for her."

She'd had it the hardest. Sophie swallowed. Yeah, Finn Kelly was a good guy. Too good. So good that he would want to be involved here because Sophie was a little like Rosie.

"What did your mom tell you about me?" she asked.

Finn blew out a short breath. But he was the always-honest one. The one who couldn't hide his feelings. "That you'd had a lot of loss in your life and that you need a mom more than you need a guy."

Sophie realized Angie hadn't really told him anything too personal. At least not in detail. She nodded. "My mom died when I was two. I lived with my grandmother for about four years after that. Then my dad came and got me. I had five stepmoms growing up. My dad just moved from one woman to the next. So I got used to loving people and then having to say goodbye."

Finn was watching her intently and she got the sense that he wanted to hug her. Which was a very strange thing to have a feeling about.

"The worst thing about it," she went on as Finn just stood there being very…*there*. She couldn't describe it better than that. Solid, strong, big, and showing no inclination to leave or even blink, "was that every time he sweet-talked another woman into falling for him and inviting us into her house and life, it was because *I* needed it. So not only did he use me to get close to them, but I was the reason he kept doing it over and over."

Sophie was appalled that she'd spilled all of that. She'd never told anyone but Angie that she felt guilty about all of that. But she couldn't stop. She supposed she could chalk it up to Finn being Angie's son and a naturally good listener. But she knew that wasn't it. She felt comfortable with Finn in a way that she couldn't remember feeling in a very long, and lonely, time.

"And I picked my third stepmom out," she blurted. "She was my fourth grade teacher, and I loved her, and he'd just broken up with my third stepmom and we were staying with a friend of his, and I was sleeping in a sleeping bag on the floor. His carpet smelled like cigarette smoke and dirty socks and so I started staying after school to work on projects and Frank would have to come pick me up because I'd miss the bus. After they'd met a couple of times, I told Frank that he should ask her on a date and…a month later we moved in with her and she became my stepmom six months later. And it lasted for five years—longer than any of the others—and I thought maybe she would be the one that stuck." Sophie took a deep breath and blew it out. "And I've felt guilty about that since I was fourteen."

Finn continued to just watch her. And she wanted him to hug her. She knew that being wrapped in those arms would make her feel very safe. For that moment she didn't care that he might only do it because he felt sorry for her. She'd bet Rosie jumped right up into his lap and licked his face and didn't care one bit if he was keeping her and giving her a home and a safe haven only because he pitied her.

But then Sophie shook her head and took a giant step back, away from Finn. She did not want pity. She didn't need it. She was out on her own now, and yeah, okay, Frank was sleeping on the couch down the hall and eating her leftovers, but she had a great place to live now and nothing smelled like cigarettes or dirty socks, and she didn't have to say goodbye to anyone she didn't want to say goodbye to. And she didn't like Finn making her feel like she *wanted* to be taken care of.

"So," she said from a safer distance, "I guess I just thought you should know that I'm very much like Rosie.

Or it will seem like I am. I'm someone your mom cares about and who seems kind of pathetic and has had a hard time. And that's what's making you feel like you want to be involved. But I'm okay. I'm able to take care of myself, and I have other people who can be there for me, and while everything you feel and do is very nice and noble, we just both have to remember that this is all just...mixed-up emotions. It's not real."

"What isn't real?" he finally asked. They were his first words in a while.

"This...attraction," she said. "This feeling that we're being drawn together. I think it's just misplaced chivalry on your part."

He took a step forward, narrowing the space between them. "And what is it on your part?"

"What do you mean?"

"Why are *you* feeling this attraction to *me*?"

Okay, so he knew it was two sided. She swallowed. "I think it's probably your arms."

He huffed out a short laugh. "My arms?"

She shrugged. "It's probably the whole carrying me away from danger the first night we met or something. But yeah."

"So it's purely physical on your side of it? While I'm feeling the misplaced urge to keep you safe and make you happy?"

Damn. The words *keep you safe and make you happy* were some of the most seductive words she could have imagined from him. But she hated that she was feeling a little like a dachshund at the moment.

"I think it feels like it's physical and emotional for both of us when really it's just"—she shrugged—"a mixture of a bunch of stuff like my daddy issues and your protective streak and us both loving your mom and maybe wanting something we can't have and that we met that first night at the fire before we knew who the other was—" She stopped as he moved in closer, and she found she was backed up against the wall. "Finn."

He reached up and cupped her face in his hands. "Yeah?"

"What are you doing?"

He leaned in. "Auditioning for the part of Tony," he said. Then he kissed her.

* * *

Well, holy hosannas, Sophie thought as Finn's lips met hers.

This kiss felt like the culmination of days of wondering and waiting. It was almost a…relief. It was as if she'd needed this and hadn't even known it.

Sophie ran a hand over the back of his head. His hair was short and it tickled her palm deliciously. He had one hand on the back of her head too, threaded through her hair. The other went to her hip, and it felt so right there that she gave a little sigh.

Sighing was clearly exactly the right thing to do, because Finn's grip on her hip tightened, and then he was pressing his body against her. Then he tipped her head to the side and deepened the kiss.

And damn. He had the part. She didn't even remember what part or what play at the moment. But Finn Kelly could have whatever he wanted from her.

He ran his hand from her hip to her shoulder and then

down again, cupping her butt and holding her still as he pressed into her. He skimmed his tongue over her bottom lip, and when she moaned, his tongue stroked over hers.

She ran her hands over his shoulders and down to his biceps, the huge, rock-hard biceps that were holding her still for his delicious onslaught on her senses, and she sighed happily. Yeah, her attraction was partly about his arms.

Finally he lifted his head and stared down at her, breathing raggedly. Long before she was ready to break things up. Disappointment and a sharp pang of need hit her, and Sophie blinked up at him, racking her mind for ways to get more of that.

Give him the lead and take the part of Angel.

Well, that was definitely one solution. Angie had written a lot of kissing into that script. In fact, in a couple of places, things went a little beyond kissing. Staring up at Finn now, Sophie realized that it would be the easiest part she'd ever played. Because, at least during those scenes, she wouldn't be acting.

"I've never done this before. How am I doing?" His voice was husky, and he hadn't let go of her yet. His big hand was hot on her butt, and she was hit by the urge to feel it with no clothes between them.

Sophie licked her lips. And watched his eyes heat. "You've never kissed a woman you barely know before?"

His lazy smile made her heart beat faster, but when he ran his thumb over her bottom lip, her heart seemed to turn over in her chest.

"I've never auditioned for a play before," he clarified.

She resisted the urge to let her tongue dart out and lick the tip of his thumb. She nodded. "Well, just so you know, typically you say words and act out a scene. On a stage. With other people watching."

"We can move this onto the stage if you want," he said agreeably. "And you just tell me the words you want to hear."

A bunch of words came to mind. *Sophie, you're amazing. I could kiss you forever. Let's take this into your office.* Wow, that was asking for trouble.

She mentally shook her head. "Probably some of the words Tony would say."

"The kissing seemed like a key part," Finn said, finally dropping his hand from her face and stepping back.

She wished he hadn't done that. She smiled, though. "There is a lot of kissing in this show."

"So it's important that the kissing is believable and good," Finn said.

"True."

"Well, I'm no theater expert," he said. "But that kiss seemed pretty believable and really damned good. Almost as if we were two people kissing in real life, totally into it and having nothing to do with a play."

Hearing her own thoughts out loud like that, Sophie took a deep breath. "No, it kind of felt like two people kissing in real life because one of them feels sorry for the other one and that one has a weakness for great biceps." Except his biceps were symbolic of something far more complicated—he was the solid one and right now, when she was feeling out of control with Frank and the money and everything going on because of the fire and the repairs and the show, solid was very appealing.

But that was all it was. And if she, or anyone else, started thinking it was more, she was going to be in big trouble.

"I don't feel sorry for you, Sophie," he said. "I understand why you might think that," he admitted. "But I don't. You're an independent, intelligent woman with a lot of people who love you. I don't pity you."

She smiled up at him. "Thanks."

"But I do want to be around you more, and yes, I do have a tendency to get involved in things that I think I can fix. I don't feel like that's all that's going on here, but I have to admit that could be part of it."

Sophie nodded. "I appreciate your honesty."

"So I think I have a solution."

Solution. Another word that she really liked. "Okay." She was open to ideas. Mostly the ones that involved more lip time with Finn. She wasn't sure, but maybe that's where this was going.

"I'll take the part of Tony. And you take the part of Angel."

"So we can keep kissing?" she asked.

"Yes," he said with a grin. "Definitely. Huge perk of this plan."

Well, she was on board so far.

"But," he continued, "part of the concern is that I'm helping out just because I'm a do-gooder. And you don't need a guy in your life and you don't like the big-family thing and my mom's afraid that she'll lose a friend if we date and it doesn't work out...so this plan solves all of that."

"I'm intrigued."

"If we do the lead roles, we can spend time together, but it's very clear what it's about. I can help the theater out, but I'm not butting into your life. I can get to know more about something that's important to my mom. We can work on the scenes without my family around so you don't have to deal with them. And everyone knows there's an end point to all of it, so, when it comes, no one's upset or disappointed."

Sophie nodded again, though slower. This all made sense. He was offering her exactly what Angie had said was important to her—a way to have the connection she wanted but inside a plan in which she knew what to expect. And there was a scripted ending. She'd see it coming, and it wouldn't hurt.

"And you get the part instead of Colin," she said, with a smile to cover that she was already dreading the end of the show. That was stupid. She barely knew him. They hadn't even started anything yet. How could she be upset about it ending?

But it felt like they had started something.

He grinned. "Icing on the cake."

"I thought maybe the kissing was the icing."

His eyes heated. "I think the kissing is the caramel drizzle."

"There's a caramel drizzle?" She was so on board with a caramel drizzle.

He nodded. "Something extra. Something sweet. Something that makes the whole thing even better."

Caramel drizzle for the win. In fact, drizzling caramel seemed like a great...

Sophie mentally shook herself. They could kiss and do the play, but they couldn't do more than that. Everything with Finn had to happen within the context of the play.

"I think it's a great plan."

"So I've got the part?" Finn asked.

He'd had the part the moment he'd walked into the

theater thinking she was her grandmother, Sophie realized. *Tony and Angel* was the right play to do, this was the right time to do it, and Finn was the right guy to do it.

She smiled up at him. "You've got the part."

"And *you're* going to play Angel?" he clarified. "That's the best way to make this work, don't you think?"

Hell yeah, she was going to play Angel. Even before that kiss. She loved the play; she loved the part of Angel; she loved being in the midst of a new show with players who'd never been onstage before. But now? To play opposite Finn as he took on his first part, in his mother's show? She wouldn't miss that for anything.

They would say goodbye at the end of the show, but she was going to enjoy the next few weeks of helping Finn discover theater, seeing Finn and Angie understand each other better, and...kissing the pants off of Finn Kelly. Not literally, of course. Probably.

"I'm going to be Angel," she told him. "For sure."

He grinned down at her and Sophie felt warm in *her* pants.

"When does rehearsal start?" he asked.

She thought his voice sounded a little husky. It might have just been the way her stupid imagination always added a little dramatic flair to everything.

"Right away, tomorrow. We don't have much time," she said.

"Okay."

For a second Sophie thought maybe he was going to reach for her. And pull her in. And kiss her again. Maybe put a hand under her shirt. Maybe...

"I guess I'll see you tomorrow," he said, stepping back.

Dramatic flair 2, reality 1.

"Okay." She gave him a smile that was only half-forced. "I'll send out e-mails to everyone letting them know what parts they got. And who got the lead."

"Oh, let me tell them," Finn said. "At least Colin."

She laughed. "You should be nicer to your brother."

"Just hold off on the e-mail for an hour or so."

She shook her head but agreed. "Fine. I'll wait till later tonight."

"Okay." He paused but finally turned and headed for the door. His hand was on the handle before he turned back. "You coming?"

"What?"

"I'm walking you out to your car."

She blinked at him. "You are?"

He chuckled. "Of course I am."

She was not used to someone being so concerned. She didn't need it. She also couldn't get used to it. But for the moment she was going to enjoy it. "Let me grab my stuff." She ducked into the office and gathered her purse and sweater and met him by the front door. He held it open for her, and she hesitated for a second, wondering if she should make a point of not touching him as she passed or take advantage of the opportunity to press close. Then again, if he was going to play Tony to her Angel, there were going to be plenty of chances to get close. Very close.

Still, she let her arm brush against his stomach as she stepped into the night. It was right there, after all. She felt the heat and hardness and fought the urge to sigh. She wondered if he was reacting at all. She couldn't really tell and didn't want to risk looking up at him and letting him see that she was enjoying the contact a little too much.

"Sophie?"

His gruff voice did get her to glance up. His dark eyes were hot and intense.

"Yeah?"

"You okay?"

She wet her lips. "Yep."

"You stopped."

"I...stopped?"

"Walking."

She had. She'd just stopped, right in the doorway, her arm against his middle. One second she'd been walking and the next she'd just...stopped.

"Oh." How could she just lose her train of thought like that? And was an automatic action like *walking* even really a train of thought? "Sorry." She managed to step the rest of the way through the doorway and out onto the sidewalk.

She thought she heard Finn clear his throat as he did the same and pulled the door shut behind him. He turned and held out his hand. "Keys?"

Keys. For the door. Right. Sophie fumbled in her purse.

She heard him sigh. "You need to have the key out when you leave and are ready to lock the door," he said. "When you're digging around in your purse, you aren't paying attention to what's going on around you. Someone could—"

Sophie pulled the key ring out of her bag and held it up. "Keys."

He shook his head and took them from her and locked the door. She waited for him to hand them back, but suddenly he pivoted, grabbed her wrist, wrenched her arm behind her back, and pressed her up against the building beside the door.

He moved in behind her, his big, hard front against her

much smaller back. He put his mouth right by her ear and said, "See? You need to be on your guard."

He was making a point. She got that. She got the point. She did. But... "I'm not sure this is the best tactic for filling me with fear and regret," she told him honestly.

Finn went still for a moment, and then he said gruffly, "No? You're not feeling like you should have made another choice?"

"I'm feeling like I'm going to be fumbling in my purse a lot when you're around."

He took a big breath in through his nose, and she was pretty sure she felt his lips against her neck right below her ear. Her knees thought so, anyway, and they wobbled slightly.

"After-hours rehearsals," he said. "We'll need some of those, right? Just the two of us?"

"Lots of those," she told him. "You're a novice, after all. Playing a lead role. You'll need lots of one-on-one time."

"That's excellent news." This time she was sure she felt his lips against her neck. "Damn, you smell good."

Then she couldn't help it any longer and she wiggled her butt against him. She was short enough, or he was tall enough, that her butt was more against his thighs than the spot she most wanted to wiggle against, but it was all still hard and delicious, and when he sucked in a quick breath, Sophie felt warmth flood her system.

And then he was gone, suddenly dropping his hands and stepping back. "So you need to be more careful," he told her.

She turned to ask what was going on and to ask him to get right back up against her—maybe front-to-front this time—when she realized some people were walking by across the street. Clearly the big cop didn't think that the sight of him pinning her against the side of the building looked as okay to them as it had felt to Sophie.

"I'll remember to only fumble in my purse when we're inside," she said with a smile.

He cleared his throat and then nodded. "Good idea."

"We could go back in right now."

He hesitated but then said, "I should probably walk you to your car."

He's the type of guy to keep a dachshund so she won't be traumatized by another move. He's the type of guy to get involved in the theater for his mom. He's the rock of his crazy family. He's a cop. He's a good guy.

She nodded. "You're not a sex-on-the-first-date guy."

"I'm not," he admitted. "I typically go pretty slow."

"Got it." She respected that, and it did seem to fit him. Finn Kelly, with his life full of people who really mattered to him and who he really mattered to, wouldn't sleep with a woman he didn't know and like and respect.

"But we're not dating," he reminded her. Or himself.

"No, we're not. We're just doing a play together," she said with a nod.

They stood simply looking at each other for a long moment. Then he held out his hand. She took it, and he pulled her up beside him as they started down the block.

"Where's your car?" he asked.

She pointed up the block. He looked around. And sighed. "I really hate the idea of you leaving late and coming out here alone in the dark."

"I'm fine. I've never had a problem. And I really do pull my keys out before I leave the building. And I do pay attention to my surroundings. I was a little distracted tonight, but I promise you, no other guy would ever get me up against the building like you did."

She swallowed hard after that, feeling her cheeks flush even just talking about the way he'd pinned her against the side of the theater. It should have felt aggressive. It should have been a great warning about what could happen if she wasn't paying attention. It should have been the lesson he'd intended it to be.

But it hadn't been any of those things. It had been hot. Period.

They stopped beside her car, and it felt like they were both hesitating.

"Are you going to unlock it?" Finn finally asked.

She pushed the unlock button on her fob. He smiled. "I like keyless. Much safer." He reached past her and pulled the door open.

She smiled back at him. "I do appreciate your concern."

"I'm overreacting. I'm aware of that. Just so you know."

"You're a protective guy. A cop. It makes sense."

He shook his head and stepped in closer. "It doesn't make sense. That's the problem."

"It doesn't?"

"I never feel protective of women like this. Other than my mother. I want people to be safe, and I'll do what I can to make that happen. But typically I trust that intelligent, adult women who have been living in this city for a while know what they're doing and will ask for help if they need or want it."

Sophie couldn't describe the look on his face. It seemed as if he was perplexed by the things she was making him feel. Well, that made two of them.

"So what's different about your mom and me?" she asked.

"I probably shouldn't answer that."

Sophie laughed. "Well, now you have to."

"Okay, my mom is...a dreamer. She believes the best about people. She thinks everything will work out if you have good intentions."

"And you think I'm like your mom."

"Aren't you?"

"I am a dreamer," Sophie confessed. "But I know not everything works out just because of good intentions."

Finn frowned and moved in closer. "You do?"

Wow, suddenly he seemed...concerned. "I do," she said. "You know that too."

He frowned harder and then shook his head. "Yeah. I do. Of course I do. I just...don't like that you feel that way."

She laughed softly. "That doesn't make any sense. That's what makes you roll your eyes about your mother. But you want me to feel the way she does? Hopeful and starry-eyed and eternally optimistic?"

Finn lifted a hand and cupped her cheek. "Yeah."

Sophie caught her breath. "Yeah it doesn't make any sense, or yeah you want me to feel that way?"

He shook his head as if he was completely confused. "Both." He ran his thumb over her cheek and then dropped his hand. "It makes no sense, but yeah, I want to think that you're blissfully ignorant of the fact that shit happens even when you do everything right."

His words seemed to slam into her, and it was a few seconds before she could respond. Because yeah, she definitely knew that shit happened even when she did everything right. "Well, I'm not as sweet and naive as that," she said, trying to sound normal.

"That's probably good," he said. "I mean, naive is not

a great thing to be. But..." He cleared his throat. "Never mind. I'm glad you're not a pushover. My mom has some trouble with that."

"Your mother is the sweetest person I know, and I wouldn't change one thing about her," Sophie said gently but firmly. "And if you and I are going to get along, you're going to have to not say negative things about my very dear friend."

He gave her an almost-smile. "I really like it when you get all prickly on my mother's behalf. It's my fourth-favorite thing about you."

"Fourth? What are the first three?" Sophie wanted to hear this list more than she wanted the leftover brownie she had waiting for her at home.

"One, that you swear like a sailor and kickbox even though you seem sweet and easygoing on the outside. Two, that you didn't cast my brother as Tony in the play in spite of him being...him."

Sophie felt her heart swell a little. She knew that Finn gave the spotlight to his brother more often than not because Finn knew Colin needed the attention.

"What's number three?" she asked.

He leaned in, his lips almost on hers. "The way you smell." Then he moved his nose to her neck and took a deep breath. "I love that, actually."

Sophie's entire body erupted in goose bumps. Him *sniffing her* made her all hot and jittery? She could hardly imagine what would happen if he touched her...*really* touched her. But she did have a fantastic imagination, after all. And she knew that she'd be imagining it later. Tonight. In bed.

"So I'll see you tomorrow," he said, straightening and giving her a smile.

"Yep. Sure. Tomorrow. First rehearsal."

"Great."

They stood looking at each other, as they'd done in front of the theater.

"Sophie?"

"Yeah?"

"You can get in your car now."

Right. Okay.

CHAPTER EIGHT

Okay, everyone, I'm going to give you a brief overview of the show and how this all works, and then Angie is going to work with the guys on the first big scene as far as stage placement and so on."

Sophie paced across the front of the stage, addressing everyone who had gotten a part in the play. Finn sat with Tripp and Colin in the row behind the bulk of the players. There were several firefighters and two or three cops as well as some of the theater regulars who wanted to be a part of raising the money the playhouse needed to get back on its feet.

Finn hadn't been to a play since elementary school, but watching Sophie move with grace and confidence, her blond hair glowing around her head and her smile bright and enthusiastic, he knew he could get used to it. If she was up there, anyway.

"It's a love story," she went on. "Tony is from a blue-collar, working-class background. He's a cop." The cops in the seats let out a cheer. She grinned. "Angel is from a wealthy family. She's been raised to be proper and to hang out with the upper crust of Boston society. One night her parents are hosting a big dinner party when they discover some of her mother's jewelry is missing. They call the cops, and one of the cops on the scene is Tony. He takes one look at Angel and he falls head over heels. This is their love story and how they each work to fit into the other's world."

She beamed at the audience. She paused and then frowned slightly, and Finn imagined she wasn't seeing a lot of beaming in return. She sighed. "There are also a couple of fight scenes and a couple of major make-out scenes."

Some of the guys sat up straighter. "Fight scenes?" one of them asked.

She nodded. "Tony's a cop, and some of his buddies are giving him a hard time about spending time with the snooty rich people Angel's family socializes with. He attends a black-tie event as Angel's date, and he gets into it with one of her old boyfriends. A few of his cop friends are the ones who are called in to break it up."

There were some whistles and hoots at that. "Attaboy, Tony!" someone called out.

"And tell us more about the major make-out scenes." This came from Colin, of course.

But Finn wanted to hear more about those too. Colin had taken the news of Finn being cast as Tony very well at Kelly's Pub last night. Of course, Finn had bought the next two rounds after he'd broken the news. Still, Colin was...Colin. He rolled with the punches and very little got him really wound up.

Finn could see Sophie's cheeks get a little pink even from that distance, and he grinned.

"Angel and Tony have a lot of . . . passion. Things between them get pretty intense."

"Let's do this thing," Travis Franklin, one of the cops, said, pushing to his feet.

The other guys followed him up onstage. Sophie stopped Finn on the steps, though. "You're not in this scene, actually," she told him. "But you and I have a scene that your mom wants to go through later, okay?"

"Absolutely." He gave her a quick grin and retreated to the seats again. He was perfectly fine with watching the rest of the guys instead of performing himself. He was going to have to get over that, of course. But he was good with easing in.

"Okay, let's start at the top of page four," Sophie told them. "We'll read through the scene, then go through the blocking."

"The blocking?" Tripp asked.

"Where you're going to stand and move," Sophie explained.

"Got it." Tripp gave Finn a look that said, "You owe me."

Finn just waved to him.

Then Angie stepped to the center of the stage. "Okay, boys, top of page four."

Sophie left the stage and came to sit next to Finn. He was tempted to stretch his arm across the back of her seat but kept his hands to himself. For now.

"What scene are we going to work on later?" he asked quietly, so as not to interrupt the read-through going on.

"Um, scene eight," she said, her eyes on the stage.

"Oh. Because I like scene four." It was the first scene where Tony kissed Angel—after pulling her back in while she was trying to climb out through the window.

Sophie looked over at him. "Scene four, huh?"

"I've got those lines memorized already," he told her with a nod.

"So you for sure want to work on scene four?"

"Yes. Seems like a great scene."

She turned her attention back to the stage. "Have you read through scene eight?"

Busted. "Um, no. Not yet. But I'll read through the whole thing tonight."

She smiled and nodded. "That makes sense."

"What does?"

"That you haven't read ahead. Because scene eight is pretty good. And I really like scene nine."

Finn reached for his script and started thumbing through the pages as Sophie chuckled beside him.

A few minutes later, he had to agree. Scene nine was going to be a favorite. It was one of the make-out scenes she'd mentioned. Unfortunately, to get to scene nine, he had to get through scene eight. That one was going to be tough. Angel and Tony were fighting in that scene, and at one point, Tony loses his temper and pins Angel to the wall. Not the way Finn had done to Sophie last night. This was much more aggressive, and he didn't like the words leading up to that action.

"Can we talk about scene eight?" he whispered to her as she watched Angie arranging the guys on the stage.

She glanced over. "Talk about it? What do you mean?"

"I'm just...He calls her a stuck-up bitch? Is that necessary?"

Sophie turned in her seat. "Yes. It's the story. Tony is a blue-collar, rough-around-the-edges guy. Angel is a high-society girl who's always gotten her way. It contrasts their personalities."

Finn sighed. "That's just not me."

"No, it's not," Sophie agreed. "That's why this is called *acting*, Finn."

"I just don't know if I can pull it off."

"We haven't even been onstage yet," Sophie told him. "It will be fine. You just need to think of something, a personal experience that is real to you, that can help you tap into that feeling of frustration and desperation. I'm sure you've experienced those things before, right?"

He shrugged. He'd pinned plenty of people to the wall at work. But they were criminals, or at least suspects, and typically they were mouthing off and needed someone to show them who was in charge. "At work, I guess."

She shook her head. "How about with your family?" she asked. "Hasn't anyone in your family ever done something or made a choice that made you want to shake them? Hasn't anyone ever pushed you into that frustration because you care about them and they're not listening and they're going to do something to hurt themselves if you don't make them see what they're doing?"

He frowned. "Well...yeah."

"That's the emotion here," she said. "Not just anger, but that feeling that they're going to get hurt and there's nothing you can do. That desperation pushes you to the point where you want to physically restrain them, to keep them safe."

"Is that what Tony's feeling?" he asked.

"You didn't read scene seven?"

He sighed. "I skipped to scene eight."

She smiled. "It's a story. One thing leads to another. Why don't you go back to scene one and give it a try?"

"But Tony isn't actually angry with her then? He's not just being an ass?"

She shrugged. "He's being an ass. But he's desperate. He thinks he'll never see her again if she walks out his door."

"Nothing else is working, so he decides to literally hold on to her," he guessed.

"Exactly. He's trying to make her see that he needs her and that he's willing to do anything to keep her."

"Got it." And he felt a niggle of understanding about his character suddenly. "And you don't worry about scenes like this at all?" he asked. "These are easy for you?"

"Not always, but I don't worry about them, no," she said.

"Because you're a pro?"

"Because I have a perfect roundhouse kick."

He grinned. That she did. "You won't let me go too far then?"

"No chance."

He hoped that applied to things offstage as well. Because he knew the boundaries here—they were spending time together only for the play—but he really did feel like he needed someone keeping him in line. He wanted to go way outside the box with this woman. Which was crazy. He was the one who kept others in line.

"Finn?"

"Yeah?"

"You should probably start on page one."

He nodded when he realized he'd been staring at her. "Well, I read through scene four. I've just got five, six, and seven to go."

She laughed. "Better get to work."

Finn flipped the pages and started to read. And he even comprehended 80 percent of it in spite of the delicious scent in the air when he was sitting so close to Sophie.

But ten minutes later, he found his full attention on the antics on the stage. His friends and coworkers were simply too distracting.

"Wow, they really suck," he said.

Sophie grinned and nodded. "They do. They're totally awkward up there."

Finn looked at her. There was a glow coming from her that reminded him of how she'd looked in the spotlight. But they were sitting in the shadowed seats now. Still, it was clear that she was in her element. "You really love this, huh?"

"Oh, yes," she said with adorable enthusiasm.

"Even when they're terrible?"

"Especially then." She met his eyes. "This is why I do this. To get people like those guys up on the stage for the first time. To show them what it's like, to push them outside of their comfort zones a bit, to get them to try something new. They won't all fall in love with it or maybe ever do it again, but if even one of them decides to come to a show because of this experience, or encourages one of their kids to try theater at school, or even just walks out thinking that they had a little fun, then this was a success."

He wanted to kiss her. Plain and simple. When she got all gushy like this and was lit up from inside, the only thing he could think about was kissing her.

He cleared his throat as memories of the kiss from last night came flooding back. "So you don't care that they could ruin the show?" he asked, not really meaning it.

"They won't," she said confidently. "For one thing, part of the draw is seeing these guys hamming it up. I don't want them to take it too seriously or be perfect. They're real, everyday guys coming in to do something nice. The audience will love it, and the more real they can be, the more the guys will love it too. And that's what I really want—everyone to leave this theater feeling better than they did when they walked in."

Wow, he really liked her.

And that might be more dangerous than wanting to kiss her.

He shifted in his seat and shuffled his script pages to cover that he suddenly wanted to drag her up onstage and demand they work on scene nine. Because if he didn't get his hands on her soon, he was going to do something stupid. Like put his hands on her out here in the seats where it was completely real.

"Hey, Sophie, you know—"

Suddenly she stood up, put her fingers to her mouth, and let out a loud, shrill whistle.

Finn blinked up at her. And all the guys on the stage blinked down at her.

"Okay, guys, listen up. The person who talks during a blocking is the director or the assistant director. That's Angie and me." Sophie made her way down the row and then down the aisle to the front of the stage.

Finn watched as the guys all quieted and shifted so they could see Sophie. His mom stepped back and let Sophie take the lead on…whatever this was. Angie had an affectionate smile on her face as she watched the younger woman, and Finn felt a thump in his chest. Angie really loved Sophie.

That was not, of course, a good reason to get involved with Sophie. In fact, it was the very reason that he should *not* get involved with her. But he did like watching them together.

He diverted his attention by examining the blackened wall of the theater on his left. It was bugging the shit out of him. He wanted the theater put back together. And he wanted to know that no one had set the thing on fire. But he also wanted to know what *had* caused the blaze. If it was faulty wiring or something, they needed to get that fixed too. He didn't want it to happen again, especially when he knew that Sophie was here alone so much.

He pulled out his phone and shot a quick text off to Chuck, who was still investigating. Now that Finn was hanging out here on a regular basis, maybe he could help get things moving. Because whatever was going on had his cop instincts riled up. And that wasn't all. The gorgeous blonde on the stage had him riled up too.

"I think we need to do some shifting," Sophie said to the guys. "Kevin, you seem uncomfortable just sitting on the chair. I think it would be better if you were up pacing."

Kevin was one of the firefighters. He was a big guy—tall and wide—and he shifted on the chair as if it didn't quite fit.

"And Dan, you're so funny. I love the expressions that you're making, but I need you up front where everyone can see them. Let's put you stage left."

Dan smiled at her as if she'd just given him a gold star and moved into position.

"Bruce, you are clearly totally at ease with the props. Let's have you and Aaron trade places. You can be the one who's doing the cooking at the counter, and Aaron, I'm going to have you take Kevin's chair. You have this laid-back vibe. I think you can slouch in that chair and deliver your line perfectly."

Sophie continued to shift the guys around to different

places and even switched some roles. Finn watched, impressed. He'd been completely distracted by her perfume and the *idea* of scene nine while she'd been seeing the big picture and honing in on specifics about each guy and his strengths and weaknesses.

"Let's run through it again from there," she said, taking a seat in the front row. "And Colin?"

"Yeah?" He gave her a big grin.

"Do you and Tripp need to be separated? You guys can't be trying to make the other one laugh the whole time. If you can't control yourselves, I'll have to make some casting changes."

Finn laughed out loud as his best friend and his brother gave each other sheepish looks and then grinned and moved apart. "We'll be good, Sophie," Colin said. "I promise."

"I'm watching you," she told him, and he nodded.

Finn settled back in his chair and took in the scene. Sophie might not have a big family of her own, but she could certainly handle a large, rowdy crowd. She had just the right combination of sweet and salty to deal with the Kellys.

Not that she would need to have anything to do with the Kellys in general, as a group, outside of the theater, Finn reminded himself. Because he was *not* going to get involved with this woman.

* * *

After about an hour, the guys were dismissed with homework and asked to be back the next night around seven.

Finn stopped a few as they headed out. "How about we make it five? Let's get some work done around here first?"

When he had a crew of about ten, he started for the stage where Sophie and his mom were chatting. "Scene eight?" he asked.

Angie nodded. "I wanted you to be aware of that scene," she said. "I thought a run-through without everyone around might be good."

Sophie squeezed Finn's arm, and he felt the electricity shoot up to his chest.

"He'll be fine," she assured his mother. "He knows it's just a play."

Yeah, he did. On a cognitive level. But he wasn't so sure that was the part of him that was going to be responding to Sophie.

"Well, let's go through it," Angie said with a nod.

Finn and Sophie took the stage and flipped to the right page.

"So, summarize the scene for us," Sophie said to him. "What's going on?"

"We're fighting," he said. And she nodded. "You're upset that I didn't introduce you to my friends when I had the chance, and you're threatening to walk out and forget the whole relationship."

She nodded. "Right. And I'm determined to leave, and you're desperate to get me to stay."

"Got it."

"Okay, so how do you want to block it?" Sophie asked Angie.

They talked through a few options, moved Finn around, had him stand next to Sophie, in front of Sophie, behind Sophie...He just did what he was told. But he was taking notes. Like noting the fact that Sophie used a very kind tone of voice and always asked Angie what she thought, but that the little blonde was absolutely in charge. She got her way on every point. Of course, it could have been that his mother was acquiescing to the more experienced director. But he had an inkling it was that Sophie was proving the old adage true—you could catch more flies with honey than with vinegar.

The Kellys used a lot of proverbial vinegar when they disagreed. Angie probably didn't even realize what Sophie was doing.

"Okay, so let's walk through it then," Angie said when they'd decided on the positioning and placement.

"Great." Sophie faced Finn. "Ready?"

"As I'm gonna be," he told her honestly. And a flash of *What am I doing?* went through his mind as Sophie started the scene.

"If that's how you feel, I'll just get out of your way," she said, starting for the door on the other side of the stage.

"I don't want you to leave," Finn read. He followed her and grasped her upper arm. "I'm sorry."

She shrugged off his hold. "You don't have to apologize. We're just...too different."

Finn glanced down at his script. "I don't care about that. I need you."

She laughed humorlessly. "You need me? You can't even tell your friends about me."

He grabbed her again. "I'll work it out. Give me a chance, Angel."

"You had your chance." She tried to pull from his grip, but he held tight and turned her, starting to walk her back to the fake wall.

"Faster, Finn," Angie said. "You're upset. You're not escorting her. You're forcing her."

Finn dropped his hold on Sophie and looked at his mom. "Yeah, okay."

Angie gave him a look. She'd said she knew he would need more time with this scene. "Again," she said.

They went over it three more times, and by the time Finn got Sophie against the wall the fourth time and pinned her hands over her head as directed, he was wound tight. Pinning Sophie's hands over her head was not something he would ever do...unless he was about to kiss her, and strip her down, and then hold her there while he thrust deep and hard and—

"I think that's enough for tonight."

His mother's voice broke into his thoughts, and he realized he had Sophie pinned to the wall quite effectively. And she was staring up at him with heat in her eyes, her breaths coming fast, the pulse in her wrist hammering under his thumb.

"Yeah, okay," he breathed. He let Sophie go and stepped back.

"Stay after," she said quietly. "We can work on this some more without your mom."

He nodded. He didn't know if she was actually offering more rehearsal or if she was thinking about a different take on the against-the-wall thing too, but he would stay after. No problem at all.

The three of them chatted about a few other points in the upcoming scenes with Angel and Tony, and then Finn walked his mom to her car.

"Are you okay?" she asked him as he opened the door for her.

"Yeah," he said. "This acting thing is just new."

"I knew that scene would be hard for you."

"Being aggressive with Sophie like that is hard," he admitted. He saw a lot of domestic assault in his line of work, and it always got to him. How people could do some of the things they did to people they claimed to love was beyond him. Even as crazy as his family drove him sometimes, he couldn't imagine getting truly physical while angry with any of them. He and his brother and cousins had wrestled and shoved, of course. The guys still punched each other in the arm once in a while. And two of his aunts would smack the backs of their heads if they swore at the dinner table. His family was physical, but it was always controlled and never motivated by anger.

"That's not it," Angie said.

"It's...not?"

"It's because those are some really intense emotions in that scene, and you're not good at public displays of emotion. And that's because of your dad."

Finn opened his mouth to respond and realized he hadn't been expecting that at all. "What do you mean?"

"Your dad was a really physical guy," Angie said. "He threw you boys up in the air, he swatted your butts when you misbehaved, he picked me up and swung me around the kitchen, and sometimes he backed me up against the wall when he was angry."

Finn blinked at her. Something niggled in the back of his mind, but he couldn't quite put a finger on it. "I remember Dad was a big guy and he filled up a room whenever he came in. He had a deep voice and a loud laugh."

And he did remember that same voice yelling at times. But he didn't remember his dad being aggressive with his kids or wife.

"He was big and loud, just like his family," Angie said.

"When he was happy you knew it, and when he was angry you knew it."

Finn frowned. "He never hit you, did he?"

Angie should her head quickly. "No, no, nothing like that. And I wasn't afraid of him. Your dad worked and laughed and yelled and loved the same way—with everything he had. He was an open book. You always knew exactly what he thought and felt and stood for. You remind me of him that way."

"Really?" Finn thought about that. People had always told him he was like his father, but he'd assumed it was in looks and build and his mile-wide protective streak and his love for his family.

"You're not loud and physical like him," she said. "But you are steady and strong and do everything with your whole heart."

"And you think I avoid being loud and physical because that traumatized me when I was little?" he asked.

She shrugged. "I don't know that you were traumatized, exactly. But I don't think you liked how...he took everything over. When your dad was around, it was hard to focus on anyone else. You like giving everyone a chance to shine."

"I do?" Finn felt the corner of his mouth curl up. He'd never really considered all of that.

"It's like you and Colin each took half of him to emulate after he was gone," Angie said with a smile. "Your brother is the outgoing, make-everyone-laugh, soak-up-the-spotlight clown. You're the rock, the one that never wavers in what is right, the one that puts all you have into things, and the one that builds everyone else up. And you've let Colin have that spotlight and be that guy."

Finn shook his head. It was true that Colin was the joker and the charmer, but Finn hadn't ever thought about *letting* Colin be that guy. "You think that because Dad always took over a room and no one else got a chance, I hang back?"

She nodded. "I do."

"But I took the part of Tony away from him," Finn pointed out.

"Yeah. That says a lot about how you feel about Sophie, don't you think?" Angie asked.

It did? Finn cleared his throat. "Maybe it just means I'm not such a giving guy after all."

"You are," Angie said. "Which is why I brought all of this up. You're one of the stars. You have to step up and take that spotlight for yourself, Finn. You're going to want to hold back and let Sophie be the center of it all, but…" Angie frowned slightly.

"But what?"

"I just realized—I've been thinking that you and Sophie are so opposite, but really, you have this in common."

"We have what in common?"

"You both want other people to feel special and to have their shot. That's her whole purpose at this theater," Angie said. "So she's going to try to make this show about you and you're going to try to make this show about her and… you both have to be willing to take center stage. Together."

Finn felt his heart thump in his chest. "Okay," he finally said. "I get it."

Angie touched his cheek. "Yeah, I think you do."

Finn watched until she drove off and then started back for the theater. He was about ten yards from the front doors when he suddenly saw movement in the shadow by the corner of the building. There was a man there one moment, and the next he'd ducked down the side of the building, taking the same route Sophie had taken the night of the fire.

Finn frowned and headed in that direction. It could be someone just cutting through to the next street, but there was a back door to the studio, and he had no idea if Sophie was as inconsistent about locking that one as she was about locking the front. He'd just make a quick check.

But as he rounded the corner, he saw the man at the back door of the theater. Finn picked up his pace, automatically feeling for his gun and then cursing when he remembered he was a civilian tonight and his gun was locked up in the back of his truck. He jogged the remaining thirty feet as the door shut behind the man. He was now inside the theater, and Sophie was in there alone. Finn's heart pounded, and he willed his adrenaline to slow. He couldn't panic just because this was Sophie. He was the rock. His mom had just said so. Though he hadn't been acting or feeling very rock steady since he'd met Sophie. He'd been acting very out of character, as a matter of fact.

Finn tried the knob and was surprised to find the door locked. Had the guy jimmied the lock? Had the door been unlocked but he'd locked it once inside? Finn didn't know or care. He ran to the front of the theater and burst through the door, making a beeline for the costume shop.

"Finn!" Sophie was just outside the inner theater doors.

"Stay here!" he told her, sprinting across the lobby.

"What is—"

Finn ripped the door to the costume shop open but found the room empty. He spun and looked up and down the hallway. He heard a noise in the greenroom and lunged for that door. He shoved it open and found a man with his jacket half-on and half-off staring at him from the middle of the room.

Finn advanced on him quickly, grabbed him by the front of his shirt, and backed him up to the wall. "You're under arrest for trespassing," Finn told him, his nose centimeters from the man's, adrenaline-filled blood pumping through his body.

"Who the fuck are you?" the man asked, grabbing Finn's wrists.

Finn shook his slightly. "You don't get to ask questions."

"Just what in the hell—"

"Frank!" Sophie exclaimed a moment later. "What the hell is going on?"

"Me? This asshole burst in here like a lunatic," the man said, looking over Finn's shoulder. "A friend of yours?"

"Yes." Sophie stalked to them and put a hand on Finn's shoulder. "You can let him go."

Finn looked from her to the man and back. "You know him?"

She sighed. "Unfortunately."

"I'm Frank," the man said. "Birch. I'm Sophia's dad."

It took a moment for his words to sink in, but when they did, Finn let go of him quickly, stepped back, and let out a long, slow breath. Well, fuck.

"Frank, this is Finn. He's the lead in our new show."

Her dad. The potential arsonist. The guy who had made Sophie sleep in a car as a kid. Finn clenched a fist, remembering the things she'd confessed to him about her childhood. He definitely wanted to grab the front of Frank's shirt again. He made himself breathe.

"Frank," he finally managed tightly, "I didn't realize you might...stop by." He hadn't known how much Frank was in Sophie's life at all, actually.

"You're the new bouncer around here?" Frank asked, smoothing the front of his shirt.

"No, I saw you come in the back door and knew Sophie was in here alone. I didn't think she was expecting anyone else, and I..."

"Came to her rescue." Frank gave him a grin. "I'm always happy to know my little girl has people looking out for her."

"Finn's here to work on one of the scenes in the play," Sophie said, a firmness in her voice that made Finn lift an eyebrow.

"Oh sure, that's fine." Frank eyed Finn. "Didn't mean to interrupt."

Finn gave him a short nod. "I'm sorry for the confusion." He wasn't sorry he'd shoved Frank around a little, though, and he should probably feel bad about that.

"Well, it certainly makes this father's heart feel better knowing you're here," Frank said.

"I'm definitely here for Sophie."

Sophie cleared her throat. "We're lucky to have Finn in the lead. But I'm sure you're not interested in all of this, Frank," she said. "We'll just head back into the theater and leave you alone."

"Oh no, I don't want to interrupt. You've got...work to do."

Frank shrugged back into his jacket as Finn wondered if he'd imagined Frank pausing before the word *work*.

"I'm going to head out and get something to eat," he told them. "I'll be back later. Probably *a lot* later."

He definitely hadn't imagined Frank's emphasis on *a lot*.

Finn had the urge to stall the man. Not because he wanted Frank's company, but because Finn knew he had a hell of an instinct. Fifteen minutes with Frank, and Finn would have a definite feel for whether Sophie's dad had set the fire. It also wouldn't hurt for Frank to know that Finn absolutely wasn't going anywhere and that Sophie would never, ever be without a safe place to sleep again.

Which was crazy. Sophie was a grown woman. She could, obviously, take care of herself. Still, Finn had a definite itch to let Frank know that Sophie was well protected.

"Frank." It sounded like Sophie was talking through gritted teeth. "You don't have to do that."

"Yeah, no need to rush off," Finn added, watching Frank carefully.

"It's fine," Frank said, moving toward the door. "I'm out."

Finn couldn't actually detain the man, and he didn't have any reason to question him directly about the fire. Chuck had already done that. But he did say, "What do you think of the new show idea, Frank?"

Frank turned back. "The show?"

Sophie had said that Frank wasn't involved in or interested in the theater. But he was sleeping here. Which meant he probably didn't have any intention of trying to burn it down again until he had somewhere else to stay. But that was small consolation. The guy had full access to the place. If he wanted to torch it, he had ample opportunity. But surely he knew that he'd be suspect number one?

Finn didn't like that he was staying here, but it really wasn't because of the fire. It was about Sophie. Finn really didn't like having Frank this close to her so much of the time.

"Yeah," Finn said, putting a friendly note into his voice that he didn't feel. "What do you think about putting firefighters and cops up onstage to raise money for a theater that caught fire?"

Frank smiled widely. "I think it's great."

"You do?"

"Sure. Should bring in a ton of cash, don't you think?"

Right. The money. Sophie had told him that Frank needed money. So even if he had set the fire, maybe the show was enough to postpone another attempt. That way Frank could get half of the box office *and* the insurance money if another fire occurred after the show was over. "I do think so," Finn agreed. "I think it's going to be huge."

"Well, maybe not *huge*," Sophie said. "Maybe a little bigger than a regular show around here."

No, Finn wanted Frank thinking the show could have a big payoff, so he'd keep his matches in his pocket. *His alleged matches*, Finn corrected himself. He didn't know that Frank had done anything but be a terrible father. But Finn's feelings on that subject were not making him forgiving toward the man in general. "Mom said that we're nearly sold out for the first show already," Finn said.

Sophie chuckled lightly. "Mostly your fellow cops and firefighters wanting to come see you guys onstage."

Finn groaned. Yeah, he should have known.

"I have high hopes for the whole thing," Frank said. "Can't wait to see it myself."

"You bought a ticket?" Sophie asked drily.

Frank gave her a wink. "I just went into the computer

and reserved my favorite seat." He grinned at Finn. "Should be some perks to owning the joint, right?"

"You got into the computer?" Sophie asked, before Finn could respond.

Frank nodded. "I have the back row, center seat, for all of the performances." He started for the door again. "And now I'm starving. I'll see you kids later."

So Frank had access to the computer. Finn filed that information away.

"Oh, hey, Finn," Frank said, turning back. "I don't suppose you have twenty bucks? I'm gonna grab a pizza but I'm a little short."

"Frank," Sophie protested.

But Finn reached for his wallet. His choices were being friendly with Frank and hoping that sometime the guy might relax and spill some important information or beating the shit out of him for ever hurting Sophie. Finn went with friendly. This time. "Sure thing." He pulled out two tens and handed them over.

Frank gave him a bright smile, and Finn suddenly saw the resemblance between Frank and his daughter. "Thanks. You're a good man." Frank gave him a salute, and then he was across the room and out the door before anyone could say anything else.

Sophie made a soft growling noise.

Finn looked around the room and took in as many details as he could. "How long's he been staying here?"

She nodded, looked resigned. "Only a few days. And it's temporary. I am so sorry that he asked you for money. That was..." She sighed. "Totally him."

"Not a big deal."

"But it is." She looked frustrated.

He crossed to where she stood. "It's twenty bucks, Sophie."

"But he doesn't need it. And he knew, within just a few minutes of meeting you, that you'd give it."

Finn frowned. "What am I missing?"

She lifted her chin and met his eyes. "He was testing you."

That tweaked Finn's cop instinct too. Was Frank here trying to get a feel for the investigation? Or here to cover something up? Or was he kissing up to the cops and firefighters in his daughter's new show, hoping for a friend to vouch for him if he found himself in trouble? Maybe Finn would pretend to be that friend and find out what Frank Birch was up to.

No, he was not objective about this case. And it had very little to do with the fire and almost everything to do with the woman now looking up at him with the bluest eyes he'd ever seen. But he didn't care.

"Testing me for what?" Finn asked.

"To see how easy it was to get something out of you."

"I had twenty dollars, and he wanted a pizza. This is not a problem."

"It's a huge problem," she said.

"I don't mind."

"Finn!" she finally said, raising her voice. "I know it doesn't make sense to you. You and your family are all about giving. All it took was for you to see that your mom cares about this place and you and your family came. And you didn't just work, but you all brought food, and music, and you made it fun. But my dad hasn't lifted a finger, ever, for this place. Despite the fact that it was his mother's pride and joy, despite the fact that I love it, despite the fact that he owns half of it."

"Sophie—"

But she wasn't done. She paced across the room. "Frank takes. That's all he does. Money, trust, affection— whatever people will give him. But he doesn't give it back. He took advantage of all of my stepmoms. He took advantage of my grandmother—taking her inheritance even though he never understood her love of this place. He took me away from every home and family I ever had. And every time we moved, he took me away from my friends, my schools and teachers, my Girl Scout troops, my dance classes, the best ice cream sundae I've ever had in my life, the only tree house I ever had."

Finn felt a huge knot tightening around his heart, and he accepted the complicated truth—he wanted to make everything okay for this woman. He wanted to take away all the past hurt and make sure nothing hurt her in the future. "I'm sorry that—"

"I know that you can't understand this, Finn. I'm glad you can't. You're lucky. But this is the reality of being around me: Frank will also be around. You just need to . . . keep your distance."

Yeah, well, that wasn't going to happen. And not just because of the investigation.

Finally she pressed her lips together, and then she pulled the door open and started down the hall.

Finn watched her go. For about twenty seconds. Then he stalked after her. Because there were a lot of things between them. But distance was not going to be one of them.

She was at her office door when he grabbed her upper arm and turned her. "Another thing about my family," he said, holding her arm and getting so close that she had to tip her head back to look up at him, "we don't let things go easily, and we can keep a fight going on all night."

"We're fighting?"

"We are," he told her, "because you basically just called me an easy target. And I'm not an easy anything." He stepped across her office threshold and then turned her back to the wall just inside her door.

She looked him directly in the eye. "You're not easy? You sure about that? Because you don't know anything about theater and have no real interest in it, but you are now playing the lead in a play. And it's in spite of the fact that your mom didn't want you to do it and your brother—who you always take care of—wanted the part."

Yeah, he was easy. For her. But she knew that. Finn ran both hands down her arms to her wrists and slowly pulled them up the wall to pin them above her head. "And what do you think that means?" He wondered if she really knew how crazy he was acting.

She licked her lips. "I think it means that you can be...rocked."

"Rocked?" He kind of liked that word. "Yeah. I definitely can. But—" he said, dropping his voice. "I want to be sure that you know who's rocking me."

She took a deep breath and wet her lips. "I really hope it's me."

She seemed perfectly fine with him restraining her hands. And that fired his blood. Not just the provocative position, but the fact that she trusted him so completely. *That* rocked him. As did the intensity with which he wanted to take care of her and make her laugh and how he wanted the right to touch her hair or the small of her back or her hand or the sweet curve of her ass whenever he wanted to. And the way he thought of her first thing in the morning and last thing at night and dozens of times throughout the day. And then there was the way he could feel his heart swell just watching her light up when someone got a scene exactly right and the way she looked at everyone with true affection and pride as they put the show together.

She rocked him. To his very core. "Nobody but you, Feisty," he said honestly.

She swallowed. Probably because of the intensity in his tone. "I hope you don't end up regretting it."

"How could I?"

Doubt flickered through her eyes, but she said, "You don't strike me as the type of guy who's happy about finding yourself in situations you never would have expected to be in."

He held her wrists together with one hand and ran the other down her side to rest on her hip. "You would be right. Usually. But it's funny—I'm pretty happy right now. And I didn't expect any of this." And he didn't even mean this moment in which he was pressed up against her. He might be completely out of his comfort zone in this theater and with this show ahead of him, but he couldn't imagine actually regretting any of it.

"And apparently, you *are* able to put me up against the wall."

Now, rather than doubt or frustration, he saw pure heat in her eyes. "Huh, look at that."

He leaned in but right before he took her mouth, she whispered, "Are we still fighting?"

"Nah," he told her huskily as he slid his hands to her ass and lifted her. "I'm thinking of a different *F* word."

"Thank God," she muttered as she wrapped her legs around him, and he groaned as he pressed into the hot, soft V between her thighs. He freaking loved the thin cotton leggings she was wearing and the loose top that allowed him to run his hand up underneath onto her bare skin. The skin that had been haunting him since he'd first seen it.

He stroked his hand up her back, holding her easily with just the one hand on her butt. Of course, it helped that she was clinging to him as if her life depended on it. Her fingers dug into his shoulders, and her thighs were tight around his hips.

And then she was kissing him as if she'd never get enough. Lips and tongues, hot breaths, soft sighs and moans were all he could concentrate on for several minutes. Several of the best minutes of his life.

She finally pulled back for air, and he trailed his lips down her neck as he squeezed her butt and splayed his other hand between her shoulder blades, holding her against him. He was already addicted to how she felt in his arms.

"Finn," she gasped as he sucked gently on her neck.

"I've been thinking about all of this gorgeous skin since the night of the fire," he told her.

"I've been thinking about your hands since the night of the fire," she said breathlessly.

"Sounds like a damned good combination." He pivoted and took the three steps to her desk. "Need some skin right now, Feisty."

"Yes." As soon as he set her down, she stripped her shirt off over her head and tossed it.

She was again in a sports bra, as on that first day here in her office, and he did what he'd obsessed about doing that day. He ran his hands down her back, stroking over the muscles on either side of her spine and then up the curve of her waist to her shoulders and to the back of her neck. He held her neck in both hands and took her mouth in a hot, deep kiss. He slid his tongue over hers while he tangled his fingers in her hair, tugging her head back and getting a low moan from her. He made love to her mouth for several delicious minutes, but eventually his hands itched to move.

He ran his hands over her curves to the thighs that he'd touched when they'd first met and that he'd been dying to touch again ever since. She parted her knees further as his palms skimmed up the insides of her thighs, and her hands went to his fly, quickly undoing the button and zipper. She ran her palm over his length, and he groaned in relief even as it ratcheted his need higher. He wanted to pull her leggings off, push his jeans to his knees, and thrust. But he also wanted to take this slow.

Sophie was not feeling the slow idea, though. She pulled back and got her sports bra off, then tossed it toward her punching bag. "Touch me, Finn." She took his hands and lifted them to her breasts.

Gladly. Her hard nipples pressed into his palms, and he ran his thumbs over them, eliciting a happy sigh from her. She ran her hands under his T-shirt and over his abs, then pushed the shirt up his torso. Finn yanked it over his head, then dipped his knees and took a nipple into his mouth. Her hand flew to his head, her fingers curling into his scalp. He licked and sucked until she was squirming. And begging.

"Finn. Please."

"Talk to me, Feisty." He straightened, his fingers going to the waistband of her leggings. "What do you want?"

He knew exactly what she wanted, but he wanted to hear it.

She wiggled as he tugged, pulling the leggings and her panties down her legs. "Take your pants off," she said, her voice husky.

But he couldn't move.

"Finn? Pants."

"Yep. For sure." He sucked in a breath. "Just give me a second."

She looked up at him, but his eyes were locked on the gorgeous view of Sophia Birch, naked, legs spread on her desk.

"Finn?"

"Just one more second."

"It's just that—"

"Soph, I've been imagining this for a while now. Just let me look."

"But you can do more than look." She took his hand and pressed it between her legs.

He sucked in a sharp breath at the wet heat against his palm. He squeezed his eyes shut as the reality of the moment came crashing in. He was going to make love to Sophie. And this was going to change everything.

But a millisecond later, he realized that wasn't true. It wasn't going to change a thing. This was the path they'd been on since he'd taken that first step to follow her into this theater the night of the fire. This was simply... inevitable.

"Damn, Sophie."

"Yeah," she breathed out. Then she reached for him. She pushed his jeans and boxers out of the way but didn't take time to just look as he had. She took his cock in hand, wrapping her fingers around him and letting out a little sigh as if just touching him was a huge relief.

He knew the feeling. But Finn had to brace his other hand on the desk beside her hip to keep his knees from wobbling as pleasure streaked through him. When his world had righted again, at least mostly, he was seized by the need to make her wobble too. So he moved his fingers. He stroked over her wetness, circled her clit, then slipped inside her tight sheath.

"Finn." Her hand tightened around him.

"Need you, Sophie."

"Yes."

"But you have to get there first." That was nonnegotiable. The chance to pleasure Sophie fully was simply not something he would, or could, pass up.

She shook her head. "Don't want to wait."

"You want to wait for this." He added a second finger between her legs as he kissed her again, his tongue stroking in rhythm with his fingers.

She arched closer, kissing him back hungrily.

His thumb circled over her clit, and she pulled back with a gasp. "Finn, please."

"Anything you want."

"I want you inside me."

"Oh, baby, I'm gonna be inside you."

That seemed to push her closer to the peak. She moaned and tightened around his fingers. Finn grinned. He leaned in and put his mouth against her ear. "I'm going to be buried deep when you come next time, Feisty," he said huskily. "But this first time, I want to feel you come all over my fingers. Then I'm gonna lick them clean while you stroke me right to the edge."

Her moan was louder, and she clenched around his fingers again.

"That's right, sweet Sophie. I'm going to hold these gorgeous hips I've been fantasizing about while I thrust deep, and you're going to think about that every time I get you up against that wall onstage. Every night when the show is over your panties are going to be wet and you're going to be strung tight." He stroked her faster, loving the way her breathing was becoming ragged and her fingers were gripping his arm. "And if you're really sweet, I'll bring you in here after you take your bows and take care of you."

Her fingers dug into his forearm and she gasped again and Finn knew he had her.

"And every time you sit down at this desk or meditate on this floor or kick the hell out of that punching bag, you're going to think about how I made you call out my name with just my fingers before taking you with my cock."

And that did it. Sophie shot over the edge with a cry, squeezing his fingers tightly.

He let the ripples fade and then lifted his hand to his mouth and did what he'd promised. He kept his eyes locked on hers as he sucked her sweetness from his fingers. Her eyes were wide, but she did her part too, stroking him firmly until he had to grasp her wrist to stop the exquisite pressure. "Now, Soph."

"God, yes." She wiggled as he reached for the condom he had in his wallet. He shoved his jeans and boxers out of the way and rolled it on and then slid his hands under Sophie's butt and pulled her to the edge of the desk.

She wrapped her legs around him, her hands on his biceps. He looked into her eyes. "You ready?"

"You can't do what you just did and not know the

answer to that question." She dug her heels into his ass, urging him forward.

And with a short huff of laughter, he thrust deep. They both groaned, and his body insisted he move immediately. The friction, the heat, the feel of her holding on to him as if he were her lifeline, the gorgeous sounds she made, the look in her eyes—Finn took it all in, and it seemed to build quickly into one blazingly bright ball of pleasure and ache and want and contentment all at the same time. But there was no pausing, no relishing. He had to go faster. He had to go harder. And Sophie was right with him.

Only a few delicious minutes later, she gasped, "Finn, *yes!*"

"Let go for me, Soph."

"I'm so close. So close," she panted.

And then satisfaction ripped through him as her second orgasm hit and she tightened around him as she called out his name.

He leaned into her, buried his face in her neck, and let go too, his own climax thundering through him as he clutched her close. He breathed deeply, taking in her scent with each inhale, letting the details—like how soft her hair was against his cheek, how she was still holding him tightly, how she fit perfectly against him—sink in. How he never wanted to be anywhere but right here. How he'd just had a deep, intense orgasm and wanted her all over again. How he'd never get enough of her.

How he wished they were in a bed where he could pull the comforter up over them, fold her in his arms, and talk with her while he let his hands wander all over this body that he wanted to memorize from head to toe. How he wanted to say sweet things like how gorgeous she was and how lucky he felt that she'd let him close like this. Close was hard for her. This was not sex-only dating, and he knew she knew that. And he wanted to eat ice cream in bed with her. He wanted to read out loud to her. In bed. And he wanted to talk dirty to her. In bed. In the shower. In the kitchen. In his truck. There were so many dirty things he wanted to say to her, do to her, hear *from* her.

Yeah, he really wished they were in a bed.

Finn finally pulled back, overwhelmed by all those thoughts and yet wanting to dive right into all of them. "Sophie—"

But just then there was a loud thump, a clatter, and then voices in the outer lobby.

No. He closed his eyes and swore.

"Sounds like Rob and Chase and the others came to do some of the painting tonight," Sophie said.

Yeah, that's what it sounded like. He sighed. "Great."

And Sophie started to giggle. The giggles quickly turned to outright laughter, and then she snorted.

He looked down at her, fighting his own smile. "Go ahead and say it." He'd been intent on getting to the costume shop when he'd thought Frank had broken in, so...

Happiness shining in her eyes, Sophie said, "You really should have locked the front door."

CHAPTER NINE

Not arson. Electric.

Finn read the text from Chuck as he made his way down the sidewalk to his family's pub a week later.

So that was that.

They could now get to work repairing the wall, and Finn could stop worrying about Frank. What a relief. But Finn had to admit that he didn't really feel relieved.

Had he wanted Frank to be guilty? Why? So Finn could lock him up and keep him away from Sophie?

Well, that was a little disturbing. And not out of the realm of possibility.

He just didn't like Frank. He didn't like that Frank made Sophie unhappy. And Finn probably liked her too much.

And he definitely needed a beer. Or five.

He hadn't seen Frank again since the night at the theater. He hadn't seen Sophie alone again since then either. It had been a week since they'd had sex in her office, and he was definitely on edge because of it. Spending time with her, kissing and touching her onstage for an audience, but not having a chance to do any of it privately, was making him nuts. But the entire cast had been working late, several of the guys sticking around to help build sets, Sophie's friends coming in to work on costumes and props, and everyone busting their butts to learn their lines. And Angie wanted to be a part of any one-on-one rehearsals he and Sophie needed. The show wasn't far off, and they weren't really ready. They were done so late at night that he wouldn't have asked if he could take Sophie home—and stay—even if his mother hadn't been there, listening in seemingly constantly.

Finn shoved the door to Kelly's Pub open. He wasn't going to see Sophie at all tonight. Sophie's friends had apparently insisted she needed a night away from the theater—and a few margaritas.

He did hope to maybe get some drunk texts from her later. Maybe even an invitation to come over. But he also knew that Maya and Kiera were Sophie's family, and he, of all people, knew the importance of time with family.

"Finn."

"Hey, Jamie," Finn greeted his cousin. Jamie was behind the bar, drying pint glasses, looking every bit the Irish pub owner. His red hair and green eyes, quick smile, and quicker temper were almost cliché.

"Burger?" Jamie asked.

As if he needed to ask. Finn always wanted a burger. "Extra fries."

Finn slid up onto one of the bar stools. He stopped in at Kelly's Pub at least twice a week. There was great food and great beer, and he liked 90 percent of the people who hung out here. And he was related to 80 percent of that 90 percent. But even if the food had sucked, he would have shown his face at Kelly's regularly because if he didn't someone would be checking up on him.

It was how the family kept tabs on one another in between huge family get-togethers. Which happened at least once a month. So it was all ridiculous. But if he stopped at the pub, he could have one of the best burgers in Boston, and he could avoid multiple phone calls and having random aunts and cousins show up on his doorstep to check on him.

Of course, they always brought food, so it wasn't all bad. Still, this was easier. Jamie and his pub functioned as the hub of family communication. Everyone tried to stop in often enough that he could keep everyone else apprised of how they'd looked, how they'd sounded, what they'd eaten, and how long they'd stayed.

Jamie pushed a beer across the bar. An Irish stout. Finn hadn't wanted to like Irish beer best. It was such a stereotype. But it really was his favorite.

"Hey, there was a guy in earlier asking about you," Jamie told Finn, leaning an elbow on the bar.

Finn took a swallow of the dark beer. "Oh?"

"Said his name's Frank. He said you met the other night at the theater."

Frank. Sophie's dad. Finn frowned. "I slammed him up against a wall because I thought he was stalking Sophie. Then I gave him twenty bucks for a pizza."

Jamie, the bartender and family go-between, didn't even bat an eye. He'd heard it all. "Well, he's coming in around six. Told him you'd be here."

"Didn't it occur to you that he might be an ex-con trying to get even with me? Or that maybe I didn't want to see him?" Finn asked, taking another long drink of his beer.

"I don't want you to get lazy," Jamie said with a grin. "I need you on your toes when you're here. What if someone comes in and tries to rob me?"

"Dick."

"Enjoy your burger." Jamie set down the plate that his waitress, their cousin Shannon, had just handed him.

Finn stuffed three fries into his mouth as Jamie moved down the bar to refill two whiskeys for the guys on the end.

Frank Birch was coming to see him. That was...weird. How had Frank known to look for him here? Though honestly, that wasn't as big a mystery as it sounded. Frank could have asked around. Finn had been a cop in this part of town long enough now that the neighborhood knew he was part of the Kelly clan that ran the best bar in the area. Hell, Finn had been behind the bar on more than one busy night.

But why would Frank want to see him? And why did Finn have the urge to put a hand around Frank's throat when he saw the man again?

"Heads up," Jamie muttered ten minutes later from behind the tap.

Finn finished off his fries as Frank climbed onto the bar stool beside him. "Finn."

"Hey, Frank. What's up?"

"Came in looking for you earlier." Frank gave Jamie a brief nod in greeting.

"Get ya something?" Jamie asked.

"Beer. Whatever Finn's having," Frank said.

Jamie filled a mug and slid it to Frank. He gave Finn a look that Finn knew was asking if things were good. Finn scratched the side of his neck. That meant, "Yes for now but stick close." All the Kelly cousins had come up with a series of hand signals when they were younger so they could communicate without the adults knowing what they were saying, and the sign language had proven just as convenient as they'd become adults themselves.

"So what brings you to Kelly's?" Finn asked Frank. It had been clear there was tension between Sophie and Frank the other night, and honestly, that was enough to put Finn on edge around the other man.

Frank turned on his stool. "You're very protective of my daughter."

"I am." There was no sense denying it. Finn knew it was obvious, and there wasn't a damned thing he could do about it.

"I wanted you to know that I appreciate that," Frank said. "As her father, I like knowing someone is looking out for her."

As her father. But if Frank was such a great, concerned dad, why did Sophie have a strict no-family rule with the guys she dated? She didn't want to get involved with the big, crazy family stuff that was the Kelly family. And Finn couldn't totally blame her. They were a handful. But he'd seen her watching them the first night when they'd all shown up to work with dinner in hand. She'd looked...wistful. She'd said he was lucky.

"Well, no worries there," Finn said. "I intend to keep a close eye on her."

"I'm glad she's got you, Finn," Frank said.

Something squeezed in Finn's gut. Sophie had him alright. Wrapped around her little finger. And it had happened quickly.

"I'd do anything to keep her happy and safe," Finn said. He made sure that his resolve was clear in his tone. He hadn't said it out loud before this, but he meant it. Completely. Even if it meant coming between her and her dad. Maybe it was fast to be feeling this way. Maybe it didn't make total sense. But it was very real.

He'd always taken his time with relationships. He'd always had plenty of time to take. He hadn't known the date when things would be over before this. Maybe he was feeling like everything was heightened and more intense with Sophie because they were packing their relationship into a month's time. The way people who learned they only had a few months to live tried to pack everything they'd always wanted to do into that little bit of time.

Or maybe it was just Sophie.

"That's what I wanted to talk to you about," Frank said.

"Sophie's safety and happiness?"

"Yes."

Finn pushed his plate back and wrapped a hand around his beer as he turned to face Frank. "Okay. Let's talk about that." He knew Frank saw how serious this was to him.

The older man swallowed and met Finn's eyes. "I haven't been a very good father."

Finn's hand tightened around his mug, but he said nothing.

"I haven't been able to settle down. I've been restless, and I've... never been able to give Sophie a stable home. Her mom died when she was only two. And I've been lost ever since then."

Finn unclenched his jaw. "Why are you telling me this?"

"She clearly likes you," Frank said. "And your mom. They're close, right?"

Finn narrowed his eyes. Frank made him suspicious. Period. His gut was solid. When it told him something wasn't right, it wasn't right. "Yes, they are."

"That's wonderful," Frank said. "I love knowing Sophie has people that care about her."

"Frank," Finn said, evenly and firmly, "what do you want from me?"

"I want you to help me get back in Sophie's good graces," Frank said. "I haven't done right by her, I admit that. But I don't think it's too late to start trying to show my daughter that I care about her and I want to be a good guy for her. I want to be in her life."

"You're not in her life now?" Finn asked, watching the man carefully. He was good at reading people. But he could also spot a guy who was good at not letting people read him. That was Frank. He was too...perfect. His look of contrition, his mannerisms, his tone of voice. It all said that he was being completely honest. And that made Finn suspicious. He wasn't the sunny optimist his mother was.

"I want to be," Frank said. "But she's not letting me close. She doesn't trust me."

"Does she have reason for that?" Finn didn't have to admit to Frank the things he already knew—like the fact that Frank had never held a job for more than six months or that the women he married usually had money or that he'd done a stint in prison for identity theft. But then again, he had a feeling Frank would expect him to have done a background check.

"She does," Frank admitted. "I always took care of her— food, clothes, shelter. She was always physically safe."

Not sleeping in your car, you jackass, Finn thought, but he gritted his teeth and stayed quiet.

"But not…emotionally," Frank said. "I moved her around a lot. I took her away from what friends she managed to make in each new place. I took her away from the stepmothers that she grew to love. It was a lot for a little girl to go through."

Finn was torn between a powerful urge to go to Sophie, wrap her up, and promise to keep her safe—physically and emotionally—forever, to promise that she'd never have to say goodbye to someone she cared about again…and wanting to strangle Frank.

He'd hurt Sophie. Now she shied away from the idea of family because, as far as she knew, it never lasted. It was easier to go without than to say goodbye over and over again. But that was keeping her from having the love, laughter, support, and comfort of a group of people who would do anything for her.

She had her friends, and Finn prayed to God that they were filling some of those gaps. But…it wasn't the same thing as having a family of her own.

It was no wonder Sophie wanted nothing to do with his family. She and Angie were close, but there was no reason to think she'd have to ever say goodbye to Angie. Unless she dated Angie's son and then they broke up.

Finn felt frustration tighten his shoulders and neck. Fuck. Sophie couldn't take any more goodbyes.

Which meant he should leave her the hell alone. He couldn't give her any guarantees. And if being involved with him would end up hurting her…he'd rather stay away. Or just be her costar. Yes, he could do that. He could help pull off the play. He had to do that. But he could keep his distance otherwise. And keep her from his family.

"So will you help me?"

Frank's question pulled Finn from his churning thoughts. "Help you what?"

"Help me show her that I'm trying to be stable, settle down, be there for her."

"How can I do that?"

Frank shrugged, and for a moment he did look legitimately downtrodden. "I need a job, a place to stay, a way to show her that she can trust me to stick around this time."

Finn watched the other man drink from his beer and then run his hand up and down the side of his mug.

"You really want to stay around Boston? Settle down here to be close to Sophie?" Finn asked.

Frank nodded. "It's time. And I have to do it, just me. No women. No new stepmom," he said. "I've depended on the women in my life to make the home and to give Sophie that sense of stability."

"And then you broke up with them and pulled that rug right out from under your daughter," Finn said, his tone tight. "Again and again."

Frank nodded miserably. "I did. So this time, it's just me."

Finn wasn't convinced that Frank was here because of Sophie at all. But if Frank didn't have a job or a place to stay, who knew how desperate he might get or what he might do? Would he find another sweet, unsuspecting single woman or widow to charm into letting him live off of her? That was his pattern. He'd never owned—or even co-owned—any of the houses he'd lived in. His wives had. And they'd all had decent-paying, solid careers. While Frank had only worked odd jobs. There had been relatively little time between one marriage and the next. It didn't take a NASA scientist to see that Frank had found women who could support him. So if he was jobless and homeless, it wouldn't be long until Frank set his sights on another woman who would take care of him.

It might not be ending world hunger or keeping the ice caps from melting, but Finn could definitely feel good about keeping Frank Birch from finding a new target. And keeping him from hurting Sophie.

He knew enough about Frank to know that the best way for Finn to protect Sophie was to know where Frank was and what he was doing. And if Sophie wanted to, eventually, ever, have a relationship with Frank, Finn could make sure it went well. And if she didn't, then Finn could keep Frank away from her.

"Tell you what," Finn said. "I can help with a job."

Frank looked up, his eyes brighter. "Really?"

"Well, you won't have a 401(k), but yeah, I can get you work."

"Great. That's all I need. I can start there and show her I'm trying."

"And you're going to have to put up with the Kelly clan." That was actually a big part of Finn's plan. Not only would he take away any reason Frank might have for hitting on a new woman, but he'd also be able to keep an eye on him, with the help of his family.

Frank actually smiled at that. "That's not a problem. I'm easy to get along with."

Actually, Finn believed that. Frank Birch no doubt was easy to get along with—when that suited his purposes.

"My cousin Gina is going to be going on maternity leave soon," Finn said. "She cooks here at the bar. You think you can handle making sandwiches and burgers and stuff?"

"I've been a short-order cook," Frank said. "No problem."

Finn thought that Frank had probably done a little bit of everything. Which could be handy. "Let me go talk to Jamie," Finn said, stretching to his feet. "You hang tight."

"Hey, Finn, thanks. I mean it. I know you care about Sophie, and I know she's pissed at me, but this is really a step toward making her happy."

Finn's gut clenched. He didn't trust Frank to make her happy. Hell, he wasn't sure he trusted anyone to make her happy. Except him.

"Listen, I'll take care of the job situation, but you'll have to prove to Sophie that it means you're really there for her," Finn said. "That's on you. I'm not going to plead your case or tell her to give you a chance or anything. You'll have to do that work yourself."

Frank nodded. "I agree. That's on me."

Finn took a breath, tamped down the feeling of what-did-I-just-do, and headed for the kitchen to tell Jamie he'd just hired Frank. Something he was probably *not* going to tell Sophie just yet.

* * *

Sophie turned a full circle in the middle of the room. The greenroom was where the actors waited in costume to go on. It was a mishmash of furniture, and the countertop that ran the length of the room under multiple mirrored panels was littered with random supplies: tissues, safety pins, needles and thread, wet wipes, black and brown markers for touching up shoe scuffs, makeup, and every color of face paint imaginable. All things someone might need at the last minute before heading into the wings.

What it did not currently have, however, was any sign that Frank was staying here. Where was his duffel? Where were the empty food wrappers? Where were the blanket and pillow she'd brought in and left for him?

There was nothing that indicated Frank had been sleeping here. A feeling of foreboding started in her gut, and she pulled her phone from her back pocket and dialed.

He'd found a new woman. Already. Unbelievable. She definitely hadn't been thrilled with him staying here and knowing all the comings and goings of the cast and crew for the show, but it had meant that he wasn't sleeping in some poor unsuspecting woman's bed, romancing her and sweet-talking her and telling her she was the center of his world so he'd have sex, and meatloaf, and cable. And not necessarily in that order of priority.

Sophie wanted to warn the woman, wanted to tell her that Frank was just using her and was never going to change and to get as far away from him as she possibly could. But right now, she just needed to know that whoever was feeding and sheltering him did *not* have the last name Kelly.

Frank answered on the fourth ring. "Hey, honey."

She gritted her teeth. The woman must be there for him to sound so happy to hear from her. "Where are you?"

"What do you mean?"

"I mean, I haven't seen you in a couple of days, and I'm in the greenroom now and it's clear that you haven't been sleeping here."

"You missed me?" he asked, his surprise almost sounding genuine.

"No, Frank. But when I know where you are, I also know where you *aren't*."

"Well, isn't that sweet." His affectionate tone was for whoever was in the room with him. Sophie could picture the look he would have been giving her if they were in person. It wasn't affectionate.

"So who did you trick into taking you in?"

"I'm staying with Joe, actually."

Sophie frowned. "Is Jo short for Josephine?"

"No, I believe it's short for Joseph."

She paused. "Didn't realize that you were desperate enough to open your options up to that point," she said drily. Maybe Frank had won a poker game or something and was letting the loser pay him back with housing.

"Joe Kelly," Frank said, his voice losing a bit of the happy-to-hear-from-you of a minute earlier.

Kelly. Sophie felt trepidation creeping up her spine. Joe was a man, but he was a Kelly. That wasn't good.

"Who is Joe Kelly?" Sophie asked, surprised to find that she was still clinging to hope. Hope that Kelly was a common-enough name in Boston that Frank had managed to befriend one who was in no way related to Finn and Angie.

"One of Finn's uncles."

Sophie felt her heart begin racing at the mention of Finn's name. And not in the usual good way. "No," she said out loud without really thinking.

"No?" Frank repeated. "Yes, he is."

And *that* was why she didn't keep a lot of hope around. Frank always managed to dash it.

"What are you doing with one of Finn's uncles?"

"Oh, I'm staying on his pullout couch," Frank said. "Joe's been living alone since his wife died, and Jamie thought it would be good to have someone here with him."

"Jamie?" Sophie repeated. "Who's Jamie?"

"One of Finn's cousins."

Oh, God. Sophie rubbed her forehead. "Frank, what are you doing hanging out with Finn's family?"

"Well, it all started when Finn and I were having a beer at the bar, and he mentioned they could use some extra help. So I agreed to take the job. And then Jamie, the manager at the bar, said that Joe had a pullout couch and said I could crash there."

Sophie wasn't sure which thing to focus on first. That Finn had gotten a beer with her father, that he'd given her father a job, that his cousin had given Frank a place to stay, or that not only was Frank back in Boston and back in her life, but he'd insinuated himself into the group of people she was falling for in spite of herself. And had just ruined any chance of her getting any closer to them. Any of them.

But, truthfully, she'd known it would come to this the moment when she'd heard him say he was back in Boston. She'd kept him away from Maya and Kiera and her other friends, and she'd tried to keep him away from the Kellys. She'd downplayed her relationships; she'd hidden her feelings. But this wasn't just Frank going after people who mattered to her. This was those people reaching out to him. It was *Finn* reaching out to him.

Because that was Finn. Frank was her father, and Finn didn't understand a family dynamic that wasn't rainbows and roses. No doubt he thought he could make Frank and her into a father-daughter version of Angie and Finn. But Finn didn't know shit about not-happy-family situations.

"How long has this been going on?" she asked, pushing the words out through the tightness in her throat.

"Oh, a little over a week."

Sophie felt the vise around her head tighten. She'd just been happy to avoid seeing Frank for the past week. It hadn't occurred to her that she should be worried. "What work are you doing at the bar?" *Please don't say they trust you with the cash register or accounting.*

"Whatever we need," Frank said. "Washing some dishes, doing some cooking. I help behind the bar if we get busy."

He was already using the word *we*? Good God. But that was part of Frank's magic. He got people to buy into the relationship because he pretended to buy in. As far as they could tell, he wanted it all to work out and was going to do his part. But Frank Birch was washing dishes at a bar and sleeping on a pullout couch? Yeah, sure, that was going to last.

She knew very well what this was. Joe's couch and the bar were stepping stones, a way of getting closer to other Kellys. Like Angie.

"And you're probably getting to know the family pretty well, huh?" she asked drily. Frank knew that she knew all his schemes and patterns. And hell, getting to know the Kelly clan wasn't hard. She could personally attest to the fact that was nearly impossible *not* to get to know them all.

"Oh, sure," he said. "They're all wonderful."

Sophie might have been the only person in the world who could have detected that tiny note of smugness in his voice, but she most certainly heard it.

Finally she dropped all pretense of friendliness. It didn't matter if Frank realized just how much she cared about the Kellys now. He was sleeping on one of their couches, for fuck's sake. So he needed to know where she stood.

"Frank, can you hear me clearly and are you paying attention?"

There was a pause on his end, as if he was surprised. "Yes," he finally said.

"You're messing with the wrong family."

"Is that right?"

"It is," she said, coolly and firmly. There was only one way she could really hurt Frank. Financially. But fortunately, money was the most important thing to him. "Because if you hurt one of them, if you so much as give one of the Kelly women a charming smile, I will make sure that you never see any money from this theater ever again."

There was another pause.

Then he laughed. Which she'd been expecting. So she gritted her teeth and waited.

Finally he said, "Really? You going to set it on fire and let it burn this time?"

"If that's what it takes to get you away from the people I care about." Shock rippled through her as she heard what she'd just said. And realized she meant it. The theater was important to her. For a long time, she'd thought it was the most important thing. It was her only happy connection to her biological family and the source of the happiest memories from her childhood. But she'd burn the damned thing down if it would keep Frank out of her life and away from the people she loved.

"I don't believe you." Frank had sobered and sounded almost angry now.

"You don't want to push me, Frank. Because I promise you, if I did burn it down, you wouldn't see a fucking penny of that insurance money." She sucked in a breath and forced herself to at least *sound* calm and in control. "But it won't come to that," she went on. "I don't need to get rid of the theater to cut you off financially."

"Well, the courts might not agree with you, *sweetheart*," he said. "I believe my fifty percent ownership is still intact."

"It is," she agreed. "And I will continue to give you fifty percent of whatever the theater brings in. But fifty percent of nothing is nothing, Frank."

"You couldn't run the theater without selling tickets," he said.

And again Sophie heard something in his voice that only she would have been able to pick up—uncertainty.

"Oh, Frank," she said cajolingly, "I can bring in enough to break even on expenses. You only get fifty percent of the *profits*."

"Ah, so you've got your sights set on Finn to take care of you then," Frank said.

Sophie narrowed her eyes. "No, Frank. I'll be taking care of myself. And only myself. Not you. Not anymore."

"You're going to have to make *some* profit then," Frank pointed out.

"Yep."

"But you're not going to share it with me?" Frank said, his voice getting harder again. "My lawyer might be interested in that."

"Your lawyer is Danny Caid, and his only credentials are that he's seen every episode of *Law & Order*," Sophie said.

"He knows lawyers."

"It won't matter," Sophie said, lifting her chin even though Frank couldn't see her. "I'll send you twenty bucks here and there to make it look good."

He laughed. "You would steal money from your own father? Really, Sophia?"

"Really, Frank," she said, letting him hear her cold anger.

"You think you could pull that off?"

"Well, I am Frank Birch's daughter. I haven't even begun to tap my manipulative, scheming, conscienceless genetics. Pretty sure I could pull off a tiny embezzlement."

He didn't say anything for several ticks. "Well, I guess I'm going to have to ask some friends for a loan then," he said. "Angie did mention that if I needed anything, all I had to do was ask."

Sophie felt her lungs freeze. "Angie?" she managed to choke out.

"Finn's mom. Lovely, sweet woman."

Sophie felt a knot begin to tighten in her gut. She recognized it, of course. It was white-hot anger. But it was now mixed with fear. And a strange desperation.

She had to keep Frank away from Angie. And Finn. And all the Kellys.

"You met Angie at the bar?" she asked tightly.

"Joe's, actually. She brought pie. Peach."

Frank's favorite. Awesome.

The anger and fear and desperation all began to roil in her stomach. Would she burn the theater down to get Frank out of her life? Maybe not. But would she do it to keep him away from the people she loved? Absolutely.

"Stay away from Angie, Frank. I mean it."

"Too late. We had a very nice, long talk at Roger's barbecue two nights ago."

Sophie opened her mouth, but she had no idea what to say.

"They asked why you weren't there and told me to bring you next time," Frank went on. "But I explained that big family gatherings aren't really your thing. Unlike your old man. I love that stuff. The talking, the sharing, the laughter. The way they're all there for one another. And they play a cutthroat game of corn hole." He laughed as if remembering the good times, but it sounded completely empty to Sophie. "You know that game? They have the big board with the hole cut out that you toss bean bags through for points?"

Yeah, she knew what corn hole was. She also knew that Frank was completely full of shit. He didn't care about family get-togethers and lawn games. He cared about nice, generous people trusting him and giving him stuff for free.

"Frank—"

"They also play cards. Pitch and poker. And they tell stories and give each other a hard time, but it's all in fun, you know? They made me feel like part of the family. What a great group of people."

Sophie felt her heart squeezing. He didn't mean it. He was making a point with her that he was already exactly where she didn't want him to be. And, dammit, where *she* wanted to be. She wanted to go to a family barbecue with the Kellys. Even Frank's reminiscing about it made her ache with want.

And that made her realize that they must think she was a terrible person. What had he told them about their relationship? Because who didn't let their own father stay at their place when he'd just gone through a bad breakup and was nursing a broken heart? She could imagine the stories Frank was spinning for them.

She could tell them that Frank had money to spend on housing, he was just choosing to mooch off of someone else instead. She could tell them that she and Frank were essentially estranged, that she'd had a rough childhood, that he wasn't who they thought he was. But they didn't know her well enough to believe her. Because she'd been staying away. And they did know Frank. They'd been around him. And she knew that Frank had won them over. Frank could be the most easygoing, fun-loving, charming, and genuine-seeming person ever. If it suited his purposes. With the Kellys it would have. He wanted to be close to that family. With good reason. If anyone would give him the shirt off their back, it was the Kellys. He'd felt like part of the family. They were taking care of him—giving him a job and a place to stay. *Son of a bitch.* Instead of focusing on just one woman to take him in, he'd hit the jackpot. He had a whole family now.

And it was her fault he'd met them.

Sophie swallowed past the dryness in her mouth. "Did you already ask Angie for money?" she asked. He had, she was sure. Just as he'd asked Finn for money for a pizza, he'd have wanted to find out how hard it would be to get them to hand things over to him.

"Oh, it just kind of came up," he said nonchalantly. Though Sophie could easily picture the scheming glint in his eye. "We were chatting about our kids and how much we love being close enough to visit them all the time, but how we don't like being a burden on them."

She squeezed her eyes shut. "How much did you ask her for?"

"Well, she understood how I hate asking *you* for help."

"Did you mention how you want me to marry her son

so that you can live in our basement for the rest of your
years?" she finally snapped.

"You better not put me in the basement, Sophia Isabelle.
I plan on having an upstairs room with my own bathroom."

"Oh, for fuck's sake! How much did you take from
Angie?" Sophie shouted into the phone.

"Don't worry. It's a loan," Frank said.

It was never just a loan. But that confirmed her worst
fears. He'd already gotten money out of the Kellys. And
not just any Kelly. Angie. The sweetest and most bighearted of any of them.

"Frank," Sophie said. "Do. Not. Do. That. Again."

"Then I guess you need to be sure I'm getting my share
from the theater."

And just like that, Frank won. As always. He had a free
place to stay, a job, and ongoing financial support for absolutely no effort at the theater, and he'd made himself
completely at home in the midst of an entire family that
would support him and help him.

But maybe when he got tired of the few demands they
might place on him—like showing up for work and being
a decent guy—and left them all behind, it wouldn't hurt
them the way it had her stepmoms.

As the thought flitted through Sophie's mind, she
latched on to it. The Kellys might feel betrayed or angry or
confused when Frank turned out to be someone other than
they'd thought. But they wouldn't be hurt. It wouldn't radi-
cally change their lives as it did those of the women he left.

Yes, that was good.

The only problem then was that *she* would still lose
them. And that would definitely hurt.

"So if the theater keeps making money, you won't need

any more from them," she said. "You'll just...sleep at Joe's and go to work."

And barbecues. Don't forget that he gets to go to barbecues.

"Well, I'll tell you what, darlin'," Frank said, his voice sugary sweet again. "I'm liking this gig. I'm just hanging out at a bar, eating burgers in the backyard and watching ball games on TV. This is way easier than trying to keep a woman happy. I can't believe I haven't stumbled upon something like this before. So...thank you. And tell you what, as long as I've got multiple Kellys to depend on, maybe I won't take off in the RV. Maybe I'll stick around."

Sophie gritted her teeth. And hung up.

She wanted to...hit something. Hard. She headed into her office and quickly changed into her workout clothes, anticipating the feel of slamming her fists into the bag. Over and over again.

But just as she'd gotten her gloves on, she heard someone calling to her. "Sophie?"

It was Angie.

One of the Kellys who had fed Frank potato salad and played corn hole with him and laughed and talked with him and included him in the family.

Sophie worked on composing herself just as Angie appeared in the office doorway. She took in Sophie's clothes. "Oh, sorry. I didn't know you were working out."

Sophie shook her head. "No, I haven't started yet."

"Is this an okay time to go over some things about the costumes?" Angie asked.

Sophie took a deep breath and blew it out. "Sure."

Angie peered closer at her. "Are you okay?"

Sophie tried to smile. She really did. She tried to

pretend she was fine. But it didn't work. She felt the frustration and worry and hurt bubble up, and she knew she wasn't going to be able to hide her emotions from Angie. "I'm . . . I just got off the phone with my dad."

Angie lowered the papers she'd been holding, and her expression grew more concerned. "Oh. Is everything okay?"

No. Her father was using Angie's family and ruining Sophie's chances of ever being close to them. Even though she didn't want that. Or she'd thought she didn't want that. Or that's what she'd said, anyway.

But that was all bullshit. Of course she wanted to be part of the Kelly clan. Who wouldn't? But especially a girl who'd never had a real family and who already loved Angie and who was, maybe, possibly, at least kind of, falling for Finn.

"He said he went to your family barbecue." She'd meant to ask about the money first. Or the couch. Or the job. But yeah, the barbecue thing bothered her. A lot.

Angie nodded. "He did. Joe brought him along."

Sophie swallowed and tried to hide her jealousy.

It didn't work. Angie shook her head, looking sorry. "You never wanted to come. You told me to stop asking."

Sophie nodded. She had.

Angie gave her a gentle smile. "I think he had a good time. He fit right in."

Sophie threw her hands up. Had Angie forgotten everything Sophie had shared with her? "Of course he did, Angie. He's an *actor*. He can fit in anywhere."

"But it was really . . . nice," Angie said. But she did look slightly regretful. "They all had a good time."

"Oh, I'm sure. He was, after all, getting free food and successfully wrapping you all around his finger."

Angie shook her head. "I knew you'd be upset, but honey, there's something you should consider."

"Oh?"

"Maybe your dad wants a family as much as you do."

Sophie felt her mouth drop open. She stared at Angie. "Seriously?" she finally asked.

"He seemed very taken with the whole environment. And it sounds to me like he hasn't had a lot of the family thing. The acceptance and fun and . . ."

"He had his chance!" Sophie broke in. "Six of them, as a matter of fact. He ruined it. Every single time. And," she went on when it looked as if Angie was about to reply, "he even told me once that he didn't want women who had children because he was trying to keep the number of people who got attached to a minimum. He knew, even before he got serious about them, that it wasn't going to last."

Sophie hugged her arms to her body and watched Angie process all of that. She hadn't told Angie those details before. But it was true. Frank had figured out that the women without a lot of family of their own would be even easier to pull into playing house with him and Sophie. Because everyone wanted family, deep down. Everyone.

She took a deep breath. "He was never sorry to leave— except for the hardship about finding a new place to stay— and God knows the women were happy for him to leave by the time it was over. So really, I was the only one hurt and sad when they broke up."

Angie gave her a smile and reached to put her hand on Sophie's shoulder. "I don't think that's totally true, honey."

Sophie shrugged off her hand, having a hard time believing she was doing it herself and seeing the surprise in Angie's eyes. "You're defending him?"

"I'm just saying that I think your dad really enjoyed his time with us."

Sophie nodded. "I'm sure. Everyone enjoys their time with your big, happy family, right?"

Angie frowned, and Sophie regretted her tone of voice. But it was painful not only to think that Frank had been warmly welcomed into the Kelly family but to know that it had been in spite of the things Sophie had told Angie. Why wouldn't Angie trust her?

Sophie took a deep breath. "Look, I know your family is amazing. I get it. And you welcome everyone in with open arms, and you make everything better for them. Your love and support inspires others, and you all band together to help whoever you can. But this is Frank. You have to believe me when I say that he's a bad guy and he's manipulative and he lies as easily as he breathes, and no matter how sincere he seemed, it was all just an act so that you would let him stay on Joe's couch and work at Jamie's bar and whatever else he can get from you all."

Sophie squeezed her arms tighter to her stomach, trying to press down the feelings of betrayal.

"I didn't know about any of that until the barbecue," Angie said.

"Frank said he and Finn had a beer at the bar together." Even saying that made a pain twinge in her chest.

"That's the story I heard too. Though Frank came looking for Finn, from what I understand," Angie said.

Ah, well, that made more sense. But didn't make it much better.

"And Frank told me you gave him money," Sophie said flatly.

Angie nodded. "But it's a loan."

"Uh-huh."

"He wrote IOUs," Angie said.

"Oh, that will—" Sophie broke off. "IOUs. As in more than one?"

"Three."

"You gave Frank money *three times*?" Sophie asked. This was completely out of control.

"He has some things he needs to do, and he said he can't ask you or take it out of the business, with the fire and everything. He knows that you're working hard to raise the money to fix up the theater."

Sophie couldn't believe it. He'd taken half the insurance money that would have repaired the theater, but he was using the fire as a reason to borrow money from Angie.

The bastard.

"Angie, Frank doesn't need your money."

"He has plans. Something he's working on that will make things better for you, honey."

Sophie rubbed the middle of her forehead as the ache there intensified. "No, he's not. He always uses me to get close to people, Angie. I've told you about my stepmoms. Every time, I was one of the reasons they thought they could trust him, or thought they couldn't throw him out, or forgave him. He took the insurance money from the fire," she told her. "And he gets money from the theater once a month. Half of it."

"I know he's your partner," Angie said.

In the very loosest on-paper sense of the word only. "Yes. And considering he hasn't paid a bill in more than a decade, he certainly shouldn't need money from you."

"If he's trying to do something good for you, something that will help you, then I have to support that, Sophie,"

Angie said. "If I can help you reconcile, even a little, with your father, it will be worth it."

Sophie's exasperation boiled over. "Angie, don't be so naive! I don't want to reconcile with him! This is why Frank wanted to get close to you and asked you for money. He can spot a victim a mile away."

Angie looked as if Sophie had just slapped her. Sophie stood breathing hard and fighting tears. She could argue that her hurting Angie was Frank's fault too, that he'd put her in this position, but she was the one who'd said the words. And if it opened her eyes and made her more careful around Frank, then Sophie couldn't regret it, even if it hurt Angie's feelings.

Finally Angie gave her a nod. "I'll just leave these here." She set the papers she'd been carrying on Sophie's desk and then turned and left.

Sophie flinched as she heard the theater door shut a moment later.

Then she made her way to the door and carefully turned the lock.

CHAPTER TEN

*F*inn let himself into the theater with the key Sophie had made him, followed the pumping bass of the music— Iron Maiden, if he wasn't mistaken—and found Sophie was beating the hell out of her kickboxing bag. She was breathing hard and sweating, so he assumed she'd been at it awhile. She wasn't feeling soft or sweet today, clearly.

They weren't having rehearsal tonight because the firefighters had drills, but he'd figured Tony and Angel could get some one-on-one time in. He'd hoped Finn and Sophie could too. But then he'd talked to his mom. She and Sophie had had an argument. Their first ever. He'd headed straight over after hearing that.

As he propped a shoulder in the doorway to watch, he realized that she wasn't completely steady on her feet and about every fourth punch didn't land square—or on the bag at all.

She dropped her arms after one of those misses and reached for the bottle of vodka on the corner of her desk.

He watched as she tipped it back, no glass needed. She noticed him as she swallowed. And instead of acting startled, she frowned and set the bottle down hard.

"You had a beer with my dad?"

Well, that had been bound to come up at some point. Angie hadn't told him everything, but she'd said that Sophie was upset about Frank being at the barbecue the other night and Angie loaning him money. Hell, Finn had been upset about Frank being at the barbecue. Finn had worked that night, so hadn't been there himself, but he'd heard all about it. How funny Frank was, how easily he'd fit in with everyone, how they now couldn't wait to meet Sophie, and all about how they couldn't believe Angie hadn't introduced her to them a long time ago.

So much for their plan to keep her away from the family.

He should have known better. Maybe on some level he had. He hadn't been shocked to learn that Frank had ended up on Joe's couch. Or that Joe was enjoying having a roommate. He hadn't been shocked to find Frank was invited to the barbecue either, once he'd thought about it.

And in spite of himself, Finn found himself smiling about it. His family was loud, and frustrating, and downright obnoxious sometimes, but it was also warm, and loving, and accepting, and generous. And yeah, okay, maybe deep down he'd thought Frank Birch could use a little of all of that. If anyone could make a man want to do better, it was the Kellys.

Finn pushed away from the doorway and crossed to the stereo and hit the power button. "We drank beers while sitting next to each other at the bar," he said, facing her.

"How is that different?"

"He came looking for me. And I talked to him once he

found me. That's not the same thing as planning to go out for a beer together."

"But you still gave him a job and a place to stay."

Finn let out a big breath. "Yeah, I asked Jamie to hire him. But the couch thing is someone else's fault." He wasn't even sure whose. He didn't know if anyone was sure who had first brought it up. It didn't really matter.

"How could you do that?" she asked, looking genuinely distressed. "We were *not* doing the family thing. And now our families are having barbecues together!"

Yeah. That hadn't been the plan. "It's just a pullout couch and a couple nights a week washing dishes."

"But it's Frank!" she said, throwing her hand out to the side and nearly knocking the bottle of vodka to the floor.

She grabbed for it as Finn instinctively lunged for it as well. The bottle stayed on the desktop without a drop spilled, but they ended up right up against one another.

She smelled like a lemon drop, her sweet lemony scent mingling with the vodka. And Finn wanted to drink her up.

"Drunk kickboxing?"

She nodded. "I couldn't decide which I needed more— punching something or getting drunk—so I did both."

"So I see." Finn eyed the bottle. "How much have you had?"

Sophie sighed. "Not enough to erase how crappy I feel."

He hated that she was upset, and he probably should have told her Frank was sleeping at Joey's when he'd heard. But he'd figured it was temporary. And harmless. "I'm sorry I didn't tell you about Frank staying with Joey."

"And working at the bar," she reminded him.

He nodded. "That too. But I just thought it would keep

him out of your hair until he leaves on his trip." And it would allow Finn to keep an eye on him.

"His trip?" she repeated.

"He said he's heading out to California in a month or so."

Sophie's eyes widened. "Finn, my dad is like a stray cat. You can't be this nice to him, you can't support him—he'll never leave."

"I'm not supporting him. We're not supporting him," he said quickly as she scoffed. "He's working at the bar."

"And what about at Joe's?" she asked. "Is he paying rent? Helping out around the house? Buying groceries?"

"It's a pullout couch. Hardly worthy of rent."

"So no, he's not helping out."

"He's only staying for a couple of weeks."

Sophie laughed but she was clearly not amused. "Do you know how he got my second stepmother to fall for him?" she asked. "She was my Sunday school teacher. He told her that he'd been laid off but had a new job starting in two weeks. And he was wondering if I could stay with her until then so I didn't have to sleep in the car with him. Because it broke his heart to not be able to provide for me." She shook her head and crossed her arms. "So of course this sweet, trusting woman said we should both stay. She had a guest room and a couch. Frank took the couch because he's such a great dad," she said sarcastically. "And then while she went to work at the bank where she was a vice president, he cleaned and cooked and did errands for her. And every night when she came home, dinner was ready, her dry cleaning was picked up, and he was reading to me on the couch." She took a deep breath. "By the time the two weeks was up, he had moved into the master bedroom, and we didn't move out for another two *years*."

Finn rolled his neck. He and Frank were going to need to have another talk about his conduct around Finn's family. Especially the women. "I don't think Joe sends anything to the dry cleaners," he said, trying to lighten the mood and trying to distract himself from the images of a tiny blond girl with big blue eyes who had been used as a pawn by her father.

"Finn," Sophie said with a deep frown. "You have to keep Frank away from your mother. And your aunts. And your cousins. And...your entire family."

"I promise you that I'm on this, Sophie."

She shook her head. "I can't believe it. He's even getting to you!"

"He's not," Finn insisted. "He's a guy who needed a couple of favors. He needed a way to make some cash, and Jamie needed some help while Gina's on maternity leave. It's perfect because your dad doesn't want anything long term."

Sophie rolled her eyes. "Well, that's the first time anyone has ever thought that it was *perfect* that Frank Birch doesn't want to commit to something."

"And you have to understand something," Finn said. "This isn't just about him. This is as much about my family as anything. Yes, he took the bar stool next to me and started the conversation. And yeah, I thought of the job. But Frank didn't have to do anything other than say yes and this snowball started rolling. My family would have gotten involved no matter if your dad was a world-class manipulator or not." Finn blew out a breath. "My family embraced the chance to take care of somebody. I guarantee that Joe loves this. He's not having cold cereal for breakfast, because somebody's bringing cinnamon rolls and egg bakes over for him to share with Frank. And I'm sure somebody cleaned his house for him before Frank moved in. And Danny finally went over and fixed the garbage disposal like he's been promising to do for two months, and Kyle and Zoe finished painting the trim around the outside windows like they were supposed to this summer. So Joe's getting plenty out of this. It's all win-win."

Sophie was looking at him like he was completely crazy. "And what are you getting out of this?" she asked.

"What do you mean?"

"You're not getting cinnamon rolls or your disposal fixed."

Finn shook his head. "Nothing. Exactly." He was taking care of Sophie. That's what he was getting out of it. He was keeping Frank out of her hair for the next couple of weeks until he hit the road. It wasn't the same thing as locking him up in jail for arson, but it kept him away from Sophie. But Finn wasn't sure how that admission would go over with her.

"You aren't using it to get on my good side?" she asked.

He laughed before he could stop himself. "What about helping Frank would make me think I would get on your good side? I do listen when you talk, you know."

She regarded him with narrowed eyes. "Nobody really does stuff for nothing."

That made him take the step that was separating them. He put his hand on her cheek. "Yeah, Sophie, sometimes they do."

She just stood looking at him as if not sure what to think.

"I know we said we weren't going to get involved with family stuff," he went on. "And I agreed with all of the reasons. But...we care about you, so we care about him. This is not a hardship for us, but even if it was, we are people you and your dad can count on."

Sophie swallowed. "You have to keep him away from your mom. And your aunts."

Finn ran his thumb over her cheek. He was going to prove to Sophia Birch that she didn't have to worry as long as he was around. About anything. "I just have to keep him from marrying any of them," he said with a slight smile. "And trust me, I will."

"But they might...You don't know how he...He's sneaky," she finally said, but Finn felt her pressing her cheek more firmly against his palm. "Your mom already gave him money."

Okay, he hadn't known that part. Finn was going to need to have a talk with his mother. "He's involved with my family now," Finn said, his smile gone and his voice firm. "That means there are rules. I know where he's sleeping, I know where he's working, I have people who can tell me what he's up to. I can keep track of him this way, Sophie."

Her eyes widened slightly.

"You have to trust me. I know what I'm doing, and I'm doing it for you."

"For me?"

She blinked up at him in an adorably tipsy way that made him want to kiss her. Of course, just being in the same room with her made him want to kiss her.

"I know you've been taking care of yourself for a long time. But I was hoping that as long as I'm hanging around anyway, you'd let me do it. A little."

Sophie swallowed. "I don't really know how to let you do that."

"Just go with it," he told her with a smile, relieved that she wasn't arguing.

"But...This show..." She frowned up at him. "I thought I was handling everything. I thought I was in control. And now...this."

"This?"

"I'm not handling any of it. You are." Her frown deepened. "Kind of."

"I am," he insisted. But he could understand that it might not seem that way. She thought Frank was manipulating Finn. He was just going to have to prove her wrong.

"Does your family hate me?" she asked.

He shook his head. "Why would they hate you?"

She pulled away from his touch and reached for the bottle. "I don't know what Frank's told them. Your mom said he was going on about how he couldn't ask me for help. Do they all think I'm a terrible daughter?"

"Of course not."

"Are you sure? They don't really..." She gave the punching bag a half-hearted slug. "They don't know how not-happy families work."

It hit him that she was right. His family had its imperfections, but in all the important ways it was...wonderful. Sophie had made him appreciate his family more than he ever had before.

"It doesn't matter," he told her honestly. "They want to be there for you."

"They don't really know me."

Because they'd agreed that was best. That was easiest. That was the way to keep things from getting jumbled up and complicated and getting emotions involved.

So much for that.

"Okay, ninja warrior, let's go," Finn said, making a quick decision that he knew in his gut was right. He snagged her hand and started for the door.

"Go? Where?"

"You're going to take a shower and then we're going to the bar."

"The Kelly bar?"

And maybe, if she hadn't had a few shots of vodka, she would have been able to hide that she was excited. But Finn saw it. "Yep. We'll get a couple of burgers and sober you up and talk."

"Will it be busy?" she asked, tripping along behind him as he led her toward the dressing rooms.

"I'm sure it will be."

"Will my dad be there?"

He tried to gauge the emotion behind her question. Did she want him to be there? "He doesn't work on Thursdays. Zoe and Hannah come in to help out."

"So lots of your family will be there?"

He stopped outside the main dressing room and turned to face her, again trying to determine if that was a positive or a negative in her mind. "Yes. It's trivia night."

"Trivia night?"

He grinned at her parroting. "Yep. There's always on-line trivia games going on, but right now, on Thursday nights, there's a nationwide tournament going on. Each bar that participates has a team, and they compete over Skype with other teams in other bars. Our pub has a team, and they're in the quarterfinals tonight." She grinned, and Finn realized that she would have probably fought this idea if it weren't for the liquor in her system. Or her father's

attendance at the barbecue. His heart ached a little as he realized that she'd felt left out.

"Do you need help in the shower?" he asked.

She raised an eyebrow. "What kind of help?"

Her smile was still sweetly tipsy but now had an added
hint of mischief, and in spite of everything else—her hurt
feelings and anger, her blood alcohol level, the fact that
they were on their way to hang out with his noisy, nosy
family—heat flooded through him, and he seriously considered carrying her into the shower and personally soap-
ing her up. He tugged on her hand, bringing her closer to
him. "Well, if you're feeling wobbly or dizzy or anything,
I wouldn't want you in there alone. You could crack your
head open or something."

"It's weird, but I am feeling a little dizzy suddenly," she
said, her voice a little husky.

She leaned in, and Finn bent to meet her lips. But the
scent of vodka hit him just before he kissed her. He brushed
his lips over hers, unable to keep from at least that much,
but then he straightened.

"How about you be really careful in there, I'll stay right
here where I can hear you yell if you need me, and then we
revisit this whole idea later after you've had some coffee
and time?"

She pouted for a moment. "You know that I'm not drunk
enough to not know that I want you in the shower with me,
Finn."

His whole body felt like it was straining toward her with
a "Please, Finn, come on, Finn, let's go, Finn." He shook
his head. "You need more than...that." He couldn't have
specifically defined what she needed, but he knew, somehow, that it had to do with his family and the pub.

"I think you are more than enough," she said softly.

And that did nothing for the urge to pick her up, carry her into the shower, and explore every inch he hadn't yet had the pleasure of getting acquainted with.

"Let me take you out." And he realized he was a lot nobler than he'd ever given himself credit for. Or stupider.

She took a deep breath. "Are we calling it a date?"

"Do you want to call it a date?" It didn't really matter what they called it, of course. Except that it kind of did. Calling it a date meant something bigger for them.

"I don't know," she said after studying his face for a moment. "Part of me does."

He nodded. "Me too."

"So maybe we'll just...not call it anything," she decided. "We'll just let it be whatever it is."

He lifted a hand and dragged his thumb across her lip. "I like whatever it is, whatever we call it."

She nodded, watching him in that way she had that made him feel as if she was vulnerable and yet wanted to eat him up at the same time.

Finally she asked, "Is this a really bad idea?"

"The pub tonight with my family?" Because standing here staring at each other, wanting each other, liking each other, was definitely not a bad idea.

"Yeah."

He shook his head. "Absolutely not. Go get cleaned up."

She gave him a little nod. "Okay. I trust you."

He watched her go and realized he'd just lied to her. It was a bad idea. For his heart. Just spending time with her one-on-one was making it hard not to fall for her completely. Having her meet his family was going to do him in. Not because they would love her—which they would—but because she needed this. And this was something he could definitely give her—family, acceptance, laughter, love. But he wouldn't want to ever stop giving it to her. It would feed something in him that had been clawing at him from almost the first moment he'd met her, to be able to give her all the things she'd been missing and wanting.

But he wasn't sure how Sophie was going to respond to him falling in love with her.

* * *

"Sophie!"

"Hey, sweetie!"

"You brought Sophie!"

That last was the only greeting directed at Finn. He smiled and watched his family literally pull Sophie into its midst. He had three aunts, five uncles, and at least eight cousins here tonight besides Jamie. Colin and Tripp were also there and lifted their hands in greeting from across the bar. With knowing smiles.

Finn shrugged it off. The minute he'd decided to bring Sophie down here tonight, he'd accepted the fact that the only way this could end well would be for him to marry her. So he'd either be nursing a broken heart in a few months...or buying a diamond.

At this point, he was okay with seeing which way it went.

He let the Kellys and a few Sullivans and a couple of Derbys overwhelm Sophie for a few minutes before making his way through the crowd and resting a hand on her lower back. "Okay, I need to get this girl fed," he told them, ushering her toward a table along the wall. Not that it kept people from moving with them and continuing to talk. But he finally got her settled and ordered from Zoe.

"The Kelly burger?" Sophie asked as Zoe headed for the kitchen.

"It's flavored with Irish whiskey," he told her with a wink. "And," he added with a sigh, looking around the bar filled with bodies and noise, "it has *a lot* going on."

"Like what?"

She was clearly amused when he looked at her again. "Cheese, bacon, crispy onions, barbecue sauce, spicy mustard, sweet pickles, and jalapenos."

She laughed. "That is a lot."

He nodded. "Like the Kellys."

She looked around too. "There are a lot of them, but it's so easy to be around them. And they don't seem mad at me. Do you think they know about the fight I had with your mom?"

Finn felt his heart thunk against his ribs. He reached for her hand for some reason. He wasn't really a hand holder but...he realized that he was. His mom had pointed out how his dad had always acted. That he had been physically demonstrative. But Finn was too. Just in a quieter way. He'd never really noticed it or thought about it with the other girls he'd dated. Maybe because they took it in stride. But Sophie always seemed surprised when he touched her. Not startled or shy, but pleasantly surprised. And she always leaned into the contact or met it with a distinctive reaction. Like now, when she put her other hand over the back of his and squeezed. With a huge smile.

"I'm sure some of them have heard. You can't hiccup in my family without everyone knowing about it."

Sophie instantly looked sad. "I hate the idea that your

mom is upset. I hate the idea that any of them might know that I upset her. I hate the idea that it will be awkward the next time I see her."

Finn squeezed her hand. "She loves you, Sophie. One argument doesn't change that. And if there's something this family knows about, it's how to get mad and get over it. Hell, you think we get along famously all the time?"

She nibbled on her bottom lip. "I know that makes sense," she said. "But my experience with arguing was always that it was the beginning of the end."

"Your dad and your stepmoms never argued until they were ending the whole thing?" He couldn't imagine that. If every single person in his family didn't have at least one argument a day, something was wrong.

She nodded. "My dad's entire job, his mission, was to keep my stepmoms happy so they'd let us stay. If he was ever upset about something, he didn't show it. And if they were upset, he just apologized. Until the end. It was like once he got tired or fed up...or they did...then it all went to hell really fast."

"Damn, babe, I'm sorry. I can't even wrap my head around that."

She shrugged. "I know it's weird now, but I didn't then."

"So what about your friends? You've never disagreed with Kiera or Maya?"

She smiled. "Here and there, but nothing big. But yeah, they've showed me a lot about how to have normal relationships."

He almost didn't say the words that rushed to his mouth, but looking into her big blue eyes, he couldn't hold them back. "Well, stick around. The Kellys love and fight and yell and laugh loudly and a lot. You'll get used to it."

She gave him a smile that he wanted to see regularly. Daily. Always.

"You still feeling dizzy and wobbly?" he asked. She seemed to be sobering up, and he wasn't sure if that was a good thing and he should ply her with coffee or if he should order a round of shots. He wanted to keep her open to being here and letting his family close. But he also wanted her to remember it tomorrow.

She nodded. "A little. But in a good way. Kind of a warm and fuzzy feeling."

Finn decided that for now, anyway, that was okay.

"Tell me about the bar," she said, eyeing the stuff hanging on the wall over their booth.

The decor was a mishmash of Irish knickknacks—everything from old pub signs to cheesy leprechauns—and family photos and heirlooms, including the gaudy hippo figurines Finn's grandmother had collected, a few old baseball trophies that his uncles had won as kids, and even the mailbox from the first house their great-grandparents had lived in.

"My great-grandfather and two of his brothers started it," Finn said. "It's been handed down through the generations. Someone always steps up to be the name on the line on the contracts, but we grow up knowing that this place is all of ours, and we all help out when and how we can."

"Who is this?" she asked of the people in the black-and-white photo hanging above the napkin dispenser.

"My grandmother's sister and her husband," he said.

Sophie smiled as she gazed at the picture. "Do you know the story behind everything in here?"

He nodded. "We all do. This is the hub of everything."

Sophie looked back at him. "That's . . . kind of amazing."

"Is it?"

"You don't think so?"

"I just...grew up here," he said with a shrug. "This is the place where the family has had Sunday dinners once a month forever. My great-grandparents started the tradition because, even back then, no one had a house big enough for everyone at once."

Sophie was biting her bottom lip, studying his face.

"What?" he finally asked.

"You take it for granted," she finally said.

He knew he did. He nodded. "Yeah, I know. I should work on that."

She shook her head quickly. "No. I think that it's... nice. I mean, it's nice to have people and traditions and history and hand-me-downs that you can take for granted. That's how it should be."

He thought about that. "You think so?"

"Definitely. I mean...it's a sign that it's all really secure, don't you think?"

He looked around the bar, taking it in from Sophie's perspective. *Secure.* That was a really good word for how he felt here. He focused on her again. "You feel the tradition and roots at the theater, right? With your grandma?"

Sophie nodded. "The only roots I have."

Finn was grateful the table was between them, because he wanted to yank her into his arms and....just hold her. Did he want to run his tongue all over every inch of her creamy skin? Hell yeah, he did. Twenty-three hours out of every day since he'd met her. But right now, he wanted to hold her and he really wanted to tell her that it was all going to be okay and that she could put roots down with him, that they could start their branch of this gigantic old tree right now, tonight.

He cleared his throat. "Let me tell you more about the Kelly clan," he said, sliding out of the booth and tugging her to her feet.

It was hard to talk over the noise in the bar, so he found that he had to get close to her ear—and fight the urge to bury his nose in her sweet-smelling hair—repeatedly during the guided tour around the bar. Finn kept her close, tucked against his side, and the feel of her arm around his waist and her smiles and laughter as he told her Kelly family stories made him want her more than even when he'd had her pressed up against the wall of the theater.

Well, almost as much.

"A broken plate and teacup?" she asked, turning away from the ceramic pieces that had been glued to the wall.

He nodded. "My grandmother. She broke those throwing them at my grandpa. She glued them up here to remind him of that argument."

"What was the argument about?" she asked, looking up with a twinkle in her eye.

An actual twinkle. He wasn't sure he'd ever seen one before in real life. He grinned. "They fought because he was spending too much time here at the bar. She put those up to remind him that the things that nourished him were at home and that, no matter how mad she got, they'd always be able to put things back together."

Sophie looked at the broken dishes again. "And now they're here to remind you all of the same thing."

"Yep. That the things that really keep us going are at home and that there's always a way to put things back together after they break."

Sophie shook her head and said nothing for a moment.

"What?" he asked.

"I just…didn't believe that families like yours really existed."

He tightened his arm around her. It wasn't the full two-arm squeeze he wanted to enfold her in—and not let her go from—but it was enough to be touching her right now. "Well, we're real."

She took a deep breath. "Very."

They were headed back to the booth when Finn noticed Zoe was bringing their food. As they slid into the booth, Sophie gave a little laugh.

"What's funny?" he asked, reaching for the ketchup.

She gave him a smile that made him want to kiss her. Even more than he'd wanted to before.

"It's just a little weird that I'm even crazier about you because your family bar has a stuffed teddy bear glued to the wall."

Finn laughed and looked over at the bear. "My uncle Nick won that for my aunt Nancy at a fair on their first date."

Sophie gave a little sigh. "God, I love this place."

Finn's chest tightened, but he pointed at her burger. "And you haven't even tasted the food yet."

They ate, and Finn turned the conversation to Sophie's memories and history at the theater. It wasn't quite as long or involved as his at the bar. The theater had belonged to her grandmother for thirty-eight years. But seeing the softness when she talked about all of it made him want to make her look like that all the time. Whatever it took.

He mentally pulled back on those reins quickly. This was what he did. He took people in—his whole family did. He and Sophie both needed to be careful here that they didn't mistake wanting each other for something else—his need to make things better and her need for family. Still, he found himself thinking about ways to prolong the night and reasons to bring her back.

The Kellys left them alone during their meal, but the moment her last fry was gone, Chloe and Hannah, two of his cousins, pulled Sophie up to the bar and had her trying a couple of the specialty shots. Finn kept his eye on her but loved seeing her with the girls. And didn't mind the idea of her being a little tipsy again. It meant he wouldn't be staying over after he took her home, but he loved the way it helped her let down her guard. Eventually she would see that she could relax around them even without the liquor. But for now, a little Irish cream wouldn't hurt anything.

CHAPTER ELEVEN

*Y*ou told Mom you wouldn't do this," Colin said as he slid into the booth across from Finn.

Finn rolled his eyes as Tripp joined them too. Colin handed him a beer and Finn realized that they had also stayed away while he and Sophie had been talking. He'd managed to be alone with her even in the midst of all of this. That was . . . something.

"I'm not doing anything."

"You're not bringing the first woman since Sarah around to meet the family?" Colin asked.

Fuck. That was what he was doing alright. "I brought Lauren around," Finn reminded him. Though why he was encouraging this conversation, he wasn't sure.

"You brought Lauren around, realized the family was going to bring her into the fold and love her and make it horrible to break up with her, just like it had been with Sarah, and that was the last time."

Finn took a drink of his beer and looked over at Sophie.

Yeah, Lauren had been the last time. Because he hadn't found another girl since who was worth the risk of hurting everyone. Until now.

So yeah, it meant something big that he'd brought Sophie here, and yeah, his mom was going to be concerned about it. But he didn't regret it. "Sophie was having a hard night. She needed to get out and have some fun."

"And, after all, this is the only place in Boston that's open on Thursday nights," Tripp said.

Finn took a drink of his beer. Tripp had a point. He could have taken Sophie a million other places. But she had needed more than to just get out. She'd needed the Kellys. And she hadn't even been given the full dose. "I can't drink for free anywhere else," Finn said.

Colin chuckled, and Tripp said, "Right. I knew there was a good reason you brought her here."

"Of course."

"And Mom will totally understand that," Colin said. "I mean, it's just a burger and a beer, right?"

"Yep." It was definitely not just a burger and a beer.

"And some harmless shots, right?" Colin asked.

"Yep." Definitely not harmless. Those shots made her less guarded, and that was probably the last thing he needed her to be.

As if to prove his point, Sophie chose that moment to glance around, spot him, and give him a big, bright, ridiculously happy smile.

"And some innocent, friendly, oh-Finn-you're-the-best stuff, right?" Colin asked drily.

Finn glared at his brother. "What?"

"You love hero worship."

"And he gets more than his share," Tripp muttered.

"That's not what this is," Finn said in a tone that should have shut them up quick.

But this was Colin and Tripp.

"Then what is it? Tell me that it's not because she's a sweet, beautiful girl that hasn't had enough love in her life and looks at you like that." Colin pointed over his shoulder without looking. Directly at Sophie.

Finn wasn't sure what to do here. Sophie was all of those things, and he did really like it when she looked at him like that. But this was not that. Okay, this was not just that. It was more. But he wasn't sure he should admit that out loud. Or even to himself.

"Sophie doesn't think I'm a hero," he said. And then he sat up a little straighter because he realized that was true. She respected him and what he did for a living, but she didn't like him because of his uniform. And he was okay with that. "I'm not really a hero anyway."

"You're a cop," Colin said. "That's not heroic?"

"It's my job, and I'm great at it," Finn said. "But I don't know how heroic it is."

"Making the city safer and the world better?" Tripp asked him.

Finn shook his head. "Come on. I don't have any major challenges. I've got a huge support system and a ton of people who believe in me and I'm following in my father's footsteps because I like to help people, but guys like us should be doing that shit, because we've got it good and had it pretty damned easy and it's the least we can do to give back."

Tripp set his beer down and stared. Colin frowned as if concerned. But neither of them said anything. Which was a freaking miracle. Because they never shut up when it came to Finn making an ass of himself.

So maybe he hadn't done that just now.

"And if anyone is a hero, it's that girl over there," he said, pointing over Colin's shoulder, also without looking but directly at Sophie. "She hasn't had support or people doing anything but using her, and she still runs a theater where she can even make you jerks look brilliant and she freaking loves it. She's also been an amazing friend to our mother, and if Mom doesn't get that Sophie deserves to be down here having fun and being loved, then Mom is just going to have to deal with it."

There was a beat of silence, and then Tripp drawled, "Holy shit."

"I know. It's amazing," Colin said, still staring at Finn.

Finn scowled at them.

"I thought it was possible, but I never thought I'd actually witness it." Tripp shook his head slowly as if in wonder.

"I'm...humbled. Truly," Colin said.

Finn narrowed his eyes further. "What the hell are you two talking about?"

Colin and Tripp looked at each other then back at Finn.

"You finally found a woman that you like more than Mom," Colin said.

"The cord has been cut." Tripp gave a solemn nod.

Finn sighed. "Fuck." He slid to the edge of the booth. "You."

Colin chuckled. "Come on, man, you gotta admit that it took a while to find a woman that you were willing to stand up to Mom for."

Finn stretched to his feet. "Fine. Go ahead and say it."

Colin grinned widely. "What?"

"That I'm a mama's boy." It wouldn't be the first time

he'd heard it, and frankly, he didn't care. Colin and Tripp felt the same way about Angie that he did. Hell, Sophie herself had been drawn to Angie's mothering. Angela Kelly was an amazing woman, and he loved her and would do anything for her. He owned that. It made him a good son. He was doing what his father had asked him to do. How could he feel ashamed of that?

Which did, in fact, make things with Sophie…bigger. Because he really would tell his mom to back off if she got upset about Sophie being here tonight. He blew a breath out.

"All I'm going to say is don't you dare make my mama cry," Colin said, pointing his beer bottle at Finn.

"If you do, I'll help him kick your ass," Tripp added.

Exactly. Angie had a mama's boy all right. Three of them. "The goal is for no one to cry," Finn said firmly.

"Even you, right, Bro?" Colin asked.

Yeah, even him.

Suddenly a chorus of voices rose up from the bar area, and they all glanced over.

"When we drink, we get drunk. When we get drunk, we sleep. When we sleep, we commit no sin. When we commit no sin, we go to heaven. So let's all get drunk and go to heaven!"

Then everyone toasted, drank, and cheered. Including Sophie.

Tripp chuckled. "One of my favorite of your Irish toasts." He lifted his own bottle and then took a long swig.

Irish toasts. Next would come the Irish jokes. Then the Irish songs. He wasn't sure Sophie was ready for all of that. Then again, she might dive right in and love every second. Which would probably be worse than her turning and running.

He headed for the bar and the woman who was making his life complicated and wonderful at the same time. "Trivia time, ninja warrior," he told her, settling his hands on her waist. He was in too deep for a few public displays of affection to rock any boats, so he might as well enjoy them.

She beamed up at him, and he laughed and shook his head. "How many shots are we up to?"

"Only three," Chloe assured him.

Sophie shook her head quickly. "Four. We had straight whiskey, then the Irish car bomb, then the baby Guinness, and now"—she lifted her glass, tossed the shot back, and smacked her lips—"the Fuck an Irishman." She turned and looked up at Finn. "That's my favorite."

Yeah, he was going to have his hands full here. Finn took in her smile, the mischief in her eyes, the way she shot the liquor as if it were nothing, the way she leaned into his touch... What had he done bringing her here?

Because he was now officially head over heels.

"There's no such thing," he said, glancing up at Jamie behind the bar with an eyebrow up and a smile he couldn't help.

His cousin held up his hands. "She insisted I make one."

"What's this got in it?" Finn asked Sophie, stepping closer and sliding his hands down to her hips. He loved how she fit against him. Whether it was her hand in his, her lips on his, or... anything else.

"Irish cream, of course," Sophie said. "Butterscotch schnapps and cinnamon schnapps."

Jamie nodded his confirmation.

"That's not already a drink?" Finn asked.

"It is," she told him with a nod that made her wobble on the stool slightly. "But it's been renamed."

"On your authority?" he asked, wanting to kiss her and get a shot of Irish cream straight from her tongue.

"Yep. Because it's smooth"—she gave him a wink—"and sweet, and hot all at once. Just like fucking an Irishman."

Finn didn't know quite what to say or do as everyone around them made a general low "Ooooh" sound and then burst into whistles, cheers, and laughter.

Well, if they hadn't been outed before, they were now. He grinned down at her and then tightened his grip on her hips, pulled her forward, and kissed her.

Really kissed her. In front of everyone.

He was sure his aunts and at least two cousins, a niece, and even an uncle or two were calling and texting his mother right now.

And he didn't care if they included photos.

Sophie slid her arms around his neck and arched closer, parting her lips, and as he stroked his tongue into her mouth, he could swear he could taste the Irish cream, the whiskey, and the schnapps all individually.

Plus Sophie. He could taste Sophie, and he was never going to grow tired of that flavor.

Finally he pulled back, licked his lips, and nodded. "I think that one's my favorite too."

She giggled and let go of him. "I hope you're not looking to fuck any Irishmen."

He pinched her butt and pulled her off the stool. "I hear they're the best in the world."

She laughed, and he wrapped an arm around her when she swayed a little. "In my experience, that's true."

Again there were whistles and big grins around the bar and he was officially the center of attention, but Finn couldn't remember having felt this...great in a long time. Though *great* seemed like too tame a word, really.

They made their way to the big tables in the back corner where the trivia game would be going on. They tried to keep the game back there so it wasn't too disruptive to the rest of the bar, but by the end of the night, everyone was playing along and shouting out answers and mocking each other for wrong guesses anyway, so it didn't really matter.

Finn put Sophie into a chair next to his and draped his arm behind her, but as the rest of the family gathered and jostled for seats, he decided that he'd already gone this far so he might as well...He reached over and pulled her into his lap, opening a seat for his cousin Ian.

Sophie didn't make a peep of protest, settling her back against his chest and her ass against his groin. Finn immediately had to shift her off the cock that was very happy to see her and was going to make that known very soon if her curves stayed where they were.

Ian grinned as he turned the chair and leaned his arms on the back. "Don't make me turn the hose on you two," he said.

Sophie giggled, and Finn could only grin and squeeze her a little tighter.

The twenty official team members took the chairs up near the big-screen TV they used to Skype with the other team. The bars took turns providing a quizmaster and tonight it was Kelly's turn. Colin had been unanimously nominated, and he took his place, near the computer and screen where he could be seen clearly by both teams. He welcomed everyone, reminded them of the rules, and then read out the first question. And the room erupted into noise and movement.

Everyone started calling out answers to their leaders, who had to be the ones to officially buzz in. Which meant that the arguing also started almost instantly. The others didn't stay seated for long, but Sophie seemed content to stay on his lap. In fact, neither of them was contributing to the answers. He leaned to look at her. She was watching it all with wide eyes. He couldn't tell if she was overwhelmed or fascinated, or both. He chuckled and rested his hands on her thighs.

"It's a little crazy," he said near her ear.

She shifted on his lap, and Finn bit back a groan.

She smiled at him. "This isn't just a trivia thing, right? They do this at family dinners and when playing cards and stuff too?"

"My family purposefully does competitive things when they're together," he said, "so they can argue and also lord the win over the losers. You should see when we play touch football in the yard."

"But they're on the same team tonight," she pointed out.

"Um, yeah," he agreed. "Supposedly."

She laughed and put an arm around his neck. Which pressed a breast against his chest. He took a deep breath and couldn't help but stroke one hand up her side, over her ribs. He didn't quite cup her other breast, but his fingers skimmed the underside and he felt her sigh.

They sat like that for a few minutes, watching the action.

"Winston Churchill," she muttered.

Finn looked at her. "What?"

"Winston Churchill said that quote, not Mark Twain," she said.

A moment later, Dan buzzed and gave the wrong answer. Finn squeezed Sophie's thigh. "You should speak up."

"Not sure I can speak that loud," she said with a laugh.

They watched the game go on, but Finn didn't hear a single question. He was too busy relishing the feel of Sophie in his arms, the warmth of her body, her sweet scent, the way she laughed at and with his family, and...just being with her. She shifted in his lap, and Finn fought a groan. His body was definitely responding to having her against it, but she seemed almost oblivious. Her attention was firmly on the trivia game and the chaos around them.

Occasionally he'd notice she was muttering answers, but she didn't say anything loud enough to be heard by the group. And Finn decided that he wanted her attention on *him*.

He ran his hand over the top of her thigh, his fingers skimming along the inner seam of her pants. She wiggled again, and he moved so that her butt was pressed against his hardening erection as he worked his fingers under the edge of her shirt. They were at the back of the crowd, and no one was paying any attention to them. He could easily cop a feel. He inched his way up, his fingertips now on the underside of her bra cup. He traced his fingers over the smooth material. Then he slid higher, finding her nipple hard behind the satin. He rubbed his thumb over it and felt her press against his fly.

"Finn," she said softly. He wasn't even sure he actually heard it so much as felt it.

He took her nipple between his thumb and finger and rolled it as he put his lips against the back of her neck. "I love holding you," he said gruffly.

She squirmed in his lap, but he didn't realize she was reaching behind her until he felt her hand on his denim-encased cock. She pressed and then dragged her palm over the firm length.

He shuddered and put his mouth to her ear. "I really love having you here with my family, but I need to get you alone soon."

She turned her face to press her lips to his. His hand slid from her breast to her stomach, and he tucked his middle finger under the edge of her jeans, rubbing back and forth across the smooth skin just behind her waistband. She trembled slightly in his arms, and her tongue slicked over his bottom lip.

Then suddenly she jumped to her feet. "No! William Shakespeare!"

The room got quiet—or at least relatively quiet—and everyone turned to look at her.

Finn wasn't sure what to do. So he sat there, behind her, and crossed one ankle over his other knee to hide his erection.

"You guys are losing," Sophie said, propping her hands on her hips, clearly not intimidated by being the center of attention suddenly. "You're not even trying to work together. You aren't listening to one another at all!"

"Uh." Colin turned to the screen. "Okay, time for our first break. Teams, be back in place in ten minutes." He pressed something on the computer that made the screen go blank. Then he looked up at Sophie. "What's going on?"

"Brian has been yelling out the answers to the science questions and has gotten the last three right, but you've all only used his answer once!" Sophie exclaimed. She took a few steps forward and pointed at Zoe. "Zoe gets every one of the pop culture and music questions right, even the oldies. You have to let her be in charge of those questions."

"In charge?" Finn's aunt Leann asked.

"You should have people who are good at certain subjects take those questions," Sophie said. "You're a team. But that doesn't mean you *all* answer *everything*. Brian and Zoe each have something they know really well. Dan knows food," she said, pointing to the leader, who grinned and nodded. "And Finn," she said, swinging to look at him, "what are you good at?"

"Uh." He was actually having a hard time focusing on anything but how much he wanted her when she got riled up. This was her feisty side. This was the real her. And she was showing it off to his family. Sure, it was because she was frustrated—and intoxicated—but as he'd said that first night, those were situations that made a person act in real, honest ways.

"Sports. He's good at sports," Chloe finally answered for him with a grin.

"And Donny is amazing at history," someone else said.

"And Caitlin knows geography."

Sophie smiled at all of them as if she was very proud. "Wonderful, so you need to work together. When you get a question in a certain category, let those people go first."

Everyone was nodding. "And," Sophie added, pulling their attention to her one more time, "I swear the next person to say Mark Twain has to buy me three baby Guinnesses. That man didn't actually say half the things that are attributed to him. So quotes? That's all me." She pointed a thumb at her chest, and everyone laughed.

The break ended, and everyone settled back into their seats, and even though Finn got his one sports question wrong—because he couldn't get his mind off all the things he wanted to do to Sophie when he got her home tonight—they were soon kicking ass.

The time started to wind down, and they came to the

final question. Colin read out, "And from the Quotes category. Who said, 'Travel is fatal to prejudice'?"

They all turned to look at Sophie, who was now standing in the middle of their group, where she'd been high-fiving and laughing and encouraging everyone.

"Sophie?" Zoe asked.

She bit her lip.

Dan leaned in. "Sophie, do you know it?"

She nodded. Dan hit the buzzer. But she didn't say anything.

"Well?" Colin asked.

She took a big breath. "Mark Twain."

They all stared at her. Then Dan hooted and gave the official answer. They swung toward the screen as if the action were choreographed, and a second later...they won the whole thing.

It took a few minutes for Finn to extract Sophie from the midst of her excited and grateful teammates, but he finally caught her wrist and tugged her down the short hallway to the restrooms and nudged her into the alcove by the back door. He immediately took her face in his hands, pressed his body to hers, and kissed her with all the pent-up desire, affection, and happiness he was feeling.

She still tasted faintly of liquor, but it had been over an hour since her last drink, and as she arched into him and wrapped her arms around his neck, Finn didn't let her blood alcohol level stop him from running his hands all over her body, her shoulders, hips, waist, breasts, ass. He filled his hands with her curves over and over, absorbing the feel of her, her taste, the sounds she made.

Until his phone rang.

He continued to make love to her mouth for several

long seconds, but the ringing was insistent and it was his work ringtone. Finally he pulled back, staring down at her. "Fuck," he breathed.

She pressed her lips together and settled back on her heels as he reached for his pocket.

"What?" he barked into the phone a moment later, his eyes still on hers.

"We've got Trosky holed up in an apartment downtown. Thought you'd want to know." The voice was that of Finn's captain.

Finn closed his eyes. Fuck. He and Tripp had been investigating Glen Trosky for three months now. They'd brought in new evidence just yesterday that would put the crooked banker behind bars, but they hadn't been able to find him. Of course Finn wanted to know. And he and Tripp would want to make the arrest.

But he knew that Tripp would also have second thoughts about running out of here after Glen Trosky if his hands were full of a hot, sweet blonde.

"Finn! Trosky! Let's go!" Tripp hollered down the hall without coming closer.

So someone had called Tripp too. And that meant Finn couldn't blow this call off. Not that he would anyway, but...Sophie shifted against him, and he realized he'd never been so tempted to let someone else handle a call.

"Finn!" Tripp yelled again from the end of the hall. Finn appreciated his friend respecting that he might have Sophie in a compromising position. "Yeah, yeah," he muttered.

"You have to go?" Sophie asked.

He nodded. "Sorry."

She smiled. "That's okay. It's your job."

"But—" He ran a hand over her lips. "I'm not sure I care."

Her smile grew brighter, and Finn realized he'd inadvertently said something right.

"Making you want to be somewhere besides with your family and at work is something."

She knew him. He nodded. "It is. And I promise you, Feisty, I want to be wrapped up in my sheets with you and nothing else or anyone else anywhere near my thoughts for about the next year and half. Just so you know."

She went up on tiptoe and kissed him quickly.

"I would drop you at home, but..." He didn't want her at her house dealing with the inevitable hangover of tomorrow alone. He could call Maya or Kiera, he knew, but he had a better idea. He knew exactly where she needed to be. "I'm going to have Colin give you a ride later," he said. "You stay and have some more fun."

"Really? Without you?"

"I know it won't be as good without me," he said with a grin. "But they're still pretty cool even when I'm not around."

She smiled. "I'd actually like to stay for a while."

"Finn! Move your ass!" Tripp bellowed from the front.

Finn grabbed Sophie's hand and tugged her back into the bar. He turned her back over to Chloe and Hannah and then said to his brother, "Take her to Mom's when she's done here tonight."

Colin nodded. "You got it."

"Your mom?" Sophie looked worried.

"Yes," Finn said. "She'll take care of you."

"But we fought," Sophie reminded him.

God, if it was the last thing he did, he was going to show

her what having a real family meant. "Yes. But now you
need her. That's all that matters."

She gave him a little nod. "Okay."

"I've got her," Colin promised.

He clapped Colin on the shoulder. "Thanks."

"Finn!"

Then he headed for the door with Tripp. "Swear to God,
man. I'm cock-blocking you the next chance I get."

* * *

Sophie rolled over, trying to dodge the sunbeam that
seemed intent on waking her up far earlier than she wanted
to be awakened. Copious amounts of Irish cream plus
yelling and cheering during trivia plus a three a.m. bedtime
were not turning out to have been a fabulous combination
of decisions.

She scooted down in the bed, trying to get out of the
shaft of morning sunlight, but her feet soon touched the
footboard and the sun was still on her face. She pulled
the comforter over her head with a groan.

Then frowned.

Her bed didn't have a footboard. And the sun didn't
come into her room in the morning. And her comforter
didn't smell like this.

She tossed the cover back and looked around. This was
not her room. She sat up quickly and regretted the move
immediately. Her head swam and pounded. Though it
wasn't as bad as she would have expected. She spotted the
sports drink on the bedside table beside a bottle of ibuprofen and a note. She couldn't make out the words from here,
but she recognized the handwriting.

She knew exactly where she was and why she didn't feel worse. Angie had insisted she down two glasses of water, ibuprofen, and a multivitamin last night before she'd come to bed.

Sophie was in Finn's old bedroom at Angie's house. Colin had brought her here, and Angie had taken her into the kitchen, plied her with hangover remedies, and then brought her upstairs, there to help her change into one of Finn's old T-shirts and put her to bed.

Sophie remembered apologizing to Angie and telling her how much she loved her, and then Angie had said the best thing ever: "I know, sweetie."

Sophie pulled her legs up and dropped her head to her knees.

She was in deep. Really, really deep. Every plan she'd made to not get close to the Kellys, to not risk hurting Angie, to keep Frank away from the people she cared about... to not fall for Finn... had all been blown to hell.

Truthfully, the not-falling-for-Finn thing had been blown to hell a while ago. But the rest of it—she'd really thought she'd been doing okay. Except for the stuff Frank kept messing with. And the fact that every time Colin or Ian or Tripp enjoyed himself during rehearsal or brought cookies in from one of their aunts, Sophie found herself loving them all more. Okay, she hadn't been doing very well with any of it.

Sophie sighed and reached for the Gatorade, painkillers, and note. She couldn't help it, waking up here felt good. She was in for a huge heartbreak. But there was no avoiding it now. Maybe she should just enjoy it while it lasted.

Angie's note told her that she'd had to head over to Sonya's house for a little bit but to help herself to anything in the kitchen. She recommended eggs and toast, and Sophie smiled, thinking that Angie probably had as much experience with hangovers that had originated in an Irish pub as she did with anything else. Sophie took a deep, contented breath. Not only had Angie taken her in last night, but she didn't feel that she needed to stick around and play hostess for Sophie. She didn't feel like a guest. She felt like part of the family. And that was enough to make tears well up.

Sophie swallowed three ibuprofen and washed them down with the fruity sports drink. Then she got out of bed and started for the bathroom. But she took her time getting there, studying everything in the room that had been Finn's while he was growing up. There were the things she would have expected—CDs, books, baseball and football cards. Then there were the things that made her smile—like the collection of plastic badges he'd evidently used to play policeman, the certificate of commendation for community service from the mayor, the photographs of him with his brother and cousins. And then there were the things that made her heart ache—the photo of him and his dad, with Tommy in full uniform, grinning and holding a young Finn who wore his father's hat; the certificate of commendation with his father's name on it for service above and beyond the call of duty; the photo of Angie, Tommy, Finn, and Colin, clearly not long before Tommy was killed; and the photo of the honor guard with Tommy's casket.

Sophie ran a finger over the photo of Finn with his family, and she acknowledged the fact that she'd never stood a chance of resisting falling in love with him.

That complicated her life immensely. She wasn't going to handle losing them all well when it was over. It seemed that maybe she and Angie could sustain their friendship, but she was going to have to insist they go back to the no-family rule once the play was finished. She wasn't sure she'd be able to handle hearing about Finn even in casual conversation.

She brought the neck of his shirt up and took a deep breath. For now she was going to wallow in it all. It seemed to her that the Kelly family had enough laughter and love that maybe even a few weeks in the midst of it could stay with her for a while afterward.

She made her way into the bathroom, found towels, and helped herself to soap and shampoo without thinking anything of it. She felt perfectly comfortable making herself at home, and by the time she stepped out of the shower, she was feeling good. Physically and mentally.

She combed out her hair, used the toothbrush that Angie had laid out with another little note—"For you"—and then slipped Finn's shirt back on to pad back across the hardwood floor into the hall. Her foot had just hit the carpet of his bedroom when she heard the sound of something metal hitting the floor. She turned to find Finn at the top of the stairs. He had a plate in one hand, a cup in the other, and a fork at his feet.

She couldn't believe how happy she was to see him. She was always happy to see him, but she felt as if last night had opened up a part of her she'd been desperately trying to hold shut. The part of her that would admit how happy she was and would even let it show.

"Morning," she said, with a big grin.

Finn looked like he was in pain. "You're wearing my shirt."

She looked down. "Yeah. It's what I slept in, and I didn't take my clothes into the bathroom with me."

Sophie watched him swallow hard. "You slept in my shirt." His eyes went to the room behind her. "In my room."

She put her hands on her hips, loving how discombobulated he seemed. "Yep."

The look in his eyes was hot and possessive as he took a step toward her... and kicked the fork across the floor. He looked down at the plate in his hands. "I made you eggs and toast. And coffee," he said.

She smiled. "Thanks. That sounds exactly like the second thing I need right now."

"What's the first?"

Sophie knew he liked her spunky side, which was a good thing. Because she was feeling very spunky this morning. She pulled his shirt off over her head. "You," she said simply.

Then she turned and walked into his bedroom.

She felt him stalking up behind her and grinned. She heard the clatter of the plate on a table as she headed for the bed, and then he was there, right behind her, his hands on her hips, drawing her back against him.

He took her wrists and brought her arms up, her hands behind his neck. She linked her fingers together, exposing her body to his touch. Finn ran his hands down her sides to her hips, squeezed gently, and then moved around to her stomach. One big palm covered her belly and pressed her against his erection while the other slid up her side, over her shoulder, and to the back of her head. He sank his fingers into her hair and then made a fist and tugged, tipping her head back to his shoulder. Sophie couldn't help her moan.

"These weren't the sheets I was talking about being tangled up in last night," he said huskily against the side of her neck, "but they will totally work."

"Finn," she said softly. She couldn't manage any more than that, but it didn't seem to matter. His hands cupped her breasts, her nipples between his fingers. He squeezed and tugged while kissing and sucking gently on her neck, until she was squirming against him.

"Need you, Soph," he said gruffly.

"Yes. Please."

"Put your foot up on the mattress."

She did, recognizing that she would do anything this man asked of her. He dropped a hand to her knee and pressed, making her leg fall open further. His other hand slipped down the front of her body until his big, hot hand was cupping her. Sophie whimpered slightly and started to move her hands.

"Let me," he ordered, his voice gravelly against her ear.

Let him touch her, pleasure her, have full access to her body to do anything he wanted? *Yes, please.*

He chuckled, the sound vibrating through her, and she realized she'd said it out loud.

She gripped the back of his neck with her hands and let her eyes slide shut, surrendering herself to whatever Finn was going to do to her.

He returned one hand to her breast, playing with her nipple and making her inner muscles clench. His other hand set about driving her out of her mind while barely doing anything. He traced his finger along the sensitive skin between her pelvis and thigh, teasing her, making her ache for more. Then he moved to the outer lip of her sex, making her writhe to get closer to the tempting touch. He finally dragged the pad of his finger over her center, but with a light touch that only made her moan in frustration. Then he switched hands, tracing that side of her body—her inner thigh, the delicate area just outside where she most wanted and needed him, the almost-there spot next to her clit, and then another light stroke over the center.

"Finn," she begged. "More."

"I'm just learning you," he told her. "I want to know every inch of you."

"There are some inches feeling very neglected."

He laughed lightly. "Well, I intend to spend lots of time there, so that won't last."

He brushed over her clit, and she gasped. "Yes. There."

"Oh yeah, lots of time," he promised sexily, his voice low and right against her neck.

He increased his pressure on her sweet spot, making her knees weak. But he had her held tightly to his body, and as he circled and pressed, she let the sensations take over. That was almost enough, and given a little more time, she knew that she would be soaring. But then he did the gentlemanly thing, having gotten a woman wound up to this point, and shifted to glide his finger into her.

Sophie moaned and let her head fall forward. "Yesss." The word hissed out between her teeth, and she moved against his hand.

"Damn, you are sweet," he said thickly. He added his thumb against her clit, and as he stroked her, Sophie felt the pending orgasm gathering quickly. "And soft."

And then he stopped.

"Finn!" she gasped.

"Oh, I'm not done with you."

"So you *are* going to finish something here?" In her defense, her tone was colored by horniness and frustration.

He laughed. "Oh, honey, I'm so going to finish something here."

"*When?*" Sophie realized she was on the verge of begging. And she was completely okay with that.

"Soon, ninja warrior," he said. "Very soon."

"You've touched pretty much everything," she said as his finger ran over her mound, tracing back and forth from one hip bone to the other.

"I have," he agreed. "With my finger."

"But I—" Understanding dawned. "Oh."

He laughed again and ran his whole hand up over her belly to her breasts again. He didn't stay there as long as she wanted him to either. He took her arms from around his neck and turned her to face him. She took in the look in his eyes as he studied her, lingering on her eyes, and suddenly she felt something that went so beyond horny and frustrated...she felt a need like she'd never imagined. And not just for his body.

Before she could fully process that thought and what it meant, Finn lowered his mouth to hers and kissed her deeply. This was so different from the first time at the theater. That had been hot and fast and incredibly sexy. But this was...more. Terrifyingly more. Like she would never be satisfied with anything less than this ever again. And they hadn't even gotten to the really good stuff. Was it possible she'd never be satisfied with anyone ever touching her besides Finn? If so, she was really, really screwed. In the not-at-all-good way.

The kiss also didn't last as long as she would have preferred, but as he pulled back, Finn pivoted to sit on the bed, her between his knees, and she forgot about worrying or analyzing or even thinking. She was just going to *feel*.

"Shirt," she said, managing only the one word.

Thankfully, Finn understood. He gripped the back of his

shirt and yanked it off over his head. She spread her hands on his shoulders and ran them down his arms and then over his chest. She understood the temptation of just wanting to touch. She could spend hours just running her hands and lips over his body. But there was an ache in her that said that touching and kissing were never going to really be enough.

"Pants," she said next.

But he shook his head on that one. "Not yet."

"Finn, I—"

"Come here." He gripped her butt in his hands and brought her forward into his lap. But that wasn't what he had been talking about. He lay back, bringing her up his body until her knees straddled his shoulders. And then he went about *really* touching her. With his fingers, his lips, his tongue, on all the places she needed him most. Within minutes she was calling out his name and soaring up and over an intense orgasm that seemed to affect every single cell in her entire body.

She had barely started to come down from it when he flipped her to her back and leaned over her.

"You are, without a doubt, the sexiest, sweetest, feistiest, most amazing woman I've ever known."

And she almost had another orgasm right then and there. His words, the look in his eyes, the intensity of his tone, all told her that he meant that with everything in him.

She clasped his face in her hands. "Make love to me, Finn."

She'd never been made love to, she knew that. She'd never had sex with a guy who actually got her. Who appreciated her, who saw things that she didn't want him to see but who liked her in spite of them. Maybe even because of them.

She knew that she was wounded and cynical, but Finn made her focus on the other stuff inside—the happiness, the hope, the way she could make other people feel. He made her want to focus on those things instead of all the things that could go wrong, the things that she needed to guard against, the risk of hurt and the idea of inevitable goodbyes. He made her want to wallow in the here and now, the idea of being cared for, of caring for other people and taking a risk because it could possibly, just maybe, turn out great.

Finn kissed her hungrily and then sat back and shed his jeans and underwear, his actions jerky as he rushed. He kicked his clothes off the edge of the bed, and she reached for him, wrapping her hand around his cock and stroking him, relishing the way he shuddered at her touch. He braced himself with his forearms on either side of her head, letting her stroke and squeeze, letting her run her hands over his abs and ass, but finally through gritted teeth he informed her, "Need inside you, Feisty."

She shifted and spread her legs, welcoming him between them. "Okay, but don't lose my place."

"Your place?"

"I've touched pretty much everything, but only with my fingers."

The heat in his gaze intensified even as he gave her a slow, sexy half smile. "Oh, I've got your place very saved."

She shivered, the emotions and desire in her making it impossible to lie still.

He lifted a condom wrapper to his mouth and tore it open with his teeth, his eyes on hers the entire time, and then, impressively, rolled the protection on with only one hand. Then he positioned himself at her entrance and slowly pressed forward.

Her back arched, and she automatically lifted her legs to link her ankles on his lower back. They groaned together as he slid slowly home. Slowly seemed to be the theme of the morning. He paused when he was as deep as he could get and then pulled out bit by bit, the friction intense and so good and yet not even close to enough.

They kissed the same way—deep and slow—and their hands also caressed everywhere they could reach in long, unhurried strokes.

The slow, steady, sweet pace lasted for another few minutes. But then Finn shifted and put a delicious pressure in a spot Sophie was pretty sure had never been touched before, and her body rejoiced, coiling tightly, squeezing him and sending heat and tingles shooting through her body.

She arched her neck and tightened her legs around him. "Oh my God!"

He paused. "Soph?"

She reached down and grabbed his ass. "Don't you dare stop. More. Please."

He laughed and then groaned as she flexed her inner muscles around him. "I'd love to make you beg a little more, but I don't have it in me," he told her gruffly.

He thrust again, deep and hard, and Sophie felt the shock waves of pleasure clear to her toes. "Yes, like that. Again. Harder."

His jaw tightened, and she knew he was holding back. "We did hard. This was supposed to be sweet and slow," he said through gritted teeth.

Sophie took his face in her hands again, meeting his gaze directly. "Remember the first night we met and you picked me up to carry me out of the theater?"

"Yeah."

"I want you to fuck me now the way you wanted to that night."

His eyes reflected surprise for about three seconds, and then he gave a little growl, slid his hands under her ass, and thrust hard. And kept thrusting hard. And fast. And deep. And Sophie moved with him, meeting each stroke and holding him tightly. The way she'd wanted to that first night too.

She went flying first, her climax rolling over her and scattering every thought. Finn was right behind her, calling out her name.

Then he buried his face in her neck and groaned.

They lay plastered together for several long minutes. Minutes Sophie spent memorizing everything about. The loose, warm feeling in her limbs, the hot hardness of Finn's body against hers, even the wallpaper in the room, and, most of all, the incredible full feeling in her chest.

So this was what she'd been holding herself back from. All this time she'd been afraid and worried and careful... she'd been missing out on this.

Then again, *this* hadn't come along until Finn Kelly had walked into her theater.

* * *

They managed to shower—not together, since that would have taken more time than they had—and eat breakfast before Angie got home.

Sophie was upstairs blow-drying her hair when Angie came through the back door into the kitchen. Finn was doing the dishes and trying really hard not to think about how much he loved the whole domestic vision he had going of Sophie and him doing all of this in their own house.

Man. The sex had been good, but had it been so good that he was ready to play house with her? Because the second Sophia Birch had so much as a pair of socks moved into one of his drawers, he was done for. He could never break up with her.

He was in love. Really, truly in love. And that meant all of the issues were solved. The only concern had been her getting attached to the family—and vice versa—if they split up. If they didn't split up, all was well.

"Good morning," Angie said, not seeming a bit surprised to find him there.

"Hi, Mom." He shut off the water and grabbed a towel to dry his hands. "We need to talk."

She nodded and moved to put her purse down on the table. "Yeah, we do."

He faced her. "I'm in love with Sophie. I didn't mean to fall for her but... I did. Completely. And I know that seems complicated, but it's not. I love her, and she'll be a part of the family forever now. So no breakups. You'll never lose her. She won't be devastated by loving us and losing us."

Angie folded her arms and studied his face. Then she took a breath and said, "I'm sorry I've been giving you such a hard time. Doing the play has made me realize that you, of all people, will love Sophie the best. A girl like her, who never had any stability or anyone to count on, needs someone like you. You've never let anyone down in your life. You are so much like your father. And I've always known that, but it's been so amazingly obvious watching you put the show together."

He appreciated that, but couldn't help but ask, "I didn't let Sarah down?"

Angie shook her head. "Marrying Sarah would have

been letting her down. And me. All of us. Because we expected you to marry for love. When you admitted that you
weren't in love anymore, you called it off. Before you got
in deeper and ended up unhappy and perhaps even breaking up down the road. That would have been worse."

"You still lost your best friend."

Angie gave him a sad smile. "Maybe she wasn't that
good of a friend after all if it was that easy to lose her. They
had to see, eventually, that you and Sarah were better off."

Finn took a deep breath. "Thanks, Mom."

"Thank *you* for being someone I can trust Sophie with,
and thank you for showing us that there's more here for
her than just you."

He frowned and shifted against the counter. "What does
that mean?"

She tipped her head. "When I lost your father, I was
devastated. But the Kellys were there for me. More than
my own family was. Sophie can't count on her dad. I was
worried about what would happen if you...didn't come
home one night. That would be way worse than a breakup,
Finn."

"You were afraid of her having to say that kind of goodbye?" Finn swallowed hard. He knew that his job was
dangerous, of course. He'd lost his father. He'd been to
an officer's funeral just two years before. But he and his
whole family of cops and firefighters believed that what
they did was worth the risks they took.

Angie nodded. "But the play, remembering how your
dad and I started, what we worked through to be together,
how happy we were...I've never forgotten that, but seeing
it come to life onstage, with you playing his part and Sophie as me, it's been...like doing it all over again. And I

know that the Kellys will be there for her, the way they were for me. If needed."

Finn straightened. "Mom..." He shook his head. "Angel and Tony are you and Dad?" A ripple of shock and then a wave of *Of course, holy shit* went through him.

She nodded. "You didn't know?"

"I guess I didn't realize."

Angie gave him a small smile as she read the surprise on his face. "You okay?"

"I'm...Yeah." He nodded. "Yeah, I'm okay."

It was weird, maybe, as he thought of the play and how it was about his parents. But it was also really...great. It was a wonderful love story, and it was what had brought him closer to Sophie, and it was going to help the theater that the two most important women in his life loved.

Yeah, it was really great.

"So yeah, Sophie," he said, "she's going to be around for a while. Like forever."

Angie stepped forward and wrapped her arms around him. "Thank God."

CHAPTER TWELVE

Sophie was putting the second layer of paint on the upper part of the wall when the back door to the theater opened.

She looked over, and her heart stuttered as she saw Finn striding down the aisle carrying several bags from the local hardware store and a cup of coffee. It was just the two of them working for the next couple of hours, and she was hoping that they both might end up with some paint streaks where other people wouldn't see them.

She grinned and started down the ladder. It had been five days since she'd awakened wearing his T-shirt in his childhood bedroom. Since then, she'd awakened wearing nothing in his grown-up bedroom three mornings out of five.

"Did you get all the stuff?" she asked, hopping from the bottom rung to the floor.

Finn was frowning as he handed her the debit card she'd given him to use for the purchase. "Yeah, I got it. But your card wouldn't work."

She looked down at the card. "What do you mean it wouldn't work?"

"The account's overdrawn, Soph."

Her heart thumped, and she felt a mixture of dread and *Of course* slither through her. *Of course* because she'd been expecting this. Dread because she hadn't wanted Finn to find out. "Oh."

"Sophie."

She took a breath and looked up at him. "Yeah?"

"What's going on?"

She sighed and shook her head. "Nothing. I'll take care of it."

"I thought the ticket sales were going well."

They were. Very well. Nearly every show had sold out since a local news station and the *Globe* had reported on the story. Not to mention the Facebook posts that had been spreading all over.

"Ticket sales are great," she admitted.

"So where's the money?"

Looking into his eyes, Sophie knew that Finn already knew the answer. "Frank," she said, simply.

"Son of a bitch." Finn hurled the coffee cup against the lower half of the wall. There wasn't much coffee left in it, but it splattered all over the new plywood. At least they hadn't painted there yet.

"Finn, it's—"

"Don't say fine," he told her.

She shrugged. "It's expected." She hated that even more than he did. Didn't he get that? But she had made sure only five thousand dollars had been in the account.

Frank had been staying on Joe's pullout couch for almost two weeks now. She knew he would be getting restless. And that when he got restless, he'd come looking for the rest of the money he needed to buy the RV.

She knew Angie had given him three ten-thousand-dollar loans. She didn't want to know that, but Frank had shared it with her. Smugly. With the insurance check, that put him at forty of the fifty thousand he needed.

She just hadn't wanted Finn to find out all of this.

"What is expected?" Finn asked.

He was going to make her say it? Fine. "That Frank would clean the account out."

Finn dropped the bags and started for the door.

"Hey!" She ran after him. "Where are you going?"

"To find your father. We need to have a talk."

Sophie grabbed Finn's arm. "There's nothing to talk about."

He stopped walking and faced her. "He stole from you. And I'm guessing it's not the first time."

"He didn't. The money's his." She took a breath. "I'd hoped he'd wait until the show was over to take his share. But he didn't steal it."

Finn shoved a hand through his hair, clearly frustrated. "But he took it all."

"He only took what was in there. I would never put everything where he could get to it."

Finn studied her eyes. "But he knew you needed all of it to finish the repairs and everything."

She nodded.

"But he doesn't care."

She shook her head this time. It hurt. But she had built up some calluses, so it wasn't as bad as it used to be.

"I fucking hate that." He reached out and pulled her close. "And after everything we fucking did for him."

Oh boy. She let him hug her for a moment, but she felt her stomach knotting. She pulled back after only a few seconds. "This is going to be a problem, isn't it?"

He huffed out a breath. "Me wanting to strangle your father every other day?"

She was completely serious. "Yeah."

He clearly hadn't been expecting her to agree. "Really?"

"This is Frank, Finn. This is who he is. And you're you. You fix things. But you can't fix Frank. You can't fix me and Frank." The realization struck her too, as she said it. This was definitely going to be an issue. Finn was going to do everything he could to get Frank to change. And it was never going to happen. "So yes, you're going to be frustrated with him. A lot."

"And you're okay with Frank being who he is?" Finn asked with a scowl.

Sophie stepped back and crossed her arms. "Of course not. But that doesn't matter. That's never mattered. If me being disappointed or angry or frustrated mattered, he would have changed a long time ago."

"So we just let him take and take and take and never give you anything back?" Finn asked.

She didn't know what to say. "That's what he's always done. He did it to *you* too, you know. Where's he been working and sleeping and eating for the past couple of weeks?"

"Temporarily," Finn said firmly.

"Bullshit."

Finn lifted a brow.

"Seriously, Finn," she said, her exasperation showing, "your family gives and gives and gives. Frank takes and takes and takes. You really think anything about that is temporary? Frank's probably feeling claustrophobic with your family being around all the time. And I think that's hilarious. He wanted to be in the midst of everything and now he is and he's probably feeling smothered. So he might be taking a break and heading out of town early, but he'll be back. My God, he found a gold mine of attention and handouts from your family."

"So by being warm and generous and welcoming, my family is setting themselves up to get screwed?" Finn asked.

Sophie pressed her lips together. Finn's family was amazing. But yeah, if there was a way for Frank to take advantage of them, he would.

"Would he steal from the bar?" Finn asked after a moment.

Sophie drew a deep breath. "I don't think so." Frank would want to come back to the Kellys in the future for a place to stay, a "loan," maybe even—as much as she had a hard time believing it—for some sense of friendship and family. So no, she didn't think he'd steal from them. "But…"

"That's why you put that money in the account, knowing he'd take it. You were keeping him from taking from the pub."

She didn't have to admit it for Finn to know the truth. She couldn't put anything past Frank. So she had changed the bank account password back to the old one and made sure there was a chunk of money—but not too much—in there.

"That son of a bitch," Finn muttered.

Her temper prickled a bit. "The thing is, you know what to expect with Frank," Sophie said. "If you would just quit being so intent on saving him and changing him and so enamored with the idea of your family somehow winning him over to the good side, then you'd just see him for who he is and you wouldn't be so disappointed."

The disbelief in Finn's eyes made Sophie take a step back.

"You're defending him?" Finn demanded. "You're saying that it's my fault that I'm pissed off? Because I expect him to be better than this? When did you start just accepting the shitty way he treats you, Sophie?"

She lifted her chin. Was she defending Frank? That seemed odd. And yet she had made a good point. You could only be disappointed in people when you expected more than they could deliver. "You're just pissed because you finally ran up against a problem you can't fix. This is stinging your ego a little, right?"

Finn's frown deepened. "This isn't about me."

"Of course it is. You think Frank should be grateful and that he should want to be a better man after hanging out with your family. Your feelings are hurt that it didn't work like that, that your family wasn't enough to change him."

"He *should* want to be a better man," Finn said. "But not because of my family. Because of you."

"Well, that's not going to happen."

"You're better than that," Finn said firmly. "Jesus, Soph, you can't let him treat you this way."

"I don't *let* him do anything. I also can't *make* him do anything, Finn," she said. "This is just how it is."

"Why do you keep letting him come around?"

"What am I supposed to do?" she asked. "He owns half this theater. He's not breaking any laws coming here."

"But he's breaking your heart," Finn shot back. "Don't

tell me that you're not hoping deep down that one day he's going to come here and realize what he's done, what he's been doing, all this time. Don't tell me you're not hoping someday he'll be sorry and that you can have some semblance of a family."

Sophie opened her mouth and then shut it again. She had been about to make the biggest confession of all to Finn. One she'd barely made to herself. One that could make her look strong...or incredibly pathetic. But finally she had to tell him.

"I don't think he'll be sorry, Finn. I don't think that he and I can ever be a family like yours. But I'm still here, in the theater his mother gave us, sharing this with him because...I want to be better than him. I want to be here where he can find me when he comes to town, I want to *stay* somewhere that matters to me, doing something that makes me proud, doing something on my own, because I want to be the things he wasn't—steady, independent, and"—she took a deep breath—"happy. God, Finn, that's all I want. I want to be happy. I want to find a place to *stay* and be happy."

Emotions flickered through Finn's eyes, but his mouth remained a grim line. "You're just going to just keep taking it then? After seeing what a real family is like, after seeing what it's like to love and take care of someone, after having people who want to love and take care of you?"

Sophie felt anger flash through her. Working to be the opposite of everything her dad had been and shown her and taught her was somehow a bad thing? Not quitting when things were tough, not running away when she got hurt, not taking the easy way out were somehow making her weaker in Finn's eyes?

"Not every family is like yours, Finn," she said quietly. "This is as much family as I have—an old theater, a bunch of memories, and a far-from-perfect father. But I can't just walk away. That's what I knew as a kid—walking away when something isn't perfect. I'm not going to do that."

"You don't have to put up with any of this," he said stubbornly. "You can be with me and be . . . happy. And stay. Be all of those things you said you wanted. Walk away from Frank and all of this. Let me fix this and make you happy."

She felt tears stinging, and she shook her head. "I would think that you, of all people, would understand and even admire me accepting him as he is and making the best of it."

Finn's expression softened slightly, but he shook his head. "I love you, Sophie, and I *don't* understand you putting up with all of this."

He loved her. Sophie felt her heart race for a moment. Then her stomach dropped. He loved her. But he also wanted to fix things he couldn't fix.

Sophie blinked back the tears as she looked into the eyes of the man who really could be her knight in shining armor. Except that she wanted to wear her own armor, and she didn't really want to ride off into the sunset. She wanted to stay right here. In the theater that was the only home she really knew.

"I love you too," she said, her throat tight. She did. So much. But Finn was a fixer, and she couldn't watch him be constantly hurt and frustrated by being unable to fix her. "And that's why I have to say that I don't think we should keep seeing each other."

His eyebrows slammed together. "What?"

"You will always want to fix this with me and Frank,"

she said. "And it will never be the way you want it to be. You need to find someone like Sarah—someone who values and understands family the way you do. Someone you can fix things for and who can let you love them the way you need to love them." Sophie felt as if her heart were being turned inside out, but all of that was true. Finn needed someone he could save.

Finn stood staring at her for several long, painful moments.

Sophie held herself tightly, willing herself not to cry, not to beg him to forget everything she'd just said, willing herself not to grab him and hold on forever.

She couldn't believe it. She was losing Finn because of Frank. But she was losing Finn because of Finn too. The world was imperfect. People were imperfect. But until he accepted that, her and Frank's crazy, stupid, imperfect relationship would hurt Finn. She had said that she would not let Frank hurt the people she loved, and now that meant pushing Finn away so that wouldn't happen.

Finally Finn gave her a single nod. "I can't keep watching you get hurt."

She let out a breath. "I know."

"And as long as he's a part of your life, that will keep happening."

She nodded. "I know."

"You should tell him to fuck off."

"I have. Repeatedly."

"But when he needs a couch, he knows the theater is here."

She swallowed hard and nodded. She wouldn't give him a couch at Kiera's because she wanted to protect her friends. She hadn't exactly offered him the couch at the theater. But once he was there, she'd realized that it might work.

"Your mom said something the other day," she told Finn. "She said that she thought maybe Frank hadn't had enough family stuff either and that he wanted it. I didn't believe her at the time. He's had his chance. But...I don't know...something about how he is with your family. It's so crazy but, maybe he needed...something else. Friends? Brothers? Mothering? Maybe it was the husband stuff he didn't want, or just wasn't good at," Sophie said. "He was crazy in love with my mom. Maybe he just couldn't do that again."

Finn shook his head. "You're making excuses for him. Un-fucking-believable."

She pulled herself up straight. "I didn't realize it until he was staying here, but maybe that's what he needs. A steady place to come to. I love the idea of him in an RV far from here. I'm not going to lie. I don't want him here every day, all the time. But..." She took a deep breath. "I know he says that he kept moving on to the next woman because of me, but then he got together with Cynthia, his last wife. He didn't need to be with her because of me. I think maybe he just needs a place to go. Maybe he wants a home too."

"He's doing a really shitty job of showing it," Finn said shortly.

Sophie couldn't disagree with that. "Maybe he's just re-alizing it. Or maybe he'll never settle down for very long at a time. And the RV is good then. But maybe if he has a place to come back to, he'll stop looking for whatever he's been looking for with all these women."

"Jesus, Sophie." Finn's tone was full of frustration and skepticism and yes, even pity.

She glared up at the big, stubborn cop she was crazy about, but who she knew she couldn't keep. "You know, I've been avoiding getting involved with families for years," she told him, planting her hands on her hips. "I've been staying far away. And then you come stomping into my life and bring this huge family with you and suddenly I'm up to my eyeballs in drama and hurt feelings and meddling. Frank and I are what we are. We've been this way for a long time. You can't fix it, and you need to stop trying."

He stared at her for a moment. Then he nodded. "Yeah, well, I guess there is one thing I *can* fix. Pissing you off right now." Finn turned on his heel and stomped up the middle aisle.

He didn't even look back as he yanked the door open and left.

* * *

"Wow, you are a dumbass," Tripp said as he tipped his bottle of beer up for a long pull.

Finn glared at him. "I'm right."

"You're not *wrong*," Tripp said, "but you're not seeing the big picture."

Finn wondered for the hundredth time why he'd called to ask Tripp to meet him for a beer. He'd wanted to talk about Sophie and the argument they'd had the night before. He'd nursed his wounds and replayed the fight over and over last night, but he hadn't come up with any solutions. So he'd called his buddy tonight. But he hadn't really thought everything through. Like that Tripp might not agree with him and might be on Sophie's side.

"Here's the big picture," Finn said. "Sophie's dad is a jerk, he took the money that she needed to finish the repairs of the theater, he does absolutely zero for her—and never has—and she still defended him when I was trying to help her."

Tripp ran a fry through the glob of ketchup on his plate and popped it into his mouth. He said nothing, though, even after he'd swallowed.

"What?" Finn asked.

"Oh, I was hoping when you heard all of that out loud, you'd realize that you were wrong."

"I'm wrong?" Finn asked. "Seriously? I'm in love with her. I want her to be happy. Frank does not make her happy. So doesn't it make sense that I would want to deal with the thing not making her happy?"

Tripp nodded. "Right. Got that part. But you're missing a few things."

Finn gritted his teeth. "Start talking."

Tripp washed his fries down and then set his empty bottle on the table. He leaned onto his forearms and met Finn's eyes directly.

"First, you're only partly pissed off that Frank is upsetting Sophie. You're also partly pissed off that you can't fix this, and you know it."

"I just want her to be happy."

"And she's not going to be happy all the time, Finn. Shit is going to happen. For Sophie, sometimes it's going to be because of her dad. But it could also be poor ticket sales, or an argument with one of her friends, or traffic. You can't make everything go right for her every second of every day. You need to deal with this or things aren't going to work."

Finn blew out a breath. On some level he knew he was overreacting. But fuck. He really didn't like Frank Birch.

"He's *always* been a shitty father to her," Finn said.

Tripp nodded. "That's another thing you need to come to terms with. That's all over. You can't change it no matter how hard you try. And being pissed off about it isn't helping anything."

Finn took a drink of beer. He didn't want to admit that Tripp was right. But his friend didn't suck at this. "Go on."

"The other thing you're missing is that Sophie is basically being a Kelly."

Finn's heart thumped. He wanted Sophie to be a Kelly. But he wasn't sure what Tripp meant. "What are you talking about?"

"She's putting up with Frank's shit because he's her family. She wishes it was different, she doesn't like it, but she's not kicking his ass to the curb. That's a Kelly thing to do."

"We don't put up with people's shit," Finn said, feeling his chest tighten in spite of his protest.

Tripp laughed. "The hell you don't. There's nothing anyone in your family could do that would make the rest of you turn your back."

Well, that was true. "But we're not pushovers," Finn said with a scowl. "We call people on their crap."

"Sophie's not a pushover either," Tripp said, with a frown of his own, and Finn got the impression his friend was feeling a little protective of Sophie too. "She calls him on his crap. But the fact that she wants anything to do with her father after everything is proof that she's got as big a heart as any Kelly."

Finn let that roll around in his head.

"She really is already kind of a Kelly, isn't she?" Finn finally asked.

Tripp nodded. "She fits right in."

She did. And that thought made Finn's heart pound. "She and I are probably going to fight about Frank whenever he comes around." And he would come around. Finn realized that Sophie was right about that. Frank might be too restless to stay, especially when he had Kellys coming out of his ears, but he'd be back.

"Nothing wrong with that, as long as you learn one of the most important things about being in a long-term relationship," Tripp said.

Finn gave a bark of laughter. Tripp had lots of relationships, but none that could be called long-term. "You know the most important things about being in a long-term relationship?" Finn asked, dubiously.

"Sure. Why do you think I'm not in one?"

"Okay, lay it on me," Finn said.

"You have to admit that you're wrong sometimes."

Finn blew out a breath. "Yeah, that might take some work."

Tripp grinned. "Well, there's always the bright side to fighting."

"Yeah?"

"Makeup sex."

His friend made a very good point.

* * *

Sophie wasn't nervous. Exactly.

But the butterflies swooped and swirled in her stomach as she approached the front door to the pub.

No, she wasn't nervous. She was terrified.

It was just dinner. With most of Finn's family. And she did believe she was welcome. But this was the test. The test to see if she and Angie and the rest of the Kellys could still be friends after she and Finn broke up.

Her stomach tightened at that thought, and it had nothing to do with fear or nerves. It was all about Finn. They'd broken up. It had been just three days ago, but she hadn't seen him since. She did know that he wouldn't be here tonight, though. He was working. Which was the only reason she was doing this. She'd resisted calling or texting. She'd resisted trying to see him at his place, or the station, or here at the pub. But she missed him. And that was the biggest reason she was nervous about tonight. Could she be with his family and not die from missing him and wanting him?

She got to the door and became aware that this was a bad idea. Maya and Kiera had convinced her to come. The dinner invitation had been issued long before she and Finn fought. But she knew that everyone inside the pub knew that they'd argued, that she'd said they shouldn't see each other anymore, and that he'd walked out of the theater. Everyone in this family always knew everything.

Maybe she should leave.

"Here, I've got it."

Finn's cousin Dan—or was he an uncle?—was suddenly beside her, grabbing the door handle, and she was stuck. She gave him a smile. "Hi. Thanks." Sure, she could pretend that she'd been hesitating because she hadn't been able to grab the door while carrying four pans of dessert.

And she suddenly realized that she'd gone way overboard. She loved to cook and she was pretty good at it and she didn't have the chance as often as she had before Maya and Kiera had fallen in love. They now spent a lot of time with Alex and Zach, and while Sophie had a chance to cook for their large group of friends once in a while, it wasn't a regular thing. So she'd gotten excited about the Kellys. And maybe she'd thought that she could win some forgiveness for upsetting Finn with her caramel apple crumble.

"What is all this?" he asked as he relieved her of the pumpkin roll and the brownies.

Brownies. That was stupid. No one made better brownies than the ones Finn's family had brought to the theater the other night. Why would she bring brownies?

"Um, just thought I'd bring some dessert." Sophie felt her cheeks flush.

"If this is your idea of *some*, you're going to fit right in here." Dan chuckled and escorted her into the pub.

"I didn't...I wasn't sure...Variety is always a good idea, right?" Sophie asked.

"Absolutely." Dan headed for the bar, where pans and pots and packages of food covered the surface. "No one here is going to complain about extra dessert."

She followed him, hoping to get the pans set down before everyone noticed her overly enthusiastic contribution to the potluck. She'd just set the crumble and the chocolate caramel decadence on the bar when she was surrounded.

"Sophie, I'm so glad you're here!"

"You brought dessert? You didn't have to do that!"

"You brought all of this? You're my favorite."

Before she knew it, she was seated at the long table with twenty family members who were all talking at once, laughing, joking, and eating enough to feed a small country. And acting as if there weren't a thing strange about her being there.

It only took about ten minutes for Sophie to realize that she'd made a big mistake. Probably the biggest of her life.

She wanted this. All of it. And she wanted the man who had given it to her.

No, Finn didn't totally get where she came from. And she was glad. She loved him, and she was so damned happy that *this* was what he knew, where he'd grown up. He'd said that he loved her the other day. And it wasn't that she hadn't believed it. She felt it too. But this…this truly proved it. The other night when he'd brought her to the bar had actually been the first time he'd told her how he felt about her. It had been subtle. It had been without those exact three words. But it had been love.

God, she missed him.

She did want a home. She wanted a place where she could stay and that would always be hers, that no one could take away. It wasn't the theater, or the house she lived in, or even the city. It was Finn.

And Frank had almost taken her away from it. Again.

But this time *she* was in charge. Frank didn't have any more power in her life than she gave him. And if she wanted Finn, then she needed to go after him. She started to reach for her purse, rehearsing excuses, and then deciding that with this group, saying "I'm going to find Finn and tell him I'm madly in love with him" was probably the best way to go.

She had just started to push her chair back when Finn's uncle Joe came banging through the pub's front door, cussing loudly.

Dan shoved his chair back and stood. "What's going on?"

"Did Frank show up here for work last night?" Joe asked.

Sophie felt her stomach tighten sickeningly at her father's name.

"No," Jamie said. "I haven't heard from him."

"Well, he moved out of my place," Joe declared.

"Well, that's okay, right?" Jamie asked.

"Sure, it's fine. If he hadn't taken two thousand dollars with him."

His words hit her in the gut and Sophie put a hand to her stomach. She was going to be so pissed if Frank made her throw up the best mashed potatoes in the universe.

"He stole money from you?" Colin asked.

"Yes!" Joe exclaimed. "And he had to go looking for it. I had that in a box in my closet."

Sophie felt Angie take hold of her hand and she looked at her friend in surprise. "Not your fault," Angie said softly and firmly.

Sophie knew that it wasn't directly her fault that Frank had stolen from Joe. It hadn't even been her idea that Frank move in with Joe. But it was her fault that Frank had pegged the Kellys as a target. She rubbed her hand over her stomach, willing it to calm.

"Do you want me to call Finn?" Gary, one of the uncles, asked.

At the mention of Finn's name, Sophie's heart clenched. Of course he was a cop who was on duty at the moment. It made sense they would want to call him about the theft. But it pained her to think that he'd be the one going after her father because he'd stolen from Finn's family.

Joe dropped into one of the chairs. "No."

"No?" Sophie asked.

Everyone turned to look at her. But she was frowning at Joe. "You should report this. He's probably still in town. He wouldn't just..." She trailed off as she realized what she'd been about to say. He wouldn't just leave. Frank Birch was nowhere near the father-of-the-year list, but he wouldn't leave town without telling her. He'd try to get money out of her as well, but he'd also say goodbye. And that meant she knew where he was.

She swallowed and focused on Joe, feeling ashamed, even though she knew deep down that she shouldn't. "If you want to call the cops, I know where my dad is." She pushed her chair back and stood, slipping her hand from Angie's. She laid her napkin next to her plate and gave a last longing look at the potatoes. "He's at the theater, and I'm sure he's waiting for me. I'm heading over there now, and I'll try to keep him there until...whoever...shows up."

Maybe it wouldn't be Finn. She could pray it wouldn't be Finn. She knew that what would hurt the most would be seeing Finn's disappointment. Not in her. He wouldn't blame her, even if she blamed herself. But he'd be disappointed in Frank, and worse, disappointed in himself. Disappointed that he hadn't been able to reform Frank and prove that family love could fix anything.

And just like that, she was in the midst of a big-time family drama. The unscripted, unpredictable, happily-ever-after-not-guaranteed kind. She knew this was part of being in a family. But she didn't want to be the cause of it.

"Sophie, you shouldn't go alone," Angie protested, shooting Colin a pleading look.

"Yeah, I'll go with you, Soph," Colin offered.

Sophie pulled her bag up onto her shoulder and shook her head. "It's fine. Frank won't hurt me."

"But—" Angie started.

"I'll call Finn," Colin said.

Yeah, she knew he would. She'd be surprised if someone hadn't already texted him. "I'm...very sorry about this."

They, of course, all protested, but Sophie didn't say anything more as she headed for the door.

CHAPTER THIRTEEN

Thirty minutes later she parked behind Frank's car at the curb a block from the playhouse. All butterflies had died. She wasn't nervous or excited or worried. She was flat-out pissed off.

The minute she stepped into the lobby, she headed for the office. Frank would want to tell her goodbye, sure, but he'd also want whatever money he could find.

She stopped in the doorway and pulled in a deep breath when she found it empty. And the door to the safe hanging open. So he'd already checked there. She whirled and started for the main theater.

Sophie yanked the door to the inner theater open and stomped inside. All the lights were blazing and she looked around quickly. Where was he?

Then she heard the sounds of someone rifling through papers. He was in the sound booth, going through the file cabinet where Finn had found her the night of the fire. Sophie's heart pounded, remembering how Finn had come after her and how he hadn't let anything deter him from keeping her safe. Well, she was going to keep him and his family safe. She'd made an important decision on her drive between the pub—the center of the Kelly family—and the theater—the center of hers.

"Frank!" she shouted before the memories and emotions could distract her.

He came to the door to the booth. "You're hiding money from me?"

She glared at him. "What do you mean?"

"I mean there's no way that you've only brought in the money that was in the safe. Where's the rest?"

She crossed her arms. "In the bank."

"Bullshit. I already cleaned that out. I know that you hide some of the profits, Sophia."

"How do you know that?" Her pulse was racing so fast she was sure he'd soon see her hyperventilating.

"Because that's what I would do. I would take money out of the proceeds and stash it so that I had enough to keep things operating before I paid out my partner."

"So you're assuming that because you would do that, then I automatically would?"

Frank rolled his eyes. "Where is it?"

"If I went to all of that trouble hiding it, why would I tell you now just because you asked?"

Frank propped his shoulder against the door. "Because it's the easiest way to get rid of me."

"Where are you going?"

"I bought the RV. Like the one I had with your mom. I'm going to travel the country like she and I planned to do."

For just a moment, Sophie's anger wavered, and she

blew out a breath. "So no more poor, unsuspecting women?" she asked.

"I told you, I'm too old for that. I did all of that when I had a little kid to take care of."

Sophie bristled. "So you blame me for not being able to travel all over?"

"I could hardly raise you in an RV, could I?"

"Did you ever care about *any* of them?" She didn't know why she'd asked that, but suddenly she really did want to know.

Something flickered in his eyes, and he straightened. "Hell no. I was avoiding that at all costs."

She felt the familiar anger tighten her chest. "But you made them think..."

"I might have led them to believe some things that weren't true, but I never promised any of them forever, Sophia."

She frowned. "You married them."

"Yep, at the justice of the peace. And never did I say 'love, honor, and cherish.'" He tucked a hand into his front pocket. "I said that to your mother. I wasn't going to say it to anyone else."

And again Sophie felt the wall around her heart cracking slightly. Damn him. "I thought we were going to be with Maggie forever," she said. "I know I was young, but I really thought you—"

"I left as soon as I felt myself falling for her," Frank interrupted.

Sophie frowned at him. "That's why we left? Because you were falling in love with her?"

Frank frowned at her. "Knock it off. None of this matters. I want to know where the rest of the money is."

And so much for the brief moment of *nice* emotions. Sophie shook her head as she remembered what she was doing here in the first place. "You stole money from Joe. You 'borrowed' money from Angie," she said, making air quotes with her fingers. "Isn't that enough?"

"You're not denying that there's more money."

"Frank," Sophie said firmly, "I'm not going to give you any more money."

He stared at her, and Sophie was afraid that she had the location of the hidden money tattooed on her forehead. She'd had to be sure that she could keep the show running no matter what Frank did with their joint account. So yes, she'd embezzled money from her company. Maybe. She wasn't absolutely sure that it was technically embezzlement. She'd looked it up online a couple of times. But since she wasn't pocketing the money for her personal use and since she was a partner in the company and wasn't taking the money from an employer, it seemed a gray area.

Or maybe she was just borrowing from the Frank Birch book of excuses.

"Fine. I guess I'll wait until the show finishes. I expect the box office to double by the time word gets out after the first show."

She'd actually expected the same thing. She knew once opening night was over, there would be an influx. Facebook and Twitter, PTA meetings, coffee dates, and workplaces would be buzzing with good reviews. She just knew it. The guys were doing a great job, but even more, they were sexy and charming and funny. The audiences were going to be predominantly female... and they were going to go crazy. The guys had put in a lot of hard work—on the theater itself and on the show. They were being brave getting up onstage for the first time. And they were having fun. They'd discovered new talents, they'd learned to work together as a new kind of team, and a few of them had even discovered a true interest in theater.

And Frank was going to expect half the proceeds. He didn't care that the money was intended for the rest of the repairs to the theater. He'd think he was entitled to half.

Hell no.

She took a deep breath. "You know what, Frank? I think that it's time for us to dissolve our partnership."

He gave a short laugh. "Yeah, that's not really how that works."

"Right. I mean, one of us would have to sell out to the other."

"And you can't afford me."

She nodded. "Or I could sell to you."

He laughed harder. "Yeah, like I want this place. And what would you do? This theater is everything to you."

It had been. But now she knew that she had something more. She had Finn. She had a family. She had a home.

The only reason the theater mattered to Frank was that it kept her here, essentially working for him. He didn't care that she had a deep emotional attachment to the place or that the theater felt like the only family legacy she had. "Or we could sell the whole thing to someone else and split the profits," she said.

"I much prefer a steady cash flow."

Sophie felt tears of frustration welling up. She'd thought she could make the theater into a place that mattered to Frank. At least a little. And she realized that she'd actually been pulling a Finn. She'd been trying to fix Frank, to fix things between them, to make something more meaningful out of what wisp of a relationship they had.

And some things just couldn't be fixed.

This was Frank's choice. He was, figuratively and literally, leaving again. As he had with Maggie. When feelings started to get involved, he bolted. So he'd started to develop some feelings for the Kellys.

Well, she couldn't really blame him.

She stubbornly refused to acknowledge the tiny voice that said it might be too late with Finn. She'd told him she didn't want to see him anymore. Well, she had to deal with Frank first. And hell, Finn might be on his way over here anyway. They could always talk after she did... whatever she was going to do with Frank.

"It would be really too bad if this place stopped making a profit," she said, proud of how steady her voice sounded despite the emotions pounding her from within.

Frank's eyes narrowed. They'd had this conversation just the other day, and it had been in the back of her mind ever since.

"There's no way you're not going to make a profit on this show," Frank said, almost as if he was warning her.

"I could stop charging for tickets," she said.

"The people who have already paid will be pissed."

"I could refund everyone." Of course, Frank had cleaned out what she had in the safe.

"Yeah, you go ahead and do that." Frank stepped down from the sound booth. "Guess you're going to have to dig into your stash either way."

Sophie watched him start for the door. He was going to leave. He was going to take the money, and he was going to hang out in Boston until after the show and take that money too. And he didn't give a crap about her or about any of the work the theater needed or the amazing things that happened here. He didn't care about the guys and girls who had stepped up and gone out of their comfort zone to help the theater recover. And he didn't care about the magic that happened here. The fact that this was the only place where she felt she belonged. Until the Kellys.

She looked to the wall the guys had finished repairing, then the stage and the set that the cast had helped her build and paint and decorate. The huge old couch they'd hauled out of the basement, the curtains Finn's aunts had made, the props that they'd all be using in four nights. Opening night.

She looked back at her father. He'd never lifted a finger, nailed a nail, swiped a brush for this place. And yet, because of this theater, she'd met Angie, and because of Angie she'd met Finn, and because of Finn, Frank had been able to steal two thousand dollars from Finn's family.

She could pay Joe back and forget the whole thing. That wasn't the point. The point was that Frank would be tied to her as long as they owned the theater together, and as long as they were tied together, there was the risk of Frank further hurting the Kellys.

And she wasn't going to let that happen.

"Or the show could get canceled," she said. Then she marched down the middle aisle. She climbed up the three steps to the stage and walked to the middle of the set. They'd built three walls of Tony and Angel's apartment. But the walls were simple plywood.

Sophie lifted her leg and kicked out hard. A perfect front kick. That knocked a huge hole in the "living room" wall.

"Sophia!" Frank bellowed.

She landed another kick, this one through one of the fake windows. And damn, that felt good. But she was going to be sore, and ruining the set was going to take too long this way.

She headed backstage. When she came back around the corner, Frank was standing in front of the stage.

"What the hell are you doing?" he demanded.

"I'm vandalizing the set." Although she thought that might be another gray area. She owned everything she was ruining.

"You think this will stop the show?"

She lifted the sledgehammer the guys had stored backstage and then swung it at the door in the middle of the set, producing a very satisfying *crack* as the wood split. She turned to Frank. "Yes. I do think this will stop the show. No show, no money. No money, no Frank."

"You're . . . crazy," he finally told her.

No. She was feisty. She swung again, cracking the wood on the third wall as well as shattering the framed photograph hanging there and sending the clock on the next wall crashing to the floor.

She kept going, driven by all the anger and frustration that had built up, the need to show Frank that she wasn't fucking around with empty threats, and the fear that she might have pushed Finn away for good.

Finally, her arms and back screaming from the effort, she dropped the sledgehammer and wiped her hair back away from her face. She couldn't swing the heavy tool anymore. But she wasn't fully satisfied. She marched backstage and grabbed a can of red spray paint. She proceeded to spray paint huge squiggly lines and X's over the set and even over the recliner and the area rug before the paint ran out and she let the can drop to the floor and roll to the edge of the stage.

Breathing hard and feeling some of the tension seeping out of her body, Sophie turned and looked around with a grin.

That slowly died. What had she done?

The set lay in ruins around her. Her shoulders hurt, her clothes were covered in tiny splinters of wood, and the red paint on her hands made it look as if she'd brutally murdered someone.

Or murdered something. Like one of the most fun shows the theater had ever put on. Like the show that was incredibly important to Angie. Like the project that had made her fall in love with Finn and everyone in his life. Like the thing that she'd just stolen away from all of those people.

"Jesus, Sophie."

She spun toward Frank. God, he always made her crazy. Why did she keep letting him do that to her?

He's your dad. He loved your mom. He took care of you the best he knew how.

She shook her head quickly, quieting all of those words that had kept her hoping all this time. She'd thought she was a cynic. She'd thought she was feisty and tough. But the truth was, she *was* soft and sweet. She did hope. She did want more from her father. She did keep thinking that maybe he'd change.

"I don't think we're going to be able to open on Thursday," she said through the tightness in her throat.

"What the hell were you thinking?"

"I'm thinking that I don't want to support you anymore. Not with this theater and certainly not with the wonderful people that I meet and get close to."

"It's your turn."

"No, Frank! It's not. Because *you* are the dad. Taking care of me and supporting me was your job, your responsibility. You weren't doing me a favor. We weren't partners in crime. I'm your daughter. I'm supposed to depend on you." She took a deep breath and then went on, unable to hold back the words. "I hurt Angie. I said terrible things to her, I got involved with Finn even though Angie didn't want me to, and we had a big fight. And yet, when I needed her, she was there. She took care of me. She loved me. Not expecting *anything* in return." She shook her head. "You've never done that. My father has only ever used me for his own gain. So...I want you to leave. I'll put the money into your account and there's no need for you to be here."

Frank looked around the set. "I get that you're trying to make a point. But—"

The anger and hurt boiled up almost before she could blink. He thought she was just trying to make a point? She'd just ruined the show for Finn and all of his family and friends and Frank thought it was just a tantrum?

Well, if she was going to throw a fit, she was going to throw a huge fit.

She stomped backstage and grabbed the box of matches from the prop table. She stalked to the couch, lit a match, and dropped it onto the center cushion.

"Sophie! Holy shit!" Frank exclaimed as the flame caught.

Sophie pulled her phone from her pocket and dialed 911.

"Nine-one-one, what's your emergency?"

"There's a fire at the Birch Community Playhouse," Sophie reported calmly. She wanted to burn the couch, not the entire theater. She gave the address and then pocketed her phone as she watched the fire jump to the next cushion. She looked over at her father. "By the way, *that's* where I stashed the extra money."

In plain sight, yet someplace no one would ever look.

Frank swore and started up the center aisle. Presumably to grab the extinguisher. Sophie descended the steps and took a seat front row, center. She crossed her legs, and as she watched the set—and a little over five thousand dollars— burn, she found that she was simply wishing for some marshmallows to roast.

* * *

"Hey," Finn answered when he saw Colin's number pop up on his phone. He'd just finished his shift and was still at his desk.

"So, um, I'm at the theater."

"Okay." Finn frowned. "What's going on?" He could distinctly hear sirens in the background.

"There's a fire."

Finn swore and shoved his chair back as he stood swiftly. "Who's there? What's going on?"

"Sophie is here. And her dad. The fire is out. It was just the couch on the set."

Finn was already jerking his keys from his pocket and was halfway to the door. "The couch?"

"Yeah."

"How did only the couch catch on fire?"

"Well, I'm going to let Sophie explain that one to you. Along with how the set got trashed."

The set had been trashed too? Finn jogged down the steps. He could tell from Colin's tone that everyone and everything was fine. But Frank hadn't shown up to work last night and had taken off from Joe's with a bunch of money. And then Frank and Sophie were at the theater together. And something had been set on fire.

Finn was pretty sure he knew exactly what had happened. "Who reported to the scene?" he asked.

"Dwyer and Konn," Colin said, naming two other police officers.

"Okay, I'll meet them all downtown." Finn slid behind the wheel of his truck and threw it into drive.

"You want them to take her downtown?" Colin asked. "Won't that piss her off?"

Finn sighed. "Maybe. But everyone is probably safer this way." Sophie would have trashed the set and lit the fire even knowing that she'd have consequences to face. Frank must have pushed her to that point. "I don't want her to be alone. Call Mom."

"Where are you gonna be?"

"I need to have a talk with her father," Finn said grimly.

"He headed out before we got here."

"I know where he is."

"Can't wait to hear this story," Colin said.

"Yeah." Finn headed for the theater, pressing the speed limit. He didn't breathe out until he pulled up behind Frank. He'd been right. Frank was still there, parked up the street, watching. Not because he cared if the theater burned down, but because he'd want to make sure Sophie was okay. Frank Birch was not a good guy or a great dad, and Finn knew that it would be years—maybe the rest of his life—before he didn't have the urge to punch Frank in the face, but he knew that Frank did care about Sophie. He just really sucked at showing it.

Finn took a photo of Frank's license plate with his phone and then shut the truck off and got out. They were far enough away from the theater and the street was busy enough that no one would notice them. Unless of course they started a brawl, which wasn't completely out of the question.

Frank saw him coming in the rearview mirror. He looked resigned as he got out.

"Frank."

"Finn."

Frank leaned against the side of his car, and Finn leaned beside him. "Hear you're leaving town for a while."

"Yeah. Thought I'd see someplace new."

"I think that's a really good idea," Finn told him.

"I suppose you're here to get Joey's money back," Frank said.

"I'm not worried about the money. I'm not even really worried about Sophie's money."

"No?"

Finn took a deep breath. "Thing is, Frank, I'd *pay* you to stay away."

Frank didn't say anything to that. Finn glanced over. Rather than the calculating look on Frank's face that he'd expected, Frank looked a little sad. So Frank didn't want to stay away completely or indefinitely. Finn had suspected as much.

Finn tucked his hands into his front pockets. "This isn't about the money you took. This is about Sophie."

Frank was quiet for a moment. "I don't know how to be a dad," he finally said.

"Yeah, I kinda got that." Finn took a deep breath. "So, here's the deal. I don't know if you really intend to just travel the country in your RV or if you're on the lookout for a new victim or if you don't really know what you want or where you're going to go, but there's something you should know."

Frank nodded. "Okay."

"In the past, the people you've walked away from have been happy to see you go. They've wanted nothing more to do with you. You've never met someone who wanted to stay in your life."

Frank said nothing.

"But you need to realize that you're about to have a cop for a son-in-law," Finn went on, "and I *want* to be involved. I want to know everything you're doing, every person you meet, everything you try. I'll follow up on you; I'll keep tabs on you; I'll always know where you are. And if you think I don't have the time or the energy or the brains for it, you really aren't that good at reading people. You've just met the one man with the right motivation to make you suffer if you don't toe the line."

Finn pushed away from the car and turned to face Frank, his hands still tucked casually in his pockets. "I'd rather you just left and never came back, but there's a part of Sophie that wants you around. Sometimes. So, if Sophie wants you here, then you'll come. And if Sophie wants you to stay away, you'll stay away. She's in charge now. Not you. And if you make Sophie cry ever again—I'll make you miserable." He met Frank's gaze directly. "Am I clear?"

Frank nodded.

Finn turned on his heel, strolled to his car, got in, and drove toward the police station where the woman he loved was sitting in an interrogation room because she'd set Tony and Angel's living room on fire.

He shook his head. He'd been right that very first night—she was a little crazy.

He was going to have his hands full with her.

And he couldn't wait.

* * *

It seemed fitting that Frank Birch's daughter would end up in jail. Sophie really should have been expecting this.

She folded her arms on top of the table in the interrogation room and laid her head on top of them. She closed her eyes and decided that there were probably worse things. This way she could avoid Frank. The theater would close, and Frank would stay away. Or if he didn't, she could put him on the list of the people she didn't want to have visit. At least that's how she thought it worked. She'd probably seen that in a movie or something.

She had no idea how much time passed before she heard the door open. She looked up, expecting one of the officers who had brought her in. But it was Finn. She sat up straight, blinking at him.

He closed the door behind him and then leaned against it with one shoulder, his arms crossed. He looked so hot in his uniform, those thick arms bulging with muscles, the belt around his trim hips...

Sophie shook her head. He was hot in uniform. But that uniform was a cop uniform and she was now a perp.

"Hey, Soph."

She tucked her hair behind her ears. "Hey."

"What's going on?" It almost looked like there was a smile teasing his mouth, but he was clear across the room and there was a shadow and... he wouldn't be smiling about this.

"Frank," she said simply with a shrug. "He always brings out the worst in me."

"Frank, huh?"

"Yeah. I'm tired of being soft and sweet. Sorry."

He pushed away from the wall and came to stand across the table from her. "Don't be sorry. I like this side of you, remember?"

She sighed. "I know it's your job and everything, but you wouldn't be the one to officially put me under arrest, right?" she asked. "I just feel like that could be a little awkward between us."

"You're not under arrest."

"I'm not?"

"No."

"But I'm"—she looked around—"In here."

"Yeah, they thought this was maybe a good place for you until I could get here. Evidently they felt there was a risk of further...feistiness. And they didn't even know about your kickboxing."

Sophie slumped back in her chair. "I vandalized the set and lit the couch on fire. Isn't that arson or something?"

He braced his hands on the back of the chair across from her, his forearm muscles bunching. And for a second, Sophie lost her train of thought again.

"It was a couch," he said simply. "And it was your couch. And I assume you're not going to turn in an insurance claim and try to profit from it. So I think you're safe from any arson charge."

She pulled her gaze back to his face. "You can set your own stuff on fire?"

He shrugged a shoulder. "Within reason."

"What about the vandalism?"

"It was a wooden play set, Soph. And again, yours. You're going to have to try harder if you want to get arrested."

She rolled her eyes. "If Frank stays in town, that could be arranged."

He frowned slightly. "He's heading out of town right now, as a matter of fact."

There was something in his tone that made her look at him closer. "Did you see him?"

He nodded. "Yep."

"And told him to get lost?"

"Encouraged his idea of getting lost. For a while."

She shook her head. "He'll be back."

"I know."

"And I'll...be like this." She spread her arms, indicating her present situation.

"Well, that's where I think you're wrong." He pushed up to his full height.

And again, Sophie couldn't help but let her gaze track down over his long, lean body. Damn, she was going to miss that. And him. And the theater. And everything else that Frank had ruined. Again.

She thought about what he'd said about Maggie but quickly pushed it out of her head. No sympathy. She was done trying to be soft and sweet. Screw that. She was feisty all the time from now on.

"I'm going to encourage kickboxing your frustrations out instead of burning stuff after this. But I get it. And I think you're going to be fine," Finn went on, "because Frank isn't going to be taking anything away from you anymore."

She looked up. "He always takes everything away."

Finn shook his head. "Not me. He can't take me, Soph. And I'm going to make sure you have whatever you need."

Her heart flipped a little, and she instantly felt the sting in her eyes. "We had a fight."

"We did. That's what families do sometimes. But, with the Kellys, anyway, it doesn't mean anything but that we've all got tempers and don't see eye to eye all the time. That's it."

"I told you I didn't think we should see each other any-more," she reminded him.

"I'm hoping to change your mind about that."

"I already changed my mind."

He gave her a little grin. "Glad to hear it."

"So that's that? We fight, then we make up?"

He lifted a shoulder. "Pretty much. Though in our case, we get to have makeup sex."

Her heart thumped, and she felt some tingles begin. "I've never done that before."

"Stick around. I have a feeling we're going to get good at it."

She couldn't help but smile, but she did say, "It will be about Frank again in the future."

Finn nodded. "That's okay. We'll get through it."

Sophie sighed. She loved the idea of getting through it with Finn. "That's sweet. But these fights could be big. He already took advantage of you being a great guy once. He'll do it again. And if he can't get you to give him stuff—which he clearly can," she added with a little frown, because really, Finn should know better, "then he'll just take it."

"You're right. He might talk me into something. He might take something of mine—money, my truck, my TV. But I don't care. The only thing that I need is you and my family.

And he can't take that." Finn moved around the edge of the table and squatted next to her. He turned her chair so she was facing him. "Tell me he can't take that, Sophie. Tell me that no matter what he does, you believe that you're a part of my family and nothing is going to change that."

The stinging in her eyes intensified, and Sophie sniffed. But she still shook her head. "People have loved me before, but he still manipulated them and hurt them, and eventually, it didn't matter how they felt about me."

"Sophia Isabelle," Finn said firmly, "I'm not going anywhere. I'm going to be here for you. Forever. And I've never not done something I said I was going to do."

Sophie felt hope bubble up. That was true. Finn was always honest.

"And," he went on, "I'm not afraid of Frank. I'm not intimidated by Frank. I'm frustrated by him, and I feel a little sorry for him. But I think he needs to know that we're going to be here no matter what too."

She groaned and dropped her head into her hands. "*Finn.* You have to stop feeling sorry for him."

He pried her fingers away from her eyes. "Soph, he's not going away for good."

She nodded, wanting to cry. "It will make you crazy."

"No. I was... not completely right... to assume I could change him."

She blinked at him. "You mean you were wrong?"

He gave her a tiny smile. "I'm still working on that."

The bubbles of hope got a little bigger.

"I tried to fix him too," she admitted. "Or tried to fix our situation. I just have to let it go." That sounded easy, but she knew it wouldn't be.

"I love that about you," Finn admitted. "I mean, neither

of us should be trying to change other people, but I love that he hasn't ruined your soft and sweet side."

"He might. If your family keeps inviting him to barbecues when he's in town," she said, her tone accusatory.

"No, you're going to be fine," he told her. "Because the soft and sweet you have in you is in spite of everything, and that means it's way stronger than some con-man dad and the guy who can't quite kick wanting to save the day. *Your* day."

"Which means you're still going to invite him to barbecues," she said.

Finn nodded. "Everyone needs a place to belong."

She narrowed her eyes, but her heart was thumping with what she knew was crazy, over-the-top love. Because how could she not love this man? "I think there's such a thing as *too* nice of a guy."

Finn lifted a brow. "Well, I have to be nice. My girlfriend burns shit down when she gets mad."

Sophie grimaced. "Sounds like a problem."

He leaned in, put his hands under her butt, and pulled her onto his lap and into his arms. "Nah. If she was soft all the time, she'd never be able to handle the Kellys. Turns out, she's just feisty enough to fit right in."

She couldn't help it. She wrapped her arms around his neck, needing to hold on. "You really think so?"

"Sophie, you were made for a big family. You see everyone individually—their strengths and what they need—but you can also bring them together into a big, productive, happy group. It's kind of amazing, actually."

"You think I do all of that?"

"It's like you're the director we've been waiting for," he said.

And she felt the tears well up. She loved him. She loved

his family. And she wanted to be a part of it. "I ruined the set. We can't do the show. Everyone's going to be upset."

"They get it. They think it's great."

"That I had a tantrum and trashed the place?"

"That you stood up to Frank."

She pulled in a deep breath. She could actually believe that. The Kellys would want her to be strong and happy first. "Well, I'm sad we won't get to put it on."

"Why can't we put the show on?"

"Uh, no set. No couch. Smoke in the theater. Some water damage to the stage. Again," she finished on a sheepish mutter.

"Piece of cake."

She gave a little laugh. "Sure."

"Everyone will head over tonight, and we'll get it back together. There's no way I'm letting a blackened couch and some red spray paint keep Tripp from getting up onstage."

"They'd do that?" she asked, her heart pounding. "Even though I'm the reason it's all a mess? For a little show that none of them really wanted to be in from the start?"

He smiled. "They'd do it for you anyway. But—don't tell them I told you—they're looking forward to the show. They're proud of it."

Sophie saw the sincerity in his eyes and grinned in spite of all her swirling emotions. It was just like how Angie had taken care of her when she'd been drunk. The Kellys were going to be there for her, even if she didn't really deserve it. Because they loved her.

"Told you that you're good at all of this," he said, squeezing her butt.

She nodded. She was still going to have to process the fact that even though she could cause them trouble, they'd still want her around, but being in Finn's arms was making everything feel very good—and very real.

He stretched to his feet and then let her slowly slide down his body until her feet touched the floor.

"Finn?"

"Yeah?" he asked gruffly, taking his time releasing her and stepping back.

"I love your family and I love the craziness and I love...being part of it."

He lifted a hand to her cheek. "Good thing. Because it's where you belong."

She belonged. The idea rocked through her, and she was suddenly sure she wasn't going to be setting anything else on fire because of Frank.

She was going to stick with kickboxing.

"By the way, I love you too," she said.

He nodded. "That's also a very good thing." He cupped her face and kissed her long and deep and sweetly.

Then she let him lead her out of the room and down the hall toward the front doors. "And maybe we can get your dad to come around and he could be here for Thanksgiving..."

She gave a little growl, and Finn stopped.

"Too soon?" he asked.

"Way too soon."

* * *

The show went on as planned four nights later.

The set was simpler than it had been before the, ahem, accident. The theater smelled faintly of smoke. There were missed entrances and botched lines.

But it was perfect.

The guys had put a fireplace into the new living room set and insisted that the smoky smell added to the ambiance. Everyone covered for everyone else when things were flubbed. And the firefighters and cops quickly realized that all they really had to do was flash their smiles and flex their muscles and the audience was happy.

And the most obvious of the issues caused the biggest cheers. When the door in the new set stuck and two of the guys had to put their shoulders into it, the audience hooted and whistled. When the window Sophie was supposed to climb through wobbled and threatened to collapse and three of the guys had to rush to keep it upright, the audience applauded. And when Finn spun Sophie around the living room and her elbow hit a candle and knocked it over, lighting the new couch on fire, and two of the firefighters rushed onstage with extinguishers, the crowd was brought to its feet.

Overall, it couldn't have gone any better.

Sophie slumped onto the smoke-and-fire-free sofa in the greenroom and propped her feet on the coffee table, feeling an incredible sense of satisfaction.

A moment later Angie handed her a cup of coffee and took the seat beside her. "Well done."

Sophie grinned at her. "You don't care that your beautiful love story turned into a romantic comedy?"

Angie laughed. "It was perfect. My life with Tommy was big and loud and fun. Just like that show."

They clinked their cups together and sipped.

Sophie rested her head back on the cushion behind her. "I just... Wow. They were amazing."

"They were amazing," Angie agreed. "I was so proud of everyone."

"Are they still out front signing autographs?" Sophie asked.

Angie laughed. "And loving every minute."

Sophie grinned. She could imagine. And good for them.

"Oh my God, I am truly brilliant!" Maya exclaimed as she swept into the room with Alex and Alex's daughter Charli behind her.

Sophie bounced up as Kiera and Zach also stepped into the room. "You are," Sophie agreed, hugging Maya. "Fire-fighters and cops onstage...who'd have thought that was the recipe for success?"

"Uh, everyone," Maya said. "At least everyone female."

Sophie laughed and hugged the rest of her friends. The room continued to fill up as members of the Kelly family came in to congratulate both Sophie and Angie. Soon it was hard to move without stepping on toes or bumping up against someone.

But finally she bumped into the hard, warm chest she'd been hoping for.

Strong arms wrapped around her as his voice rumbled in her ear, "Good show, Feisty."

She turned and slid her arms around his neck. "Ditto. You were the perfect Tony."

"I felt very connected to the part." He kissed her but pulled back before things got too hot and heavy. "It was the perfect first role...and the perfect one to retire on."

Sophie smiled up at him. "This is it?"

"I think I might be better behind the scenes. And in a supporting role for the theater owner."

"I loved having you onstage," she said. "But you really are good at the supportive stuff."

He leaned in to kiss her again, but before their lips touched, Sophie heard, "Next time we do a musical!"

Colin had just entered the room. Finn groaned, and Sophie snorted. "Looks like someone got bit by the theater bug," she said.

"Spotlights and applause," Finn said with a nod. "Right up his alley."

"Well, we have some work to do before we can go that big," Angie said. "But I've got some ideas."

Sophie unwrapped herself from her friend's son and turned to face Angie. "You do?"

"Yes. And I'm going to reinvest my twenty percent into the physical building for the first year. We'll replace the seats and carpeting first."

Sophie frowned slightly. "Your twenty percent of what?"

The room had quieted, and Angie gave her a huge smile. "My twenty percent ownership in the theater."

Sophie shook her head. "I don't understand."

"I loaned your father thirty thousand dollars," Angie said.

"Right." Sophie's heart started thumping even though she wasn't sure why.

"Well, when I called in his IOUs, right before he decided to pack up and leave town, he didn't have the money. Or," Angie said, "he wasn't willing to repay the money, anyway."

Sophie felt Finn's hands settle on her shoulders, and she appreciated his touch. "That sounds like Frank."

"Well, I informed him that the IOUs he wrote were legally binding contracts according to my nephew the lawyer," Angie said. "And then I offered to take shares in the theater as payment. So I'm now a twenty percent owner." Angie stepped forward and took one of Sophie's hands. "Your dad isn't your equal partner anymore, honey. You're the majority owner of the Birch Community Playhouse."

Sophie stared at her as thoughts rattled around in her head, the realization sinking in slowly. Angie had freed her from being Frank's equal partner. "Angie—" Sophie's voice caught. She cleared her throat. "I don't know what to say."

"Say you're happy about it," Angie said, squeezing her hand. "This was my idea from the second I offered him the first loan. But I couldn't tell you about it. I didn't want him to realize what I was doing until he was in over his head, and I knew he'd get suspicious if you weren't stressed out about the whole thing. I'm sorry to make you worry."

Finally it fully sank in. Sophie grabbed Angie and hugged her tightly. "Angela Kelly, you are amazing!"

Angie pulled back and gave both Sophie and Finn a look. "I thought I was naive and innocent."

Sophie laughed. "No, ma'am. I stand corrected. You just outmanipulated Frank Birch. *That* takes feistiness."

Angie grinned a grin that was so much like her oldest son's that Sophie caught her breath for a moment.

"Well, thank you very much. I always thought I had some sassiness in me." Angie gave her a wink.

Finn laughed. "I'm a little concerned about an increased level of sassiness in you, Mom."

"Then look out," she said with another big smile. "The Birch Community Playhouse is now in the hands of two of the most...vivacious...women you know."

"I don't know how to say thank you," Sophie told her.

"Just . . . stick around." Angie lifted her gaze to Finn over Sophie's shoulder. "And love us."

Sophie felt her eyes stinging, but she nodded.

Angie leaned in and gave her a kiss on the cheek. "You don't have to thank me for having your back. I'll protect you and help you however I can, whenever I can."

Sophie sniffed as Angie moved off into the crowd and conversation started again.

Finn's hands slid to her waist, and he pulled her back against him. "By the way, that runs in the family," he said against her hair.

She turned in his arms. "Which part?"

"All of it."

"The part about me wanting to stick around?"

"Uh, yeah, you're not going anywhere. You're mine."

She let out a happy sigh and snuggled into him. Because she was, no doubt about it, totally his.

Zach Ashley is an EMT who lives to save people, while Kiera Connelly is a graphic designer who prefers to hide behind her computer. When disaster strikes and Zach must rescue Kiera, there's an instant attraction. The two don't agree on much, but despite their differences, they have one very important thing in common: they are crazy about each other.

Please turn the page for an excerpt from *Completely Yours*.

$\mathcal{I}$ like the new troll spell and the expanded fairy kingdom, but what happens if you get through the forest without finding any gems?" Aimee asked.

"You'd have to avoid all of the paths to *not* find one eventually," Kiera pointed out.

She and Aimee were sitting in a coffee shop about four blocks from where Aimee and Zach lived. It was officially twenty-four hours after her concussion, and Kiera was feeling good as long as she kept ibuprofen in her system. They'd agreed to meet here while Zach worked. Maya and Sophie had been, predictably, thrilled when Kiera had told them she was going out for the afternoon. They didn't need to know that she was spending the time showing Aimee some of the new Leokin designs she'd been working on. Though Kiera had to admit that getting someone's reaction in real time, in person, was actually pretty fun. And when it was a hardcore Leokin girl like Aimee, it was also very helpful.

"But the witches and even some of the elves would be able to avoid the paths and make it through the whole forest," Aimee said.

Kiera nodded. Aimee had a point. She typed a note about Aimee's observation into the chat window she had open with Dalton.

"Dalton says we could distribute the gems with the moonsky flowers in the forest," Kiera read to Aimee a moment later. Witches and elves were the only ones who could see moonsky flowers and benefit from their powers.

"That would work. But the gems will be too big to be hidden in the moonsky flower bushes," Aimee said.

Kiera typed another note to Dalton, then made a few tweaks to the gem graphic. She sent it to Aimee, who opened it in her e-mail program immediately.

"Yes, that's perfect."

Kiera grinned at her. "Awesome." She typed, "Aimee approved" into the chat window. Dalton sent her a thumbs-up.

"I can't believe it," Aimee said, sitting back in her chair.

Kiera looked up. "What?"

"I'm hanging out with Kiera Connolly, chatting online with Dalton Sagel, and giving input into new Leokin stuff. This is awesome."

Kiera was flattered by Aimee's admiration. But she was also worried. On the one hand, she didn't want Aimee to get too attached to her. This whole thing was going to be over in a few weeks. On the other hand, if Aimee was more open and friendly with Zach because he was dating Kiera, then it was a good thing.

Ignoring all of those confusing thoughts, Kiera gave Aimee a smile and focused on her work. Leokin was always the answer when things got confusing in the real world.

Her phone started buzzing, and she glanced over. Zach was calling. She frowned and reached for the phone.

"Hello?"

"Hey, Princess."

His deep voice made shivers dance through her. "Hi."

"Where are you?"

"At the coffee shop near your place."

"What are you doing?" he asked.

Kiera narrowed her eyes. "Talking to your sister."

"Great. I thought I'd swing by after my shift and say hi."

She knew that Zach had told Aimee he'd be by around four. She'd been hoping to see him. She leaned back in her chair, trying to make her tone nonchalant. "Okay."

"Everything going well?"

"You're checking up on us?"

"No. Just thinking of you and wanted to say hi."

She wasn't sure she believed him, but she couldn't help that her heart flipped a little at that idea. Still, she didn't want to encourage quick calls "just to say hi." She hated talking on the phone, and unimportant phone calls interrupted her work flow, and, most of all, this whole thing with her spending time with him and Aimee had been his idea. If he felt he needed to check in all the time, they needed to rethink their plan.

"You still there?" he asked.

"Yep."

"And everything is okay."

"Yes."

She was sure the short, one-word answers drove Zach crazy. He was a talker. But she wasn't.

"You're not very talkative," he commented a moment later.

She smiled in spite of herself. "No, I'm really not. I don't like talking on the phone."

"Oh." He sounded confused. He probably was, she thought, her smile growing. Zach was clearly an extrovert who didn't get introverts.

She heard him sigh.

"So if I want to check in, say hi, make plans..."

"Text me," she said cheerfully.

She imagined the exasperated look she'd already seen a few times from him.

"Okay," he finally said. "But I will see you later. And you'll talk to me in person, right?"

"Within reason," she agreed, wondering if her grin was evident in her tone. She wasn't sure why it was fun to poke at Zach. Maybe because he seemed so sure that he knew exactly how things should always go. She liked shaking up his expectations a little bit.

"Right. Okay." He sighed again.

"See you later," she said.

"Yep. See you."

She chuckled as she disconnected with him.

"So you didn't mention anything to Zach about me meeting up with my WOL friends, did you?" Aimee asked.

Kiera looked up. "No. Why?"

"He won't like it," Aimee said. "But I've been thinking about doing it more and more. You think it's okay, don't you?"

Kiera frowned and moved her hands off her keyboard. "I understand that you feel close to them even with having never met them," she said. She and Pete and Dalton were close and worked well together in spite of living three thousand miles apart. "And I don't think meeting them is a bad idea. Why wouldn't Zach like it?"

"He doesn't get the online friendship thing."

Just then her phone rang with a text. From Zach. She rolled her eyes but opened it.

Is Pete your boss?

He wanted to know about Pete? She typed back. *Yes. And one of my best friends.*

So you're not in love with him?

She laughed. *No.*

Good.

She stared at the word for a moment.

Then she forced herself to concentrate on Aimee. "But this would be in person," she said about the meeting with her online friends. "Wouldn't Zach like that you were moving it into the real world?"

Aimee shrugged. "Yes and no. He'd like that I was being more social, getting out. But he wouldn't like to know how close I've gotten to them and that they've been helping me through everything."

Kiera frowned. "Why not?"

"Zach likes to be the one I need for everything," Aimee said. "He likes to be the one everyone needs for everything."

Kiera had no idea what to say to that. It didn't shock her. But she didn't want someone all mixed up in her stuff. Zach's wanting to be involved in everything all the time should be a mark in the con column. So why was it kind of attractive?

Another text came in. She was surprised to feel her heart flutter at the sound.

Have you had your heart broken before to the point that it made you hole up in your room for two months?

She shook her head. She wouldn't have personal conversations with him, but he thought she'd tell him personal things via text?

But as she thought about it, she realized this was a lot easier. She didn't have to see the other person or think about what they were seeing in her face. And she knew already that Zach would keep pushing.

Yes. Her breakup with Mitch had messed her up for longer than two months.

What happened?

First love. Mitch. Very controlling. Tried to change everything about me.

Kiera hit send before she thought about it or read it over. She couldn't believe she'd told him that. But maybe it was good for him to know where she was coming from. Their relationship was just a temporary, mostly fake thing. But it wouldn't hurt for her to put all her cards out there.

Change you?

She took a breath. *Hated all my hobbies, didn't want me to spend time with anyone but him. Wanted me to change my hair and the way I dressed. Wanted me to lose weight.*

You told the bastard to fuck off?

She smiled. Essentially that was exactly what she'd told him. *Yes.* She hesitated over her next words. But she ended up typing them anyway. *So he moved on to Juliet.*

Who's Juliet?

She was my best friend, Kiera told him, feeling the familiar stabbing pain in her chest.

What did she do?

Became his perfect woman.

And when he'd insisted that she needed to lose weight too, she'd developed an eating disorder that had landed her in the hospital. Kiera had gone to try to talk her into leaving him, to let Kiera take her home. But Juliet had chosen the emotionally abusive asshole over her best friend.

But you stopped it? Got her away from him?

His question made Kiera's heart squeeze. *Tried. And failed.*

He took a long time to answer. *I know how bad that hurts.*

She didn't know what to say to that. Juliet had met Mitch because of Kiera. If Kiera hadn't gotten involved with him, he would have never had Juliet on his radar. Kiera knew that, in part, Mitch had gone after Juliet because he'd wanted to get back at Kiera for rejecting him. So yes, she felt somewhat to blame. But Juliet had made her choices. Kiera had given her an option for getting out, and she'd turned Kiera down. It did hurt. But there was nothing she could do about it. Besides try to keep anything like that from happening again.

Something about Zach's answer nagged at her, though. Was Zach talking about his relationship with Aimee? He was trying and failing to help her? She never delved into other people's personal angst and drama, but suddenly Kiera needed to know.

"What have your friends been helping you through?" she asked Aimee hesitantly.

Aimee looked up from what she'd been doing on her computer. She blinked. "Getting over my sister."

Kiera felt a trickle of foreboding go through her. "What do you mean?"

Aimee sighed. "I don't know. I can't explain it. Even before Josie died, Leokin was this place where I could...get lost. And then after she was gone, it was the only place I felt like myself."

Kiera froze.

She didn't move or make a sound.

Holy crap.

She glanced up, but Aimee was concentrating on her own computer screen.

Kiera held her breath. Aimee had lost her sister? Zach had lost his sister? This was definitely messy family stuff. Was Aimee not handling it well? But Kiera knew...Aimee was immersing herself in the game to avoid everything.

Kiera got that. She so got that.

Aimee sniffed and shifted on her chair. "I feel bad sometimes, but I never had a sister in Leokin, so I didn't miss having a sister there. That made it the only place I wanted to be. I missed having a sister *everywhere* else."

Kiera felt her eyes stinging but kept her gaze firmly on her computer screen. What did she say now? Dammit, she was so bad at this stuff. She had to clear her throat before she asked, "Was your sister into gaming?"

"No, she was in a band. A rock band. She played guitar and sang. She was awesome."

Kiera could hear Aimee's smile, and she looked up to catch it.

"They were coming home from a gig really late one night, and Hunter, he was the bass player and the lead singer, was driving. He was so cool." Aimee's voice trailed off for a moment. Then she said, "He fell asleep at the wheel and crossed the center line into oncoming traffic."

Kiera blinked and forced herself to breathe as she stared

at her screen, where the stream bubbled happily by the tall trees and long grass of the meadow.

Kiera had to say something. And the thing was, she kind of had something to say. She didn't have any siblings, but she'd had someone she'd thought of as a sister. And she'd lost her. Not to death. Juliet had chosen to leave Kiera's life. Not the same thing exactly, but Kiera knew the pain of losing a loved one and knowing your life would never be the same.

But she was out of practice. Since Juliet's betrayal, Kiera had made a firm habit of staying out of people's business and keeping them out of hers. She believed that people needed to make their own decisions and their own mistakes.

Condolences weren't the same thing as advice, though. "I'm really sorry about your sister, Aimee."

"I miss her every day," the younger girl said softly.

"You'll miss her every day forever," Kiera said honestly. "But thinking about her won't always squeeze your heart so hard that you can't even take a deep breath."

There was a long pause, and then Aimee said softly, "That's exactly how it feels sometimes."

Kiera nodded. "I know."

Aimee swallowed hard. Then she gave a little nod and inserted her earbuds into her ears.

Each got absorbed in what was on her screen, and Kiera ignored all thoughts that went anything like, "Did I do okay?" "What's she thinking?" "Did I mess that up?"

She'd told her the truth. And Aimee wasn't her responsibility. Kiera knew the girl was hurting, but she had a big brother who was amazing and protective and sweet. He was taking care of her, Kiera was sure.

It took only about five minutes for her to get lost in her work, and they sat together quietly for nearly twenty minutes before she heard, "You girls are in so much trouble."

Kiera recognized the voice immediately, and her gaze flew to the clock in the corner of her computer screen. *Dammit.* He was early.

Kiera looked up to see Zach standing next to the table. He had his hands on his hips and was watching her with an eyebrow up and an expression that looked partly exasperated and partly amused.

He looked sexy.

She had an inkling that if she found him sexy when he was exasperated with her, she was going to be finding him sexy a lot.

"You said four o'clock," Aimee said, looking guilty.

Kiera wanted to kick her under the table. She needed to not look guilty.

"I said four o'clock because I intended to show up at three thirty to see what you were up to," Zach said. He kicked the empty chair out and sat. "I knew you'd be on your computers."

"We never said we *wouldn't* be on our computers," Kiera pointed out, surreptitiously closing the window she'd had open to work on new graphics.

She and Aimee were together. In person. In a public place. It was more social than either of them had been in several weeks without being coerced. So why did Aimee look guilty for their being caught on their computers? Why did Kiera *feel* guilty?

"I knew you would be. You've been away from it for a whole day. You were probably dying," Zach said drily.

Kiera couldn't deny that she'd been eager to get back

online. But she also couldn't honestly say she'd been completely away from it for a whole day. She'd checked in when she'd first gotten home. But her head had started hurting within two minutes. She didn't want to admit that either. So she just didn't say anything.

"When you said you were getting together, Maya, Sophie, and I assumed it was to, you know, talk to one another and do something together," Zach said.

Kiera snorted.

"You talked to Maya and Sophie?" Aimee asked.

Zach's eyes were on Kiera, but he answered his sister. "No. I'm guessing. But Maya and Sophie were led to believe you and Aimee would be doing something other than sitting across from one another, each on your own computer, for three hours straight, weren't they, Princess?"

She really liked when he called her Princess.

The truth was, Maya and Sophie had probably assumed that Kiera was going to see Zach today. They didn't know about Aimee. Kiera shrugged. "I didn't go into any details one way or another with them."

With his gaze on her, Kiera felt hot—probably still the guilt—and wiggly, as if she had an itch she couldn't scratch. Zach looked huge on the tiny wrought iron chair, and when he stretched his long legs out, he took up far too much space. Too much of *her* space. He was crowding into Kiera's area under the table, as if he was trying to be sure she took note of him. She could hardly help it. He linked his fingers together, resting them above his belt, and she also couldn't help that her gaze went to his big hands, and his flat stomach. Then below his flat stomach.

"Good to see something can pull your attention from your computer screen."

Her gaze snapped up to his. And the knowing smile below his gaze. *Dammit.*

As she met his eyes, *He's lost his sister* went through her head. The thought jolted her. He'd distracted her with his early arrival. And his grin. And how great he looked in uniform. But now that she'd remembered, she wanted to hug him.

And that was so uncharacteristic that she actually reached for her coffee cup to keep from reaching for him. Her empty coffee cup. She pretended to drink from it anyway, grateful there was a lid so he didn't know she was faking.

Kiera cleared her throat. "Aimee and I have had a nice time together," she told him. "Just because you happened to walk in at a moment when we were each checking in on the computer doesn't mean that you know for sure we haven't been chatting this entire time."

"Have you been chatting this entire time?" he asked.

"We—"

But he was asking his sister. Kiera had to squelch the urge to kick her again.

Aimee sighed. "Not the *entire* time. But we never said we wouldn't be on the computers."

"Exactly," Kiera agreed quickly. "We're not doing anything wrong."

Just then a beeping erupted from her computer. Her alarm. She scrambled to get it shut off. When she looked up, Zach was smirking. "If you weren't doing anything wrong, why did you set a timer?"

"That timer could be for anything," Kiera told him.

He nodded. "Interesting that it went off with just enough time to get your computers shut down and packed away before I was supposed to get here."

She was busted. "I had some work I had to do today. Whether or not that makes you and Maya unhappy," she informed him. "But Aimee and I have spent the time together and we did chat and I will readily admit that this was nicer than working alone in my room in many ways."

"In many ways?" Zach repeated. "Not in every way?" But he seemed more amused than judgmental.

"Well, I'm in real clothes instead of pajamas," Kiera said.

She probably should have expected the way his gaze tracked down her body with that comment, but she hadn't, and she felt the wave of heat that went from her scalp to the soles of her feet as his eyes roamed over her.

"And I've only had one bowl of cereal today," she added.

Zach nodded. "Poor girl."

She couldn't help the little grin she gave him. "The struggle is real."

Zach pushed back from the table and stretched to his feet. "And I haven't seen you in your pajamas yet, but I love the jeans. Let's go."

Yet. He'd said *yet* about seeing her in her pajamas.

"Are we going home?" Aimee asked, starting to gather her stuff.

"I've got a game."

"Basketball?" Aimee asked.

Zach nodded. "You two have been doing the computer thing all day. So now you have to put in some time of *actual* socialization."

"You play basketball?" Kiera asked Aimee.

The girl shook her head. "No. He does."

Yeah, Kiera remembered that. And that she knew almost nothing about the game.

Kiera watched Aimee tuck her computer into her bag and stand.

"Well, I guess I'll see you?" Aimee asked.

"Definitely."

Zach stood simply watching her.

"What?" Kiera asked.

"Let's go," he repeated.

"Go?"

"To my game."

Kiera felt her head start shaking. "No, that's okay. I don't really like basketball."

He gave her a slow smile. "Yet."

Kiera opened her mouth to protest, but then a crazy thought flitted through her mind. *Why not?* She'd gotten a lot done today, she was actually a little ahead on things for now, and...she was willing to watch a basketball game to spend some time with Zach.

Crap. She was in trouble.

Kiera got to her feet and pulled her bag up on her shoulder. His gaze ran over her again. "Yeah, this view of the jeans is even better."

Kiera felt herself blush. And was glad she'd worn the jeans instead of the yoga pants she'd had on first. *Damn.* She wasn't dressing for Zach. She was *not*.

Thirty minutes later they pulled into the parking lot of a YMCA. Kiera blinked at the front of the building. She realized she'd been expecting Zach to play in an expensive rec center or a members-only gym. Zach held the door for Aimee and Kiera. As she passed him, she looked up, noting the huge grin on his face. She felt a little flip in her stomach.

She liked seeing him so lit up. She tried to tell herself

that it was because she'd just learned that he'd lost his sister in a car accident and that it was nice to see him happy about something. But she knew that wasn't the whole truth. She just liked seeing him happy, period. Even before she'd known about Josie.

But thinking about Josie made her want to hug him again. Well, that and the memory of how great it felt to be pressed up against him in general.

"Gym's down that way," he said, stopping at the doorway to the men's locker room and pointing. "Grab a seat. And be sure to whoop and yell loud."

She grinned up at him. "I won't know when to whoop and yell, Zach."

"Whenever the orange ball goes into the basket on my team's end of the court," he replied with a shrug.

"How about I just sit in quiet awe of your athletic prowess?" she offered.

He chuckled, and the sound made her smile grow.

"I can definitely handle having your eyes on me for the next hour or so, Princess."

Yeah, she was pretty sure she could handle that too.

Zach startled her by leaning in and giving her a quick kiss. She stared up at him as he straightened.

"Been dying to do that since I walked into the coffee shop," he said. Then he turned and headed into the locker room with his gym bag.

Kiera drew a deep breath. It was show for Aimee. She was supposed to think they were really dating. But the look in his eyes had seemed real to Kiera. She needed to be careful about not getting too caught up in their story herself.

She followed Aimee into the gym and up onto the bleachers.

"So you know a lot about basketball?" Kiera asked.

Aimee shrugged. "Yeah, I guess. I was a cheerleader for my high school team for three years."

Kiera looked over at her, surprised. "Really?"

"Oh yeah. Before…everything happened…I was a cheerleader, homecoming queen, really social and popular. The whole thing. That's why Zach's so freaked out."

Kiera turned her attention to the court and to the few guys already out there warming up. She could kind of see why Zach would be concerned with his sister's complete personality one-eighty, actually.

"Hey, speaking of being social," Aimee said.

Kiera looked over. "Yeah?"

"I've decided to meet my Leokin friends who live locally. I was wondering if you'd go to the coffee shop with me next Saturday. We're going to meet there and I thought it might be nice if you were there too, just to, you know, be sure it's all fine."

Kiera nodded immediately. "Of course. I think that's a great idea, actually." She was happy Aimee was getting together with her new friends, but was also glad she was being safe about it.

Aimee gave her a big smile. "Thanks."

"No problem." She glanced at the court again, then started to look back at Aimee. But something snagged her attention.

Zach. Who had just walked out of the locker room. Without a shirt on.

Her eyes widened as she took him in. Broad shoulders, sculpted arm muscles, wide chest and hard abs. She easily conjured the feel of all of those under and against her last night. The baggy gym shorts didn't keep her from appreciating his firm butt and muscled thighs and calves either.

This just might be the best hour of her life.

"Right, Kiera?"

She heard Aimee's voice but didn't turn her head. "Um, what?"

Aimee laughed. "How about I ask you again later?"

"Yeah." That would be great. She supposed.

The game started, and Kiera settled in with a happy sigh. Sweat-slicked, tanned skin moving over bunching shoulder, back, and ab muscles should not have been so mesmerizing. But damned if basketball wasn't suddenly her favorite spectator sport.

* * *

Zach walked Kiera to the train station after the game so she could catch the train back to Cambridge. Aimee was with them but was hanging back, clearly trying to give them some time alone. He smiled to himself. Man, this plan was brilliant. He got to spend time with Kiera and help his sister at the same time.

They stopped by the entrance to the station, and Kiera turned to him.

"Come back to my place for a little while," Zach said before she could speak. "It's early." He should be hoping she'd come over so he might have a chance at more time with Aimee, but truthfully, it was the peck on the lips he'd given Kiera before his game that made him ask. The quick taste hadn't been nearly enough.

"I should get home," she said. "I'll see you later this week, though."

"When?" he asked.

Aimee had stopped about a half block away, and Kiera gave her a glance. She was leaning against the wall, her head bent over her phone.

"Wednesday?" Kiera suggested.

Wednesday was three days away. He needed to see her before that. "I work the next three nights."

"I thought your goal was for me to hang out with Aimee," Kiera said. "Keep her from being holed up in her room."

He nodded and moved in to brace his hand on the railing beside her hip. "But it's a win-win when we can both spend time with you."

"True," she agreed easily. "But Aimee could come over and hang out with me one of the nights you work."

Zach searched her face for a moment. "I can come pick her up after my shift ends at ten."

"Great," Kiera said quickly. Almost eagerly. Then she cleared her throat. "I mean, sure. That's fine."

He couldn't help but grin. He liked the idea of Kiera being eager for him.

"Thanks for coming to my game." He'd loved having her there. And every time he'd glanced up into the stands and seen her watching, he'd felt a kick in his chest.

She laughed at that. "Did I have a choice?"

"Don't tell me you minded," he said. "Your eyes were glued on the game."

The way she looked up at him from beneath her lashes was adorably hot. "I enjoyed it. But you and I both know that I wasn't watching the game."

"No?" He shifted closer to her.

She shook her head. "I was watching *you*. And enjoying the fact that you're a total geek about basketball."

He frowned slightly. "I'm not a geek about basketball."

Kiera nodded and grinned. "Oh yes, Zach Ashley, you definitely are."

He liked basketball. Loved it, even. But he'd never been called a geek in his life. "Maybe our definition of *geek* is different."

She lifted a shoulder. "I've seen how sports fans act when it comes time for a big game or event. They throw parties and they dress up in the team's colors and jerseys. Some even paint their faces. And they go out there and revel in being a part of something that makes them so happy. That's geekiness, Zach. Passion for something. Passion that you give time and energy to. The crazy way they yell at the refs and the way they go nuts because one team manages to put a ball where the other team doesn't want it…that's not acting, but it's also not *really* them. It's part of their personality. A part they only let out on certain occasions when they're around other people who share the same passion."

She paused, and Zach knew exactly what she was going to say next.

"That's how I feel and act about Leokin."

He sighed. He supposed she had a point. "I never thought of it that way," he said. "And I definitely didn't realize that all pretty much makes me a cosplayer."

He started to shift away, but she reached out and grabbed his forearm. "It was really hot watching how into it you got."

Zach lifted an eyebrow. "Yeah?"

"Yeah." She wet her lips and stepped closer to him. "You were so happy out there. It was sexy to watch you having such a great time. You were laughing and shouting and putting everything you had into it. It's clear you love it. You were intense, but relaxed at the same time."

He nodded slowly. "I feel different out there. All I have to do is concentrate on the game. All the other... stuff fades away."

She gave him a soft smile. "I'm glad."

"And now you like basketball," he said.

She shrugged. "I like watching you like basketball."

Something about her words made him stop and think. She'd lit up when she'd been talking about common interests with the injured while he bandaged them up. He'd seen the same thing in both Kiera and Aimee when he'd walked into the kitchen last night. There had been something in their faces and voices that had said they were in their element.

"Princess," he finally said, "I think it's possible that I'd like watching you like just about anything."

She smiled and then stepped forward and wrapped her arms around him.

Surprise quickly morphed into something he wouldn't have expected. Affection. He enfolded her in a hug that made him feel content and restless at the same time. Holding her felt good. But he wanted so much more.

She pulled back after a moment and looked up at him.

"What was that for?" he asked, not ready to let her go yet.

"Been dying to do that since you walked into the coffee shop," she said.

Then she stepped back, gave Aimee a little wave, and disappeared into the train station.

ABOUT THE AUTHOR

Erin Nicholas is the author of sexy contemporary romances. Her stories have been described as "toe-curling," "enchanting," "steamy," and "fun." She loves to write about reluctant heroes, imperfect heroines, and happily-ever-afters. She lives in the Midwest with her husband, who only wants to read the sex scenes in her books, her kids, who will never read the sex scenes in her books, and family and friends who say they're shocked by the sex scenes in her books (yeah, right!).

You can find Erin on the Web at:
  ErinNicholas.com
  Twitter @ErinNicholas
  Facebook.com/ErinNicholasBooks

Fall in Love with Forever Romance

SUGARPLUM WAY
By Debbie Mason

The *USA Today* bestselling Harmony Harbor series continues! As a romance author, Julia Landon's job is to create happy-ever-afters. But she can't seem to create one for herself—even after a steamy kiss under the mistletoe with Aiden Gallagher. After a bitter divorce, Aiden has no interest in making another commitment; he just wants to spend quality time with his daughter. But with Christmas right around the corner, both Aiden and Julia may find that Santa is about to grant a little girl's special wish.

Fall in Love with Forever Romance

TOTALLY HIS
By Erin Nicholas

In the newest of *New York Times* bestselling author Erin Nicholas's Opposites Attract series, actress Sophie Birch is used to looking out for herself. When her theater catches fire and a cop scoops her up to save her, she fights him every step of the way...even though his arms feel oh-so-good. Finn Kelly can't help but appreciate how sexy the woman in his arms looks...even if she's currently resisting arrest. But when Sophie finds herself in trouble again, can Finn convince her to lean on him?

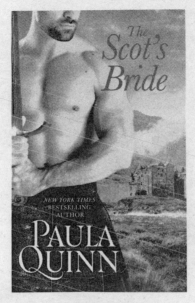

Fall in Love with Forever Romance

BACK IN THE GAME
By Erin Kern

Fans of *Friday Night Lights* will love the heartwarming Champion Valley series by bestselling author Erin Kern. Stella Davenport swore she'd never let anything get in the way of her dream—until sexy, broad-shouldered Brandon West walks back into her life. Brandon knows that love only leads to heartbreak, but Stella is a breath of fresh air he didn't even know he'd been missing. When she's offered her dream job in Chicago, will he be willing to put his heart on the line?

LETHAL LIES
By Rebecca Zanetti

Long-buried secrets and deadly forces threaten Anya Best and Heath Jones as they hunt down the infamous Copper Killer. Will they find love only to lose their lives? Fans of Maya Banks and Shannon McKenna will love Rebecca Zanetti's latest sexy suspense!